HOMECOMING LOVE

RAFAELLA DUTRA

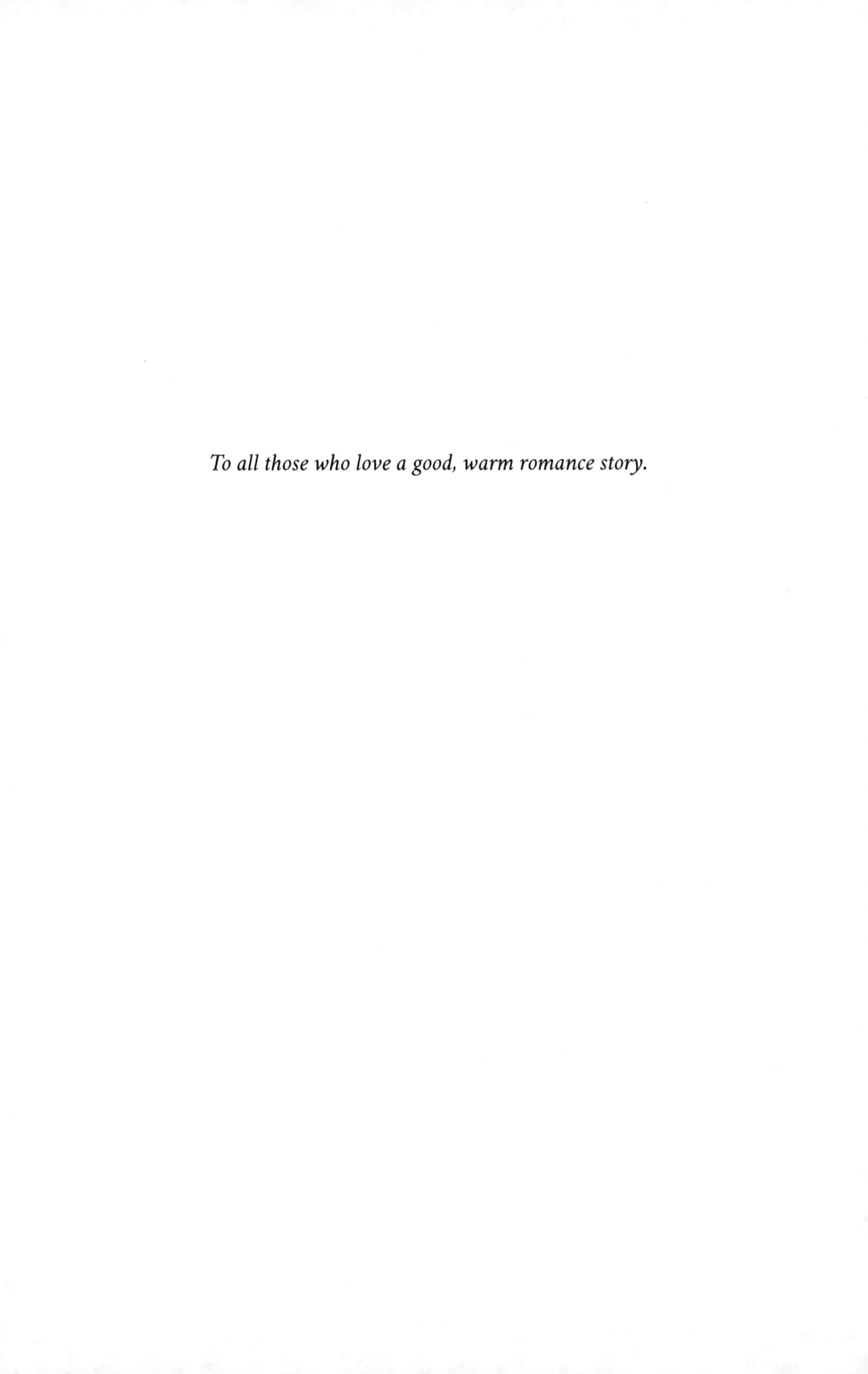

To all those who love a good, warm romance story.

CONTENTS

CHAPTER ONE

Your brother's wedding should be considered a happy day, right?

But for me, it's not.

In fact, I'm dreading it.

Not because of my brother—or his fiancée, for that matter, I do like her—but because I know who will be there, and that's something I'm not looking forward to.

I have what people call a rotten picker—for men, that is.

Every single guy I ever hooked up with or had a fling with were stupid assholes.

Except one. Spencer Bailey.

And he is precisely the reason why I'm not excited for my brother's wedding.

I'm definitely not ready to see him again.

But to tell my brother that I won't attend his wedding because I'm afraid to face my ex would be pathetic.

Even for me.

And I'm not that person. I'm not someone who runs from problems. I face them head on. Or at least, that's what I like to think I do.

Well, I guess if you're ready for some drama, then my life is definitely the right place for you to find it.

"Stop looking at me like that," I burst to my sister, Lauren, rolling my eyes and tossing my pillow at her. "I've already told you several times that I'm fine. And if anything, you should be taking my side on this. I don't have to remind you of the reasons why this sucks."

"I was just checking on you to make sure you're okay." Lauren tosses the pillow back at me before pulling her light brown hair into a ponytail and fixing her firefighter uniform. It still astonishes me how she can look so pretty wearing a uniform—and before 8:00 A.M. That should be considered a crime. "And honestly, we have, like, thousands of cousins coming to the wedding. Maybe you won't even see Spencer. Let alone bump into him."

She is right about that. We do have a big family. Mom and Dad have, like, countless siblings, which takes us to countless cousins and so on....

"Whatever," I mumble, frustrated. "What are you even doing here? Don't you have to go to work? I don't even know why you moved out in the first place if you are here pretty much every day."

"Well, last time I checked, this is still my parents' house. I can come by anytime I want. And I moved out because I wanted to be closer to the fire department. I can sleep a few more minutes since I don't have to drive there."

I groan, too frustrated to find a proper answer for her. At moments like this, I regret not having my own space.

But honestly, I went down that road several times before, and none of those times could I convince myself that paying rent while my parents own this huge ranch was a good idea. They give me enough privacy; I have my own room. I don't meddle in their business, and they don't meddle in mine, and I get to help them with some of the bills. It's a win-win situation.

"I'll be going now. Are we still on for picking up the dresses tomorrow morning?" Lauren asks with her hand already on the doorknob.

"Yeah, ten A.M. sharp. Otherwise, I'll leave without you," I answer, flashing her a grin and tossing the pillow back at her. She dodges it and turns on her heel, vanishing from my sight before I have the chance to tell her off.

I sigh, falling back on my bed and staring at the ceiling. I really don't want to complain about my life or anything—I'm not that person. I don't mope. I have a good life. I don't even have the right to complain.

But my family bringing up this problem all the time is making me poke at that wound again. It took me so long to close it, to put it behind me. I thought I'd never have to see Spencer again. Or at least, when I had to see him, that it wouldn't bother me. Wasn't it supposed to be the way this should go?

I shouldn't be worried about seeing Spencer. It should mean nothing.

In fact, Lauren is right, I might not even have to talk to him. The party will be filled with guests, friends, and family. Why would I pay attention to Spencer?

Truth be told, from the way things ended between us, I doubt he'll talk to me even if I trip and fall on his lap. Which I hope with all my heart doesn't happen!

I'll be the bigger person here. I will swallow down my pride, hold my head high, and go through this moment politely, pretending he didn't shatter my heart into tiny little pieces that no one was ever able to put back together.

"Hayden Jenkins! Breakfast is ready! Come on!" Mom yells from downstairs, her voice reverberating through my room even though I have the windows and the door closed. She's this kind, tiny little person, but she can be so loud when she wants to be. It's insane. "I know you're up! You sister just told me, so hurry up or I won't save you any pie!"

Geez, the nerve of this woman to threaten me with pie. Ugh!

"Coming in a second, Mom!" I yell back, tossing myself off the bed. I don't bother changing out of my pajamas, just pull my hair up into a messy bun and rush down the stairs, feeling the delicious smell of dough and coffee hit my nostrils.

"Good morning, sunshine!" Dad greets me as soon as I step into the kitchen. And that's when I realize it's crowded.

Ryan, Alice, Chad, Mom, and Dad are all gathered around the table, with all sorts of fruits, cakes, bread, and Mom's delicious apple pie—which is already being destroyed by Chad—in front of them.

"Is it someone's birthday today? Why are we having pie for breakfast anyway? Isn't that for special occasions only?" I ask, a bit grumpy. Did I mention I'm not a morning person?

"Always a delight, Hayden. Calling her sunshine is a bit contradictory, isn't it, Dad?" Chad teases me while shoving a forkful of pie into his mouth and grinning at me.

"Will you leave some of that for me, or will you eat it all by yourself?" I push him on the shoulder when I pass by him to get to my spot at the table. "Good morning, Alice." I flash my sister-in-law-to-be a smile, trying to be polite since she doesn't have to put up with my morning mood.

My family is another story.

"Today is a special occasion, sweetheart. Your brother is getting married, and only God knows when I'll get the whole family together like this again. It's a pity your sister won't be joining us," Mom explains.

I want to roll my eyes and tell her she's being overdramatic, because even though Ryan is getting married, I'm positive he won't stop coming over to eat her food. He already moved out a while ago, and he still shows up pretty much every day. Just like my other two siblings.

"Lauren said you were grumpy this morning, but I didn't think it'd be this much," Ryan chimes in, raising his eyebrows at me.

"And I have all of you to thank for that, don't I?" The words fly out of my mouth before I have the chance to think about it. I wasn't planning on discussing this with anyone—not even Lauren, but the annoying girl pretty much forced it out of me—but now that I let them in, they won't let it go.

Ryan's brows arch even more, and I feel everyone's eyes on me.

"Are you still upset that I invited him?" Ryan asks cautiously, his brows creasing into a frown. "I thought you were over it. It's been what... six years?"

"Seven. And I *AM* over it. You are the ones bringing it up every time and not letting me forget about it."

Me and my big mouth! I should have let it go, pretended I'm not freaking out.

"Honey, it's not like your brother could get away with not inviting him. The Baileys have been our friends for years," Mom tries to meddle in.

I know she has the best of intentions, but I don't want to hear it. Honestly, I don't want to have this conversation with any of them.

I appreciate their concern. They saw how broken I was when Spencer and I ended things. I'm really thankful for them being there for me all of those years ago, but now, it's just weird to talk about this.

"I am fine, okay? I can behave, if that's what everyone is concerned about," I tell Ryan and Alice, flashing her another smile when I see her brows creasing in a concerned way. "I won't ruin your wedding, I promise."

Alice shakes her head at me, dismissing me with a comforting smile, but I know better than that. Everyone is afraid of me getting drunk and telling Spencer to shove all of his success with his career up his ass.

"You know that's not what I mean, Hays. I don't want you to be uncomfortable at my wedding," Ryan continues.

He's conflicted, I can tell, but it's hard to pretend I'm not dying inside either. Even though I'm doing my best to tell them that I'm fine, only I know how the prospect of seeing Spencer again is keeping me awake at night.

"I won't be. There will be hundreds of people present. I won't even have to be close to him." I repeat what Lauren said to me earlier. It is a huge possibility indeed. Seeing Spencer from a distance and having to talk to him are two different things.

I can feel Chad's gaze on me, but I don't dare look at him.

Obviously, I never wanted his friendship with Spencer to get off track, so I tried the best I could to keep any information from getting to him, but he's not stupid. Even though he doesn't know what happened between us, I know he's worried about us being in the same room again. I can't blame him.

My mother clears her throat, pouring more coffee for Alice and my dad. "Alice, dear, is there anything else you need help with? Oscar can drive us around, and I can leave the bakery for a few hours."

I'm so grateful that she changed the subject that I almost let out a sigh of relief. I finally get to my breakfast, putting everything I can grab on my plate, but my stomach is telling me it's not a good idea. I'm suddenly not that hungry anymore, but dismissing my mom's delicious food would be a waste—especially her pie.

Alice shakes her head, her perfect blonde locks swooshing over her shoulders. "Oh, not at all, Norah. You already did a lot by letting me skip work today. Everything is settled. Ryan just has to pick up his tux. Right, baby?"

Ryan makes a noise similar to a grunt, his mouth too full to reply without getting chastised by Mom.

"Well, I hate to interrupt this family bonding moment, but I have to go to the newspaper before I get fired." I rise from my seat, taking a last sip of coffee and waving goodbye to everyone.

I rush to the sink to wash my plate and mug and run upstairs to get dressed, not feeling very enthusiastic about work today. However, I do want to get out of the house and avoid the pitiful stares I'm getting from my family. I won't be able to handle another day filled with questions about Spencer and how I feel about seeing him after seven years.

You'd think it's weird that I never saw him again after he left to study in LA, especially with his sister still living in Missoula. Back then, I used to find excuses to come home from college every week or two–doing the laundry in the dorms was a pain, and I missed my mom's food more frequently than not–but whenever I heard Spencer would be back to visit his family and hang out with my brother, I managed to stay at Poppy's—my best friend—or at the dorm, so I didn't have to risk bumping into him.

Half an hour later, I arrive at the newspaper and take a deep breath before walking inside, preparing myself for the day.

Poppy spots me as soon as I cross the threshold and rushes toward me, her long, wavy auburn hair bouncing up and down.

"Isn't it lame that we work at the local newspaper, and all our boss wants to know about is your brother's wedding? She wants ME to write an article about it, as if people don't have more important things to read about," she complains when she approaches me, her beautiful green eyes rolling up as she tells me the news.

"Seriously?" I ask with a frown. "Does she really want you to cover the wedding while being completely drunk and not in control of your mental faculties?" I tease, laughing at her shocked face. I drop my head back when I see her discreetly flipping the bird at me.

"You're ridiculous," she mumbles, annoyed. "I'd think this is stupid if I were you."

"I do," I agree, pulling myself together. "But it is what it is. It's a small town; people like to talk. Besides, you can do this with your eyes closed."

"What about while being hungover? Because that's how I'll be after tomorrow. Or maybe I'll be comforting your whiny ass after you realize you lost the most handsome man this town ever saw."

I halt in my steps, turning to look at her. "Meaning?" I challenge with clenched teeth.

Poppy tosses her hands in the air in a surrendering pose. "You know what I mean... I know you last saw Spencer in another lifetime, but can you imagine how hot he must be now, at twenty-eight? Girl, I don't envy you."

I shrug, biting my tongue and preventing myself from telling her to fuck off. "It was his loss, not mine."

"That is true." Poppy concedes, nodding eagerly at me.

"Besides, he can be as hot as he wants. I couldn't care less," I carry on, too pissed off to stop now. "I bet all he can find in LA are women wanting to take advantage of him and his stupid position at the record label."

"And do you think he's complaining about that?" Poppy teases, nudging me in the ribs.

"It must get tiring some days, don't you think? Spencer used to want a big family. I don't see him giving up on that. But again, what do I know? I thought I knew him, and I was damn wrong." I head for my office, Poppy hot on my tail.

"Sorry, girl. I was just joking to ease the mood, but I guess that was a bit cruel of me."

"It's fine. I'm just overreacting. My family went all 'intervention' on me this morning, and they've been cornering me ever since Ryan announced he was going to get married. I'm still having a hard time handling the idea of seeing Spencer, and they're not helping," I muse, finally getting to my office. I toss myself into the chair behind my desk, leaning back and closing my eyes.

"Shit, that must have sucked. And I totally understand why you feel this way. You're not overreacting. You're just being cautious and protective of your heart. What's wrong with that?" Poppy asks, sitting across from me and holding my gaze.

I sigh. "I hate to be this person, but I just can't shake this bad feeling. I don't know what to think or feel. Seems stupid to be thinking about this after so long, don't you agree?"

"No, I don't. Every person feels different about different situations. Only you know what you went through, even if we were all there to watch it. But you have nothing to fear, okay? I'll be there with you the entire time. And if you need my 'come-and-rescue-me' superpower, all you have to do is blink. and I'll punch him in the face."

I chuckle, shaking my head at her. Poppy is such a loyal and reliable friend. I have no doubt she would do what she says if I ask her to.

But she is right. I have nothing to fear. I'll be there, enjoying my brother's big day, pretending Spencer isn't there, and it will be over before I know it.

But fate is a funny thing, isn't it? It never really goes the way we expect it to.

Neither does it fail to surprise you—for better or worse.

CHAPTER TWO

he next morning, Lauren and I go out to pick up our maid of honor dresses. Since Alice doesn't have a sister, she chose us both to stand up with her. Her brother will be Ryan's best man alongside Chad.

Lauren and I picked two simple, but incredibly beautiful, silk olive green dresses. After the ceremony at the church, we'll go back to our family ranch where the reception is being held. I wasn't so sure about it at first, but now I can see it's actually a good idea. I know every single shortcut in there, and if I want to—or need to—I can hide or escape to the house in no time.

"Aren't you glad Alice picked a color that looks good on both of us?" Lauren asks, admiring herself in the mirror while we do our final fitting to make sure there isn't anything to be sewed or fixed before we take them home.

I admire myself too, seeing the fabric hold my curves in the right places. I do look nice in it. My chestnut-brown hair doesn't stand out as much as Lauren's, but I like the way it accentuates my fair skin and the freckles on my nose—which I'm actually fond of.

I ignore the way my brain reminds me of how much Spencer used to love my freckles too and nod at Lauren. "Yeah, green suits us."

I can see Lauren's eyes darting from my face to the floor and back to me, as if she wants to say something but is not sure if she should. She has a good heart and is compassionate. She's a good sister to me. We've always been close, and I trust her with all my heart, even if sometimes she can be super nosy.

However, I can tell she's genuinely worried about me, so I take a deep breath and decide to address this in a serious way for once.

"I am okay, pony." That's what I've called her ever since she was three and begged Dad to get her a pony for her birthday. It began as teasing, but eventually, it became a thing between us, and she started calling me that too. Now, it's just a loving nickname we use with each other. "Really."

"I know you are! It's just that…" She sighs, turning to look at me face-to-face instead of through the mirror. "I remember how this was a terrible period for you, and I don't want to see you go down that hole again."

I smile fondly at her, grabbing her hands and squeezing them. "Look, I know you're all worried about me, and I do appreciate it. But I'm stronger now. I won't let him get to me. And I promise you that, if I feel somewhat sad or uncomfortable, you'll be the first to know, okay?"

"Okay…" Lauren finally seems convinced, and I drop my shoulders. "It's a promise. You tell me, and I'll punch Spencer in the face and take you away from the party, hear me?"

I chuckle, nodding at her. "Poppy said she'd do the same thing."

"Poppy knows the deal," Lauren adds with a shrug, turning her attention back to her reflection in the mirror. "I love you, pony. And you can count on me any time. You know that."

I smile at her, ignoring the sudden lump forming in my throat. Lauren and I don't normally show affection toward each other, rather choosing to show our love through bickering and teasing, but I know she loves me and will do anything to see me happy. Just as I am there for her no matter what. Knowing I have Poppy and Lauren on my side is enough for me to put my fears and insecurities behind me and focus on the day ahead.

This is an important moment for my brother and my family, and a guy shouldn't be able to ruin this for me. So, with this renewed determination in mind, I take off my dress and head back home with my sister so we can start getting ready.

The ranch is pure chaos by the time we return, and after checking if anyone needs my assistance, I go to my bedroom to take a shower and get my hair and makeup done. Lauren rushes to her old room, saying she'll meet me when she needs help with her eyeliner—something she can't get right no matter how many video tutorials she watches.

Thankfully, I'm skilled at that.

It takes us three hours to be completely ready and waiting by the front door.

"We're going to be late," Dad complains, waiting by his truck with the driver's door open. "Just get in and let's go!" He slides behind the steering wheel, and I climb onto the back seat.

"Where's Chad?" Lauren asks, following me while staring back at the house, searching for our brother.

"He's picking Ryan up, remember?" I answer as we watch Mom walk out of the house looking like a Hollywood queen.

She gets inside the car. When Dad kisses her in front of us, Lauren and I fake vomiting, and after that, we finally head out.

People say that weddings make us emotional and thoughtful, and well, they aren't lying about that. It's inevitable to imagine certain scenarios when you cross those beautiful old wooden doors and spot the colorful glass windows around, the painted ceilings, and the majestic and ethereal architecture of the church.

I would be lying if I said I never imagined being the one walking down this aisle. I lost count of how many times in the past I pictured my wedding day with Spencer. I don't regret that. I was too in love, completely infatuated by him, so I really thought we would one day be husband and wife.

But life had other plans for us.

As Mom and Dad walk to the back of the church to meet Father

Joseph, Lauren and I head toward Chad, Ryan, and Poppy, who are gathered in a corner, talking enthusiastically.

"Hey, guys. What's up?" Lauren greets them as soon as we approach them.

"Everything all right?" I ask, taking in their faces.

"Yep," Chad replies with a grin. "Just giving Ryan the last chance to run away from this. I can distract Mom and Dad, and you can distract Alice."

I throw my hands up, smiling at them. "Don't count on me for that, bro. Alice can be really scary when she wants to be."

"You're not wrong about that," Ryan muses in a low voice. He seems a bit nervous, fidgeting with his fingers.

I look around, making sure no one is close enough to hear us, and stare back at him. "You're sure about this? It would be okay if you aren't," I say softly.

Chad and Lauren nod eagerly. Poppy remains quiet, and I know that even though she's known my family since forever, she doesn't feel like this is a conversation she should be part of.

Ryan kindly smiles at me, and warmth spreads through my heart as I realize this is it. My oldest brother is getting married and starting his own family. This gives me a bitter feeling, knowing life will be somewhat different now. I always struggle with changes. Ryan doesn't live at the house anymore, so it's not like it will be a drastic change, but still... The realization that he will have his own family now weighs on me.

"I'm sure of it. Alice is the love of my life, and I can't wait to marry her," he replies. "Thank you for being so supportive, though. All of you," he adds, glancing at our siblings. "It means a lot to know I'll have you all by my side no matter what."

"Of course, man. That's what we're here for," Chad remarks cheerfully, patting Ryan on the shoulder. "Just don't show up at my place when Alice sends you to sleep on the couch. I might have someone over."

"Ew, Chad. You should man up and stop being such a playboy," Lauren complains, rolling her eyes like she's repulsed. She lowers her voice. "No one will ever want to marry you when you have your dick inside a different woman every night."

Chad seems offended for a moment, but then widens his grin, turning to Poppy. "Poppy would marry me, wouldn't you?"

She chuckles, unbothered by his flirtation. "Of course. In your dreams I would."

I cover my mouth with my hand, preventing a loud laugh from coming out. Chad's expression is priceless, and we all have to do our best not to make a scene inside the church.

Our bonding moment is soon interrupted when Mom and Dad rush us to the entrance so the ceremony can start. I notice immediately that Spencer isn't around. I'm starting to wonder if he decided not to come. It can't be a comfortable thing for him to do either.

As I walk down the aisle to get to my maid of honor position by the altar, I spot Spencer's sister, Aubrie, with her husband and daughter, and I briefly nod at them. They have always been nice to me, and there's no reason for me to be anything but kind to them. They didn't break my heart and throw the pieces to the wind like Spencer did.

By the time Alice shows up, looking divine in her white perfect princess wedding dress, my brain gives me a break and forgets about Spencer. For a moment, all I can pay attention to is this beautiful bride walking toward her husband-to-be, looking as happy as I've ever seen her, the future ahead of them so uncertain, but at the same time, so secure.

If the expression on my brother's face is any indication of how much he loves her, I believe they will be fine.

But then, something shifts my focus. In my peripheral vision, I can see someone sneaking in through the side door, walking toward one of the last pews as careful and silent as a person could ever be.

And I make the mistake of turning my head to see who it is.

My heart immediately begins to race as I spot those piercing blue eyes I used to love so much. It's been seven years since I last saw him, but he's only gotten better. More handsome, more muscular, more... perfect.

Shit.

Of course, Spencer would get better with time. At seventeen, he was already considered a freaking super model. His athletically built body is even bigger now, more muscular and toned. I can tell even with all the layers of his suit covering it. His chiseled jawline is as sharp as ever. He now has a bit of a stubble covering it, making him look more mature and grown up than I remember him ever being.

I don't remember ever seeing Spencer in a suit before, or maybe I did. At his parents' funeral, perhaps? But in that situation, I was definitely not in the mood to notice how handsome he was in one. His dark hair is a bit longer too, a bit messy but still presentable, as if he's trying to be both professional and casual at the same time.

And there it is, his dimpled smile.

God, how can one man be this perfect?

I hate that he's gotten more handsome with time.

Spencer sits on the pew, being cautious not to make any noise or disrupt anyone else watching, and that's when I notice it—the woman coming in behind him and sitting by his side, her dazzling smile blinding me.

Spencer brought someone. A woman. To my brother's wedding.

I feel this rage boiling inside me, even though I have no idea why this bothers me so much.

Maybe because he should have been more thoughtful than to bring a date to his ex-girlfriend's brother's wedding?

Perhaps he doesn't care about me enough to think I would care that he brought someone else. It's been seven years, after all. I shouldn't be mad or annoyed by it. But for some reason beyond my comprehension, I am.

I shake my head discreetly, trying to divert my attention back to the ceremony taking place in front of me.

My gaze meets Chad's from across the altar, and by the way he's looking at me, his brows slightly creased, I can tell he also spotted his friend walking in. And he also noticed my reaction. I really hope I didn't make it too obvious. The last thing I need right now is to prove them all right. I said I'd be fine, and I intend to be exactly that.

I just need a bit of champagne to help me.

For the rest of the ceremony, I do my best not to take my eyes off the couple getting married. I can feel my palms sweating as I hold Alice's bouquet, but I don't dare make a move. I almost let out a sigh of relief when we're finally allowed to walk out of the church. As soon as I'm free of my maid of honor duties, I rush toward Dad's truck, praying that I don't bump into anyone on the way.

I just need to get to the reception. I'm not someone who usually drowns herself in alcohol to forget a problem, but tonight I will be.

There's no way I can get through this evening sober. Not if it means I might have to talk to Spencer and be introduced to his girl-friend. Or wife.

Oh, God!

She can't be his wife, right? Chad would've mentioned it to me if his best friend—my ex-boyfriend—had gotten married. He'd have gone to the wedding himself.

Unless Spencer eloped. But that doesn't sound like something he would do. But again, what do I know about him? I'm a completely different person now. He might be as well.

I'm overthinking it, I know. I'm cursing myself as to how easily I'm influenced by his presence. In the end, I've ended up doing exactly what I was afraid I'd do—freaking out about Spencer.

"Girl, it looks like you've seen a ghost," Poppy notes as she walks toward me. I'm leaning against Dad's truck, waiting for them to stop greeting the guests so we can drive home for the reception.

"I kind of did, didn't I?" I mumble in a low voice.

"I'm so sorry, girl. I know this must be really hard for you," she says sympathetically, squeezing my arm.

"How are you doing, pony? The nerve of this guy to bring a date." Lauren shows up, the frown on her face warming my heart. It makes me feel really good to know I have them backing me up.

"I mean, it's been several years right? He wouldn't expect me to be annoyed by him bringing a date to my brother's wedding." I'm trying to convince myself of that, but it helps to know my sister feels the same way I do.

"Whatever. He should be more considerate," she adds with a grimace.

"I agree. But hey…" Poppy turns to face me completely, grabbing me by the shoulders and forcing me to look at her. "Tonight is about your brother and your family. Screw Spencer and his Gigi Hadid-wannabe girlfriend. We're going to celebrate and drink our faces off."

I chuckle, grateful for them. "Thanks, guys. It means a lot to me that you're all so supportive and not thinking I'm being a bitch about this."

"Are you kidding?" Lauren widens her eyes at me as if everything I've just said is utter nonsense. "You're not being a bitch about anything, and you're entitled to feel the way you're feeling."

Lauren can be so mature sometimes it astonishes me. She's always been the goofy, social butterfly in the family—alongside Chad—but it still impresses me when she has these moments of wisdom and maturity. I should be the one being mature about it all, but well, I guess I'm not.

Mom and Dad finally appear, and we get to the party before Ryan and Alice finish taking photos outside of the church. Needless to say, the first thing I do when I walk inside is grab a glass of champagne. The ranch is starting to get filled with people quickly, so I try my best to keep myself occupied, greeting family members I haven't seen in ages and engaging in conversation with some old friends.

Either it's the champagne or the atmosphere around me, but I manage to relax and enjoy the party. The music also helps a lot, and I dance until my feet start to hurt. At this point, I'm already drunk. Not out of my mind, or unable to stand upright, but slightly happy and giddy.

"I think I need to pee," I say to no one in particular since the music is really loud and Lauren, Poppy, and a few of my cousins aren't really paying attention to me.

"What?" Lauren asks, not looking at me but tilting her head to the side so she is nearer.

"I am going to the bathroom!" I yell close to her ear.

"All right, do you need me to go with you?" She turns to face me, her brows raised while she waits for my answer.

I shake my head, dismissing her with my hands. "Of course not. I'll be right back."

Lauren nods, returning her attention to the waiter passing by with a tray filled with glasses of champagne. I ponder grabbing another one, but my bladder is hurting at this point, so I turn on my heel, heading to the closest bathroom.

Thankfully, it's unoccupied. By the time I leave and stop in front of the sink to wash my hands, I'm a bit surprised at my reflection in the mirror. My hair is a little sweaty and messy, not to mention that the hairstyle I put together for the ceremony is far gone by now. My makeup was worth every penny because it's still intact. But for some reason I can't point out—maybe it's something in my eyes that looks a bit glassy and distant—I look like shit.

I shake my head, slapping my cheeks lightly to shove some sense of reality back into my brain. I would try washing my face with cold water, but that'd ruin my makeup for good, and I'm not ready to go to bed yet. So, after straightening my dress, fixing my hair, and applying some lipstick, I feel ready to return to the party.

But when I decide to take a shortcut through the back door into the kitchen, I encounter the only person I have been avoiding the entire night.

Spencer Bailey.

CHAPTER THREE

It's not like I can pretend I don't see him there.

He's literally in my way.

Spencer leans against the fence outside of the kitchen door, one hand shoved in his pants pocket and the other holding a glass of whiskey—or whatever that amber liquid may be.

I freeze in my tracks, unsure of what to do. He hasn't noticed me yet, but if I walk back inside the house, it'll be too obvious that I'm trying to avoid him. I don't need to be this pathetic in front of him. I look around, trying to spot his skinny blonde sidekick, but she is nowhere in sight.

He is taking in the surroundings, almost as if he's checking if everything is still the way he probably remembers it being in the past. And when he turns his head to the other side, that's when his eyes find me.

I take a deep breath, preparing myself for the next moment.

There's no escaping, no turning back now.

Spencer looks slightly surprised when he spots me, but he does a better job than me by hiding it almost immediately.

"Hayden," he simply says. His tone is even, free of any suspicious indicator that he's uncomfortable by seeing me. But it still does something to me to hear him say my name after all this time.

"Hey," I reply, afraid that he might notice the awkward silence if I take too long to answer.

"I—wow, okay…" He clears his throat, starting to show signs of his uneasiness. "I prepared myself for this moment, but I wasn't expecting it to be like this."

I fight the urge to frown. He prepared himself for this moment? What moment? Seeing me? Why does he look so unsettled? Am I crazy to think he isn't as cool with it as I thought he was?

"How have you been?" he finally asks, composing himself.

I shrug, trying to dismiss the tension in my shoulders. "Fine. You?"

Spencer nods mildly, stepping away from the fence and taking a step forward. It's evident he is not taking any chances by approaching me, unsure of how I'll react, and I appreciate him for that. I'm also not sure how I'd react if he came too close. "I've been all right. It's been so long…" he trails off, looking at me expectantly.

"Yeah, seven years," I point out, as if he doesn't know. Maybe he's forgotten though. Maybe he hasn't been tracking it like I have.

"Seven years," he repeats, lowering his voice.

This is so fucking awkward. I had imagined this scenario in my head so many times before, and in all of them, I'd tell him the truth to his face, show him how he hurt me, how he shattered my heart and left me here, alone, with no hope for the future, with this hatred in my heart that I can't forget. And now…

Now, I can barely think. I have so many things choked down my throat, and this is the perfect opportunity to say them, but I can't make myself do it.

Spencer looks at me with his piercing blue eyes, expecting me to say something, but I can't.

And I can't make myself move either.

"You look happy," I finally mutter, and I curse myself inwardly.

Of all the things I had to say, I said he looks happy?

What the fuck is that supposed to mean, Hayden?

Spencer chuckles, or forces out a chuckle. It doesn't match his expression, though. He does not look happy. Instead, he looks... despondent?

"I am happy to *BE* here," he emphasizes, looking around with a melancholy expression.

"Yeah... Hm, well, I think we should go back to the party, huh? Your date is probably missing you, and I told Lauren I'd be back soon..."

I hate myself. Why can't I get a hold of my tongue for once in my life? Now, he's going to think I'm jealous.

Phenomenal job, Hayden.

Spencer looks taken aback, his eyes widening almost imperceptibly. But I know him too well to miss it, no matter how hard he tries to hide it from me. That's one of the things that apparently didn't change about him. Spencer always tries to hide his true feelings. He doesn't normally allow himself to be vulnerable with others. And there are some traits that are noticeable in his body language that always give him away.

You just have to know where to look.

"Look, Hayden... I wanted to talk to you since, you know...things happened so fast, and we—"

"Let's not do this, Spencer." I cut him off. I don't mean to sound rude, but the words come out harsher than I intended. "I'm glad you managed to come to the wedding. Everyone is really happy, especially Ryan and Chad. Thanks for doing that for them."

"Of course, I wouldn't miss it for the world," he mutters.

"Good. I'll head back now." I point in the direction of the party and resume my walk, circling the house and focusing on putting one foot in front of the other without stumbling and falling.

My brain is full of a whirlwind of thoughts and memories, and I feel slightly nauseated. Damn those glasses of champagne.

Why do I feel so unlike myself? I expected this moment to be awkward, but this is something else.

It takes me a second to pull myself together, and when I finally find Lauren and Poppy, they are no longer on the dance floor, but rather, they're engaged in a group chat with Chad, Ryan, Alice, a few cousins of ours, and… Spencer's girlfriend.

Great! Just what I needed right now.

Poppy waves at me to come over, and I ponder pretending I haven't seen her for a moment. *Do I really want to bond with Spencer's girlfriend?* However, I can't run away from this. The party is almost over, and soon, I won't have to worry about Spencer, his girl, or anything related to them. I'll be back to my normal, boring life, and it'll be as if nothing happened.

I grab a glass of champagne on my way there, taking a huge gulp from it, and by the time I get to their circle, the glass is almost empty.

It takes me a while to understand what they are talking about. Some words stand out to me, but I can't force my brain to make sense of what they are saying. Everyone seems entertained by something Chad is babbling about, but I'm too busy looking around and trying to spot the waiter again to grab another drink.

That's when I spot him, Spencer, standing right behind. I smile at the waiter and grab two glasses at once while Spencer joins us. His girlfriend flashes him a smile and wraps her arm around his waist, and I feel some stares being thrown my way, but I ignore them, taking another sip from my cold champagne.

"Girl, you might want to take it easy on that, or you'll have a hell of headache tomorrow," Lauren whispers in my ear. But honestly, at this point, I don't care.

"Yeah, I already have one, and it has nice legs, arms wrapped around my ex-boyfriend, and you conspiring with it." I shoot her a hard glance, my eyes narrowed.

My sister shrugs, looking sorrowful. "They ambushed me and started talking about this stupid game where they met each other. What should I have done? Leave?"

"Exactly," I murmur, more to myself than to her.

"Is everything okay, though? You took a while to come back from the bathroom," she points out.

"I bumped into you-know-who on my way back," I reply, focusing my attention on some guests on the dance floor. I look at Lauren when I hear her gasp, and the way her jaw drops almost makes me want to laugh out loud. I would if I wasn't so pissed and buzzy right now.

"You…talked to him? How did it go?" she urges me, doing her best to keep her voice low with all the excitement clearly bubbling inside of her.

"Can we not talk about it here? He's literally right in front of us," I note, rolling my eyes at her.

Lauren looks ahead, and then at me, nodding. "Yeah, and he's looking at you."

I gulp, ignoring the weird sensation in my stomach. I shouldn't like hearing that Spencer is looking at me while he has his bimbo glued to his torso, but alcohol is giving me the green light tonight.

"That's funny, Hayden once did a two-week internship in LA for this newspaper. Have you met?" My ears perk up when I hear my cousin, Sara, mentioning my name, and I look up to see what they are talking about.

"You did an internship at the *Los Angeles Times*?" Spencer's girlfriend asks me, sounding and looking way too excited for my taste.

"You've been to LA?" Spencer shoots at the same time, looking surprised and somewhat…offended?

I clear my throat, looking at Poppy and Lauren for some emotional support. They are both watching the scene with their breath held, and Chad's eyes are going from the couple to me and back to them as if he's watching a tennis match. "Hm, yeah… It was just for two weeks though. Why?"

"I worked at the *LA Times* for a few months too. Maybe we met at some point? Millie Carlton? Ring a bell?" the girl presses with amusement..

"Ah, I don't think so. Sorry," I say with a forced smile. "Like I said, it was something really quick."

My eyes fall on Spencer, and by the way he's looking at me with a huge frown, I know what he's thinking. I went to LA and didn't contact him. Honestly, that was an opportunity that came up during college, and at that time, I did everything I could to become a great journalist. Not taking the opportunity would have been stupid. And truthfully, I never even considered the possibility of bumping into Spencer back then. Los Angeles is huge, after all.

And what did he expect? That I'd call him after years and tell him I was in the city, so we should go out for a drink and catch up like old times?

Ha! As if!

"So, Spencer, what have you been up to? I met your sister at the bookstore the other day, and she said you got some billionaire contracts at the record label recently. Does that mean we officially have a rich friend now?" my cousin Phil asks.

Spencer looks away from me, chuckling and taking a sip of his whiskey. "Nah, I'm not as important as my sister seems to believe I am."

"That's not true, baby," Millie chimes in, and God, have I mentioned I hate her voice? "Record labels have been fighting over him for years now. Everyone wants a piece of him."

I think I'm going to vomit. My head is spinning like a fucking tornado, and my stomach feels really nauseated. I believe I won't be able to keep everything inside for much longer.

"I think I'm done for tonight," I tell Lauren and Poppy in a low voice, but by the way Ryan, Chad, and Spencer dart their gaze at me with worry coating their faces, I assume I didn't speak as low as I intended.

"Is everything okay, Hays?" Ryan asks somberly.

"Are you feeling well?" Chad adds with a frown.

I roll my eyes dramatically, dismissing them. "I'm…fine. I just had too much to drink, and I feel a bit sick. I'll head inside. Nothing to worry about."

I turn to leave, and my heels get stuck on the soft grass beneath me, making me stumble and lean on Lauren for support.

"Oops, sorry, pony." My voice sounds so high-pitched and annoying right now, I must be drunker than I realized.

"Hayden," Chad calls me in a serious tone. "I'll take you inside."

"I'm okay. It was nothing. I don't need help getting to my room. It's not that far."

"You can barely stand upright," he argues. "Judging from the number of glasses you've drained in the last ten minutes, I wouldn't be surprised if you fell headfirst up the stairs."

"Whatever." The word comes out of my mouth in a funny way, and I laugh at myself. "Sorry, guys. If you'll excuse me…it was lovely to see you all. Ryan and Alice, I'm so happy for you. I really am. I love you."

Alice smiles fondly at me, trying to hide her amusement by seeing me drunk while covering her mouth with her hand. Ryan looks at me with a gloomy expression, but I don't care. I didn't do anything to ruin his wedding–like I promised. Getting drunk and being taken to my room isn't exactly making a scene.

"Do you need help?" Lauren and Poppy ask at the same time while Chad wraps his arm around my waist and forces me to stand still. But instead, I feel myself leaning more and more against him, his supportive body serving as a wall to my lazy and sluggish one.

"Nope," I reply, allowing Chad to take me inside. The effect of the alcohol escalated so quickly that I didn't even realize I was this drunk until I notice people watching me being chaperoned to my room by my brother.

The silence inside the house makes me feel a bit less anxious and nauseated, even though I still feel like I might puke at any moment now.

"You might want to swing me a bit less," I warn Chad as he takes me upstairs.

He sighs, shaking his head. "Geez, Hays, why did you have so much to drink?"

"What? It's Ryan's wedding!" I retort. "I am happy for him and was celebrating. Didn't *YOU* drink?"

"A couple of glasses. Not the whole bottle."

"Well, I might have drank more than that," I point out with a chuckle.

"You're going to feel like shit tomorrow," he notes.

"I kind of already do," I tell him, flashing him a wide, forced smile while he opens the door to my room. I escape from his arms, walking inside and heading toward the bed, stumbling a bit as Chad closes the door behind him.

I toss myself on the mattress, not caring to take off my heels or dress, and too tired to care about my makeup. I can worry about that in the morning.

"Hays," Chad calls to me softly. I feel the mattress shifting as he sits down close to me, but I can't gather the courage to open my eyes and see how he's probably looking at me with his judgmental eyes.

"Don't judge me, brother. I'm already doing that for the both of us," I say before he starts a conversation I know I'm not ready for. "I'm really sorry, you know? I never meant for it to be this way."

Chad is the one person I avoid the most when the topic is Spencer—for obvious reasons, and he knows that. I feel bad because I love him, and we've always gotten along so well, but I can't allow myself to be completely honest with him. I don't want him to resent me for ruining a lifetime friendship.

"You have nothing to be sorry for. And I would never judge you. Why would you even say that?" he asks.

"I know you're worried, but you don't have to be. Your friend seems happy, and so am I. There's nothing to be concerned about. I'm fine."

There's silence in the room, and for a moment, I wonder if he left. But I'm drunk, not deaf, and he certainly isn't so quiet as to leave the room without me hearing the door being closed.

"You don't seem fine, Hays. I know seeing him after so long must suck for you, and I am really sorry that you have to go through this," he states carefully. I knew he was trying to muster the courage to bring up the subject, but this is certainly not the right moment for me.

I force my eyes open, finding Chad looking at me with pain engraved on his face. It makes my heart ache, but what can I do? It's not like I wanted any of this to happen. In fact, if I could go back seven years ago, I might have done things differently. But now, well, it's too late.

"Why is everyone so worried about me, huh? I'm not that weak. I might have been once, but I'm not the same person I was anymore, okay?" I say, anger starting to get the best of me, my voice rising up an octave. "I know I looked pathetic back then, but that's just life." I choke down my tears I didn't even realize were coming. And Chad seems to have noticed that too because he looks slightly surprised.

"Hays, I—"

"It sucked, and I tried to hate your friend for so long... I just couldn't. But I don't need...to be reminded of that every time his name comes up...not by my family, anyway," I carry on, sobbing and choking on my own words, failing to get a hold of myself. I knew that champagne would be my doom. "No one seems to...care about Spencer...because he probably never suffered the...way I did, right?"

Chad doesn't say anything, but rather, pulls me into a tight embrace. His hands caress my hair while he tries to calm me down with soothing shushes. I hate crying. Especially in front of others. Maybe I've been too stressed out and didn't realize my anxiety piling up with everything going on lately and the prospect of seeing Spencer again for the first time in years. Alcohol must have helped me loosen up, but I should have stopped a few glasses ago.

"I am so sorry," he whispers. "I really am."

"It's not your fault," I tell him.

"Still, I wanted to do something to protect you, but I... I didn't know what to do," he confesses. He sounds so hurt, sorrowful even. It makes me feel bad for him. I never blamed him or even thought he had picked a side. I'm not unfair, and I never tried to make him feel bad about his friendship. That's why I never talked to him about this.

"You didn't have to do anything, Chad. You're my brother, and I love you." I pull back from him, feeling more composed now. I wipe my wet cheeks and take a deep breath before continuing. "I'd never forgive myself if you resented me, or if you thought I wanted you to pick a side. I would never do that. I hope you know that."

"Of course, I do." Chad seems to be pondering something for a moment, and I almost think he'll give up, but then he straightens up and stares at me with a hooded gaze. "And don't think you're pathetic because you suffered, Hays. Spencer wasn't in a good spot either, I can tell you that much. I've never seen you two look so wrecked, and it killed me to watch it and not be able to do anything."

It's the first time I've heard him say anything about how Spencer dealt with that moment in our lives. I don't know why it surprises me to know Spencer suffered as much as I did, but it does.

"I know you've been avoiding him, and you have every right to do so, but I think you might have to rethink your methods. I don't want you turning into an alcoholic every time you end up in the same room as him," Chad teases, nudging me in a playful way.

"Why do you say that?" I frown at him, not following it. "I won't become an alcoholic for drinking at my brother's wedding. And after today, I won't have to see Spencer again, so you have nothing to fear."

Chad shifts uncomfortably on my bed, scratching his neck and messing up his hair.

"What?" I press, feeling the nausea coming back.

"Well, Spencer just told us that he'll be staying in town for a while," he replies, the words coming out of his mouth in slow motion.

"Meaning? For a while as in a couple of days?"

This can't be happening.

Chad shakes his head, and I gulp down.

"No. As in for good. He's moving back, Hays."

CHAPTER FOUR

I have just enough time to jump from the bed and rush to the bathroom before I let out all the champagne into the toilet. I'm glad I also managed to close the door behind me so Chad doesn't have to witness this humiliating moment in my life.

"Hays, are you okay?" His voice is muffled by the closed door, and I'm still too nauseated to give him a coherent answer, so I just grunt instead, hoping he takes that as a 'yes.'

I wait a couple of minutes to make sure there's nothing left inside me, and then I get up from the floor, brushing my teeth and wiping my makeup off with a cleansing wipe. I feel a bit better now and ready to go to bed. I should get out of this dress and put on my pajamas, but I don't feel keen to do that. Maybe it won't be that bad to sleep in this.

I open the door to find Chad offering me a glass of water and an aspirin, the corner of his lips curled up in a grin.

"It'll make you feel better in the morning," he explains, handing me the pill.

I gulp it down, thanking him while heading for my bed. I decide against changing, and just toss myself on top of the duvet.

"Thanks for taking care of me, Chad," I murmur, my voice dragging and my mind starting to drift off.

"Anytime, sis. Call me if you need anything. I'll be outside."

The dreams I have—or should I call them nightmares?—make me toss and turn in my bed the whole night. In a couple of them, Spencer and I are still together, and we're so happy that it's frightening enough to make me sabotage our relationship and end things between us. In a few others, there are flashes of scenes where Spencer cheats on me with Millie, her annoying voice and stupid smile haunting me until the morning. But the one that stays in my head the entire day is a pretty vivid one—but it isn't just a dream, it is a memory. From when Spencer and I were still in high school.

I was at the end of my sophomore year by the time Spencer first caught my attention. He had been friends with Chad for a while since they both played on the football team, but I was younger than them, so I barely frequented the same places and parties. But on that day, everything changed.

Spencer noticed me. In a different way than just as his best friend's little sister. I was invited to this after game party, and I made sure to bring Poppy with me so I wouldn't feel left out. But Poppy hooked up with this cute guy she knew from math club, and I was left alone. Until Spencer came to my rescue.

He said he saw me standing there alone, and these parties were known for being dens of sharks preying on lonely girls, so he was doing my brother a favor by keeping an eye on me. Chad had gotten sick the previous day, so he didn't play nor came to the party.

And well, that was the first time Spencer and I spent some alone time together, and by the time he took me home, we shared our first kiss.

My entire life changed after that day.

Waking up isn't an easy thing to do. Partially because of these dreams, and partially because of the horrible hangover that hits me. Good thing I don't have to work today.

I ponder staying in bed, but I know Ryan and Alice will leave for their honeymoon later, and we all planned to have a family lunch before their departure. Also, I'm sure the ranch is a mess after the party last night, so Mom and Dad must need all the help they can get. Reluctantly, I force myself out of bed, heading for the shower. I step out of my maid of honor dress and into the shower, feeling the warm water cascading down my hair and back, washing away the irked feeling I have from yesterday.

While I wash my hair, I replay the scenes from the wedding, trying to fill in the voids left by the alcohol. My conversation with Spencer was awkward, to say the least, but I can't push away the small signs I spotted on his face whenever he looked at me.

He seemed hesitant, regretful, restrained…

And whenever Millie was close to him, hugging him or whispering things in his ear, he didn't look happy. Not in the way I remembered him being with me anyway.

Was I imagining it? Am I reading too much into it? Was I seeing what I subconsciously wanted to see?

A part of me was so angry at him for showing up like this, with someone else, trying to engage in a conversation about our past as if it had just happened. Another part of me, though, ached for him. It was like he never left. When I saw him there, standing alone, leaning against the fence, it was like no time had passed. It was like we were young again, and he was there, waiting for me so we could go out on a date to watch the stars and stay awake all night talking about our plans for the future.

A future we were supposed to share.

For a moment, all I wanted was to run to him, throw my hands around his neck, and tell him I never stopped loving him. That no matter what happened between us, it was in the past, and we could forget about it and move on.

But that's impossible. Not only because now he has someone else, but because there is a lot of emotional baggage involved—things that were said and done that neither of us can pretend never happened.

I step out of the shower, drying off and getting dressed. I grab a pair of jeans, a white shirt, and my old, worn out caramel cowboy boots. My hair is wet, and I consider blow drying it before leaving, but I'm in a bit of a rush, and I desperately need a cup of coffee, so I leave it wet. I grab my sunglasses, phone, and car keys before heading toward the door.

The commotion already happening in and out of the house catches me a bit off guard. I don't know what I was expecting, but it was definitely not this. It seems like the ranch was turned upside down during the night. There's a lot of people cleaning and organizing things, but still, it takes me aback for a moment.

"Hayden, sweetheart. How are you?" Mom comes rushing when I cross through the kitchen door. Breakfast is on at the table, but there's no one around other than her and Dad apparently. She hugs me tightly, pulling away to check my face and analyze me. "Are you feeling well? Chad told us you got sick last night."

"I'm fine. Just had too much champagne," I tell her with a smile. "Morning, Dad."

"Good morning, sunshine. Sunglasses, huh?" he teases, handing me a cup of coffee. The aroma of it is enough to boost me up.

I take it from his hand, taking a sip of the hot liquid. It immediately makes me feel better.

"Sit down and grab something to eat. You'll be good as new," Mom encourages me, pulling the chair for me. I do as she says, grabbing a waffle and shoving it into my mouth.

Since I had nothing to eat last night—which explains why the champagne had such a strong effect on me—I'm starving. Despite the buzz around the house, the kitchen seems relatively quiet without my siblings around.

"Is the rest of the family still asleep?" I ask, looking around to search for a familiar face.

"Ryan and Alice went home to pack and will be back for lunch. Lauren is sleeping in her old bedroom, and Chad went back to his apartment," Dad explains while reading today's paper. "Who wrote this article about the wedding?"

I snap my head in his direction, impressed at the speed that Poppy managed to have the article done. "Poppy was supposed to do it. What does it say?" I ask, curiously looking over his arm, but I can't read anything from this angle.

There's apparently a picture of the newlywed couple, but other than that, I have no idea what she wrote about.

"Yeah, nothing too revealing. Nothing about the groom's sister vomiting all over her brother while he took her to bed because she couldn't walk by herself," Dad jokes.

My jaw drops, astonished by his provocation. "I didn't vomit on anyone. Chad is such a liar!" I counter, huffing.

"I am no such thing." Chad walks in through the kitchen back door, looking refreshed and showered. His light-brown hair is wet, and he's wearing a flannel shirt and jeans, ready for whatever chores Mom throws at us. He grins at me, stealing the waffle from my hand before sitting across from me.

"You two should have been the journalists in the family," I snarl, rolling my eyes at him and Dad. "Lying suits you both."

Dad shrugs, unbothered, and my brother chuckles while Mom pours him some coffee.

"How did you sleep after you flushed your stomach down the toilet?" Chad asks, staring at me from over his cup.

"As good as one could considering I drank all the champagne from the party."

"Goodness, Hayden! Why did you drink so much?" My mom sounds shocked. What is the deal with everyone scolding me for drinking at my brother's wedding?

I look at her with narrowed eyes and smirk. "You're one to talk, Mom. From what I heard, you weren't a saint when you were young either."

"For your information, young lady, at your age I was already a mother. I didn't drink all the alcohol I could get my hands on," she retorts bitterly.

"Yeah, but you did when we were in college," Dad chimes in, his eyes still focused on the newspaper.

The outrage is evident on Mom's face, and Chad and I laugh, dropping our heads back while Dad pretends he didn't say anything.

While they bicker, Chad and I finish our breakfast. Eventually, Lauren walks in, looking just as bad as I feel. The only difference is that she is still wearing her dress. Her makeup is smeared across her face, making her look like a panda.

"Glad to know I'm not the only one feeling embarrassed today," I say, getting to my feet and grabbing my keys. Lauren flips me off since our parents aren't looking, and I laugh. "Is there anything for me to do downtown?"

"Yes, as a matter of fact, there is. I need to return these containers to the bakery. Could you drop them there for me?" Mom gets up and walks to the kitchen counter where three big boxes are piled up.

"Sure."

"Need some help, Hays? I can go with you," Chad offers.

"Yeah, if you're free."

"I also need you to pick up the roast chicken at Bob's restaurant. He said he'd prepare it for me since I won't have time to cook lunch today," Mom explains, handing me one of the containers..

It's really heavy, but I'm used to it, having helped at the ranch my entire life. Heavy lifting is just a daily chore around here, so it's not a problem. Chad joins us and grabs the remaining containers before we head to my car. It was Dad's before he got his new truck, but I'm so attached to it that even though it's old and begging for a makeover, I can't seem to be able to get rid of it. The paint is chipped, and the seats could use a new leather cover, but I like it the way it is.

Chad and I climb inside, and I start the car, driving off. We remain quiet for a few minutes, but it is not an uncomfortable silence. I know Chad is not judging me for what happened. He told me that yesterday, and deep down, I always knew he isn't like that. But I still feel bad about it.

"Sorry about last night," I finally say, my voice so low I wonder if he hears me.

I feel his eyes on me, but I keep mine on the road ahead.

"You have nothing to apologize for," he replies. "I know you were drunk, but I appreciate you opening up to me. We've never talked about it, and I respected you and your space, but it felt good to finally get it off my chest."

I shoot him a sideways glance, unsure of what to say. "Yeah, I guess you're right. Thank you for being such a good brother to me, and a good friend to Spencer. I know it wasn't easy for you, but I appreciate you not making things harder for us than they have to be."

Chad huffs, somewhat frustrated. "How can you be so kind-hearted? You should be blaming me for keeping my friendship with him, not thanking me for being nice to him."

I chuckle, finally reaching Mom's bakery and parking in front of it. "What can I say? That's how our parents raised us."

"Yeah, not me. I'd be cursing you if you stayed on my ex's side," Chad adds in a joking tone.

We take the containers inside the store and place them under the counter. While we're closing the door, two women who work at the city hall pass by us, so engaged in conversation that they don't even notice our presence.

"Did you hear he's coming back to Missoula?" one of them says cheerfully. "I wonder what made him want to return. He was success-ful, wasn't he?"

"Yeah. I wonder what it's going to be like now. The Jenkins girl must be devastated. I heard he took a date to the wedding?" a woman I recognize as Mrs. Hudson adds.

Chad clears his throat, drawing their attention to us. The look on their faces is laughable when they realize I'm the one they were talking about.

"Oh, hi there, kids. I heard your brother got married last night. Congratulations!" Mrs. Hudson mutters, evidently embarrassed that she got caught gossiping about us.

"Thank you," I reply with a wide smile. I'm not fond of small town gossip, but catching someone off guard is always so much fun. "I'll be sure to pass along your best wishes to him, Mrs. Hudson."

Chad and I nod, leaving them to it as we head back to the car. The two women leave in a hurry, eager to vanish from our sight.

"Congratulations my ass," Chad murmurs when we climb back inside.

I laugh, driving us to Bob's restaurant. I park in front of it, waiting for Chad to run inside and grab Mom's chicken so we can get back to the ranch for our family lunch.

"This city is pathetic with all this gossiping," Chad complains as soon as he gets back to the car.

"What happened?" I ask, driving us home.

"All everyone is talking about is Spencer's return. Like...why do they care? It's no one's business." He huffs, staring out the window.

"Speaking of which..." I begin, taking the opportunity to satiate my own curiosity. Last night I didn't have the chance to ask Chad about it, and now seems like a good moment. "What is the deal with him returning anyway? I thought he was successful and rich. Why would he leave LA and come back to Montana?"

I feel Chad's darting gaze turn toward me, but I keep my eyes on the road, not wanting to give myself away. I know he's probably thinking I'm interested in Spencer's life, but truth be told, I'm really just curious. It makes no sense that, after seven years, he'd return with no explanation at all.

"Apparently, he's tired of the big city life. He'll keep working from here while trying to start his own label," Chad replies matter-of-factly.

"He wants to start his own label?" It's hard to hide the surprise in my tone. Not that I don't think Spencer can do it, but only because I never thought he'd one day return to Missoula, let alone start a business here.

"Spencer has the money and contacts for it," Chad points out. "I don't see why it wouldn't work. He'd be closer to his family and friends."

"Right..." I concede.

This is my main reason for remaining in Missoula my whole life. My family means everything to me. I couldn't see myself moving to a completely different city, away from everyone I loved, to start anew. I wasn't brave enough to do it, and honestly, I wouldn't change my decision if I could go back in time. Maybe I would've handled things in a more mature way, but what did I know when I was seventeen?

"Is Millie coming with him?" The words sound too inquisitive for my taste. But I can't help it.

Chad shifts uncomfortably on the seat beside me and clears his throat before answering me. "Well, I think Millie is what we'd call a fling. So, no, I don't think she's coming with him."

I frown, suspicious. "A fling?"

"Why are you asking me these things?" Chad retorts, a bit bothered.

I gasp, darting an ugly stare in his direction. "What? I'm just curious. What's the big deal? You're his best friend. Who should I ask about it?"

"No one?" he suggests in an obvious way. "Why are you so interested in what he's doing? You're not…still into him, are you?"

I hit the brakes, frustration seeping into me.

"What is wrong with you? You're the one making a big deal out of this," I snap back, infuriated by his accusation.

"I just asked a question. You didn't have to almost kill us." Chad runs his fingers through his hair, equally irritated. "It was an honest question, Hayden. You overreacting like this makes me believe I may be right."

I open and close my mouth several times to give him an answer, but no words come out of it. I want to tell him he couldn't be more wrong, that not even in a million years, and if the salvation of humanity depended on it, I'd never get back with, or even consider, a life with Spencer again.

But, deep down, something within me holds my tongue, preventing me from speaking.

I can't still be into Spencer. That would be the stupidest mistake I could ever make. And that's saying a lot.

"Good Lord, you still like him," Chad utters in a whisper, his voice so low that I barely hear him.

"Shut up!" I burst, turning away from him and speeding up. Suddenly, all I want is to be away from Chad and his judgmental remarks. I know he's not technically judging me, but still… I don't like the way it makes me feel.

"Hays…"

"I said shut up," I repeat through clenched teeth. "Don't you dare speak about this with anyone, or I'll kill you."

I mean…what's the point in trying to deny it? Chad can read through me from miles away. I can keep lying to myself. I can tell him, and whoever else wants to hear it, that Spencer is in my past, and he means nothing to me anymore… but who would I be kidding?

I guess this was evident all along. Maybe that was the reason my family was so worried about me seeing him for the first time in years. They knew it'd hit me hard and make me realize that all the feelings I buried seven years ago are still here, dormant, but just as powerful as before.

Realization hurts like a physical blow.

I still love Spencer. Maybe I'm not in love with him anymore, but it's just a matter of time.

I know it.

And probably everyone else around me knows it too.

CHAPTER FIVE

The rest of the day is uneventful—as much as it can be when it comes to my family.

Lunch with everyone is nice, and I get to hear all about the party that I missed. No one brings up the ex-boyfriend topic, which makes me utterly grateful, although I have to ignore Chad's glances at me every once in a while when someone mentions Spencer or his family. But since it has nothing to do with me, I don't even flinch when I hear his name.

And because I slept poorly the night before, I retreat to bed earlier than usual, taking the opportunity to rest since I have to go to work tomorrow.

A week flies by, and eventually, the wedding buzz dissipates, bringing back my calm and peaceful days. I get to work in the morning, leave before the sun is down, go for an evening jog or horseback riding, and then return home for dinner. Sometimes, depending on their work schedule, Chad and Lauren join us back at the ranch, but mostly, it's just me, Mom, and Dad.

I miss the house being crowded, even though I don't say it much. It's fun to tease my siblings about having the place all to myself, but the truth is, this huge house feels so lonely without them. I wish Chad and Lauren would come back. I mean, our parents' room is on the other side of the house, and it's not like we don't have enough personal space.

I guess I just want to have more people around me every day.

On Friday night, as I'm leaving the newspaper building, I ponder inviting Lauren or Poppy over for some wine and a good chat, but I know Poppy has a date with this guy she met online, and Lauren is on duty until midnight, and I doubt she'll want to do anything other than crash in her bed when she's done.

I'd call Chad, but considering our last brother-and-sister chat last Sunday, I'm not sure I want to spend alone time with him. I know he'll pry about Spencer, and I'm not in the mood for it.

In fact, I'm trying to forget he's moving back to town. I haven't seen or bumped into him the entire week, and from what I heard, he went back to LA to grab his things, so he should be showing up sometime soon. I'm trying to be at peace with that. From now on, the possibility of me seeing him on a daily basis is huge.

As soon as I step outside the newspaper building, the cold evening breeze hits me. It's not winter yet, but it is starting to get impossible to be outside without a coat. A cloaked figure leaning against a car parked on the sidewalk catches my attention, and it takes me a few seconds to realize who it is.

Me and my big mouth. Did I summon him through my thoughts?

"Spencer? What are you doing here?" I ask, approaching him while wrapping my arms around my body to protect myself from the wind. Or maybe I'm trying to convince myself that the chills running through my body are related to the weather and not from seeing him again.

He looks so casual, dressed in gray sweatpants and a hoodie, and it reminds me so much of his teenage self. I curse myself inwardly for noticing how hot he looks now, more mature and handsome. This is not the time or place for me to have dirty thoughts about anyone. Especially not Spencer.

"Hey, I was hoping I'd find you," he replies, seemingly a bit flustered.

I try to hide my shock, but my face must give me away because he flashes his cute, dimpled smile at me, and I almost forget how to speak.

"Okay, did something happen?" I finally say.

"Not really. I just wanted to talk to you. We didn't have a chance at the wedding, and honestly, I don't think that was the right moment. I apologize for trying," he confesses with a shrug, shoving his hands into his pants pockets, looking a bit uneasy.

I shake my head, dismissing him. "It's fine. I shouldn't be so bitter about it either, so I'm sorry about that."

Spencer chuckles, his eyes piercing my soul as he stares at me. "You had every right to. It wasn't fair of me. So… can we talk?"

I look around, considering his offer.

Should we? If I go with him, what will we even talk about? Is there anything left to say? What would that even mean?

But it's so hard to say no to him when he's looking at me expectantly.

Ugh, how can he be so irresistible?

"I guess so," I concede.

Spencer opens the passenger door for me, and I hesitate. "My car is parked right there." I point at the corner where I found an empty spot close to the supermarket earlier today. I was planning on stopping there on my way out to grab that bottle of wine I've been dreaming about, but I guess my plans have just changed.

"I can drop you off here later," Spencer suggests. "I think it's wiser to go in just one car."

"Fine." I sigh, surrendering to his offer and climbing inside his fancy, shiny black car.

Spencer closes the door and circles the vehicle, and in the meantime, I notice how good it smells in here. In fact, I'm taken on a trip down memory lane as his cologne hits me like a slap in the face. He always smelled so good, so masculine, even when he was young.

I close my eyes for a second, allowing myself to be encapsulated by his scent and my old memories. The click of the driver's door being opened brings me back to reality, though. Spencer gets behind the wheel and looks at me with an amused glint in his eyes as he fastens his seatbelt.

"Any particular place you want to go?" he asks.

"Not really. I thought you had it all planned out when you came to meet me?" I tease, knowing his methodic, organized habits are probably something that haven't changed over time.

"Touché. I was just making sure you had a say in this," Spencer notes, starting the ignition and driving off. "But since you don't, I might have a suggestion."

For most of the drive, we sit in absolute silence. I want to say it is uncomfortable, or at least awkward, but surprisingly, it's not. Of course, my brain is convulsing with so many thoughts running around like birds trapped in a cage, but that's on me. I don't know what to expect from this conversation. I have no idea what Spencer can possibly want to talk about.

It's been so long. Will he even bring up our relationship? What would be the point?

I know where he's taking me before we get there. It used to be OUR spot by the river. It's a public space, but people don't normally go there, not at this time of the evening anyway.

I'm not sure how I feel about it. Is he doing this on purpose to bring back old emotions, or is he just honestly thinking this is a nice place for us to talk?

Am I reading too much into it?

Spencer parks the car close to the riverside, and we silently head to where we used to sit under this lonely willow tree. It feels natural heading there, even though I have avoided coming here for the last seven years. For a moment, it feels like I'm back in high school, coming here with Spencer after he won a football game and was up for a little private celebration.

Those were the good old days.

We remain silent for a few more minutes, both of us probably gathering the courage to open Pandora's box, secretly hoping the other does it first. However, he invited me to come and talk, so he should be the one to start it. Right?

But I'm getting annoyed and anxious with all this quietness, so I clear my throat and give him a side eye.

"So, what did you want to talk about?" I pry cautiously.

Spencer scoffs, amused, his dimpled smile making me momentarily distracted.

"What?" I squeak, confused.

He shakes his head, leaning against the tree trunk. "It took you longer than I expected to break the silence. You would have never endured the silence for so long in the past."

He's got me there. I was definitely not a patient person back then. In fact, I'm still working on that, but I like to think that I have improved somewhat in the last decade.

"Yeah, well, I guess people do change," I muse, crossing my legs and staring out at the river. The weather is chilly, but for some reason, I don't feel cold anymore. I guess having Spencer by my side warms me somehow.

"I'd like to think so," he adds, more to himself than to me.

I snap my head in his direction, creasing my brows at his remark. "What's that supposed to mean?" I do my best not to sound accusatory or defensive, but judging by his reaction, I didn't succeed.

Spencer throws his arms up in surrender, widening his smile at me. "I was talking about myself. I'd like to think people are capable of changing and improving themselves."

"Why do you say that?" I know what he means, but I want to know why he'd say it about himself.

"I'm not a fan of who I was in the past. I mean, I guess that's not completely fair, but I wish I could have done things differently," he explains in a low voice, his eyes focused on me.

I suddenly feel vulnerable. Why is he looking at me like that?

"What's the problem with the old you? I liked him," I confess, although I'm not entirely sure why I let my guard down so quickly. I should be walking on eggshells right now, not allowing myself to be comfortable around him.

Spencer's lips curl slightly in a smile, but he drops it almost immediately, his face becoming stoic again. "I don't like the way I handled things between us. I've always regretted it, and I was too much of a wuss to come back and talk to you, to set things straight."

"I don't think it'd have mattered," I say genuinely. "We said a lot of shit to each other, and we were both pretty hurt. It might have made things even worse if you'd tried."

"Do you honestly think that?" He frowns at me, clearly surprised by my answer.

"Of course. I don't know about you, Spencer, but I was a mess. After everything we said to each other, I didn't want to see you, think of you, or even hear about you," I burst, diverting my gaze toward the river again. This is a sensitive topic for me, and I can't put it all out there while looking into those beautiful blue eyes of his. And if we're supposed to be honest during this conversation, I must clear my mind so I say all I have to say.

In fact, I've been keeping this locked up for so long that, now that I'm allowing it to come out, I fear I won't be able to stop.

"Huh… so you did hate me," he mutters.

"Didn't you hate me?" I turn to look at him, finding him with a painful expression as he stares back at me. "I mean, how could I not hate you? You broke my heart! You said I wasn't ambitious—"

His eyes widen in shock, his jaw dropping. "I never said that!" he counters in disbelief. "Don't put words in my mouth, Hayden. Where did you get that from?"

"You did!" I yell, turning to face him completely now. It's hard to gesticulate while seated on the ground, but I'm too nervous and mad right now to get up. "You wanted to go to LA because you had dreams, and apparently, mine weren't as big as yours."

"I asked you to come with me. Does that make me a bad person?" he asks, bewildered.

"It does! Because you knew I would never go. You knew what my family meant to me and that I never planned on leaving them behind… the ranch, none of it."

Spencer huffs, running his fingers through his hair in frustration. "You're being completely irrational. How can you misinterpret my invitation to move in with me and start a life together in another city as me thinking you're not ambitious?"

"I don't know, okay? I was barely twenty. What did I know about life? All I knew was that I wanted to be with you, but you never considered my dreams," I spit, not caring to sound stupid or reasonable.

Truth be told, it's been so long, and so much happened back then, that it's hard to keep up with details. Lots of what was said might have been altered in my brain with this much time.

"You're being unfair," Spencer points out, sounding hurt. "I always supported you, Hayden. And you can't pretend all of this was on me. You were pretty mean back then too, remember? You accused me of some stupid shit that you knew damn well I'd never do to you."

"Like what?" I press, anger boiling inside me.

"So, that you don't remember, huh? We tried long distance because I insisted we do, since you didn't want to go with me. And every missed call was a reason for you to accuse me of cheating on you," he says, exasperated.

"So what? What did you want me to think? You were miles away from me and never answered my calls."

"I was studying. Or working. Or playing," Spencer retorts bitterly. "You had your own life here, and I never complained about it."

"Yeah, right… You know what? I knew this was a huge mistake." I get up, too frustrated to remain seated.

"Where are you going?" Spencer asks, joining me.

"I'm going home. What else is there to say? We aren't going to agree on this, Spencer," I tell him, allowing my self-control to return.

My heart is beating rapidly, and I don't know why I'm so worked up. Everything that happened seems like it was in another lifetime. It shouldn't hurt this much anymore. It shouldn't even matter. But since this is the first conversation we have had since, maybe it's okay to let all the frustration, hurt, and pain out so we can finally move on.

"Look, I know things weren't easy between us, but I don't want you to hate me forever, Hayden." Spencer takes a few steps forward, standing in front of me. I fight the urge to take a step back, keeping a safe distance between us, because the truth is, I don't trust myself around him. No matter how much I'm mad at him, the effect he has on me is way stronger.

If he decided—for some crazy, delusional moment—to try and kiss me, I wouldn't think twice before letting him. My entire body screams for him. My entire being is aware of his presence, of how much I need to feel his skin, his touch, his lips. Anything that would give me a glimpse of what I used to have.

The way he looks at me, so tenderly, but also so filled with passion and longing, it only makes everything harder. How am I supposed to trick myself into believing I don't want anything to do with him when he stares at me like this?

"I don't hate you, Spencer. I never really did," I confess in a whisper. He doesn't deserve to know that, but I guess it's necessary to put it out there so we can both turn the page.

The frown in his forehead softens, giving way to a beautiful expression of relief. "I'm really happy to know that. I am truly sorry for everything that I said or did to you, Hayden. But I wanted to talk to you and set things straight so we can at least be around each other. Now that I'm coming back, I was thinking that maybe we could try to be friends and..."

Shit, am I being friendzoned? Me being friends with Spencer? Does he really see that happening? Is he so unbothered by me that he doesn't even flinch to make a suggestion like this? Or am I the stupid one to still harbor feelings for him after so long?

"Do you really want us to be friends?" I let it escape before I realize what I'm saying.

I see him gulping, his Adam's apple bobbing up and down as he considers my question. His eyes search my face, looking for something I can't quite figure out.

I wonder what is going through his mind right now. What exactly am I expecting him to say? That he still loves me? That he still wants us to be together?

Get a hold of yourself, Hayden. Stop being such a loser, waiting for something you can't have.

"Would that be such a bad thing?" Spencer finally asks, but the way his voice shakes doesn't go unnoticed. He doesn't look as confident as I thought he'd be.

"It clearly doesn't seem to be for you," I retort sharply.

"I just thought it'd be the best thing to do since we might bump into each other more often once I'm back," he explains.

"Right. I can be polite and treat you nicely if that's what you're concerned about. I won't make your life difficult."

"That's not what I meant, Hayden, and you know it," he adds, frustrated.

"What is it then, Spencer? Why are you suddenly so eager to be friends with me after seven years without even caring how I've been?" I snap.

"Because I miss you!" he shoots back. "I miss talking to you and having you in my life. I thought being friends was the only way to have you around. And you're wrong to think I never cared about how you were. I always knew what was going on in your life, Hayden. Always."

CHAPTER SIX

Ever since Spencer told me he'd been keeping track of my life from afar, my entire world shifted on its axis. Apparently, he always managed to hear from his sister, my brother, and even from my own mother how I was.

I didn't know whether to feel flattered or betrayed, but I didn't have anything else to say to him that day.

All I could promise him was that I'd try, but honestly, I don't think I will ever be okay with just being friends with Spencer. I still care about him too much not to get that line blurred from time to time.

After we both realized our conversation was over, he took me back to grab my car at the newspaper, and I drove home, suddenly feeling mentally and emotionally drained.

I tried to bury myself in work during the next few days, not allowing myself to think too much about what he said to me. Or how he looked at me. I don't want to fool myself, but whenever I allow my brain to go there, I can't pretend I didn't see the same glint in his eyes that I used to see when we were dating.

But who am I kidding? Of course, Spencer doesn't see me that way anymore. I'm the only one stuck in the past.

It's understandable that he missed me, though. We were together for a few years, and he was pretty much part of my family. He'd been friends with Chad for a while, and his parents were somewhat close to mine before they died in that tragic accident.

It isn't because he secretly still loves me.

Right?

Anyway, even though I try to focus on anything else and distract my thoughts from going back to Spencer, it's hard to do when I have a friend named Poppy Bennett glued to my heels pretty much 24/7. If it isn't enough to have to listen to her prying into my personal life during my free time, I also have to deal with her questions during work hours.

Apparently, I haven't given her enough information on the whole situation with Spencer, and regretfully, I have to admit that's my fault. I shouldn't have told her that I went out with Spencer to have a conversation in the first place. Now, whenever she can, she tries to ask me more about him.

"Don't you have anything better to talk about? Why is my high school relationship that's been over for more than seven years so important to you?" I ask for the hundredth time this week.

"Because we live in this small town where nothing cool happens," she says matter-of-factly, pouring herself some coffee while we spend our break time together in the newspaper's break room. Thankfully, it's otherwise empty today, so I don't have to worry about our colleagues overhearing stuff that doesn't concern them. Being around small town people is already bad enough, but hanging out with small town journalists turns one's life into a reality show. "Spencer's return is pretty much the coolest thing that's happened in five years," Poppy adds, adding more sugar than she should to her coffee.

"What happened five years ago?" I ask with a frown, trying to access my memories to remember something significant happening.

"Mr. Collins found out his wife was cheating on him with the florist guy?" Poppy replies in a questioning tone, creasing her brows at me in disbelief. "Girl, what the hell? Are you sure you're a journalist?"

I dismiss her with a roll of my eyes, not wanting to give her more ammunition. "That was a nice time to be around," I muse with a chuckle, remembering how worked up everyone in town was, taking sides and thinking they had a right to judge the Collins and their marriage. In the end, they ended up getting back together and moving out of Missoula, knowing no one would ever allow them to forget about those dark times in their lives.

They did the right thing if you ask me. A few times, I wished I had moved out of here myself so I wouldn't have to listen to anyone talking about my breakup with Spencer. They should just get a hobby instead of making one out of our lives.

"Isn't your break time over yet?" Our boss walks in, stomping her heels on the hardwood floor, and narrowing her eyes at us.

Kayla Baldwin is what I call a hard pill to swallow. She's in her late thirties, often seen as overdressed and caring too much about her image. She is really beautiful, but her personality spoils everything for her. She's self-centered, annoying, and for some reason I could never understand, she hates me.

Or at least that's what it always feels like. Good thing I'm so good at my job, otherwise, I'd be working at the ranch right now and not here. It doesn't mean she makes my life easy, though. Whatever chance she has to make things harder for me, she will embrace it without blinking. And I have to clench my teeth and swallow my pride every time to avoid being fired.

"I wonder how you'll ever take my place one day if you don't give it your all, Ms. Jenkins," she muses, pouring herself a cup of coffee and smirking at me and Poppy. "And you, Ms. Bennett. Don't you have an article to write for me? I need it on my desk by five. Do you expect it to write itself?"

I want to tell her that I couldn't care less about her position, but I decide against it. It's never a good idea to indulge her more than I have to.

I see Poppy gulping her coffee—grimacing at the hot temperature—just so she doesn't have to answer.

"It'll be ready in no time, Ms. Baldwin. Hayden is already revising it," Poppy answers, her jaw tense.

"Speaking of which, Ms. Jenkins," Kayla turns to look at me with an evil glint in her eyes, "are you all set to cover the Sentinel High School celebration this year?"

Ah, the celebration. I was kind of expecting to forget about it. Sentinel High School is throwing an anniversary party this year, and all current and graduated students are invited. So, that means my entire class—and also my brothers' and sister's.

Don't get me wrong, I'm looking forward to returning to that place and celebrating. But now that Spencer is back, I'm not so sure I want to relive that time of my life. Almost everyone who will be there was present in our lives when we were together.

"Yes, we should have the article ready just in time for the morning's paper on Sunday. Right, Poppy?" I glance at her, knowing she is the one responsible for writing it. If there's one thing she is good at, it's writing an article in record time—even after a couple of drinks. It amazes me to this day how dedicated she is to her career.

I often find myself pondering if this is really what I want to do with my life. In all honesty, I don't love my job anymore. It's been like this for a while now. All I ever wanted was to be able to publish my novel and live off it. I know this is a huge dream, but for that to even be considered a possibility, I'd have to finish writing it first.

And that's proven to be harder than I imagined it would be.

A few years ago, I started putting together some ideas for this romance I wanted to write, but inspiration was short and I ended up forgetting about it. But maybe I should try it again. I don't see myself working here forever, and even though I know there's a lot for me to do at my parents' ranch, I don't see myself being happy with that life either. Maybe one day, when I'm close to retiring, but definitely not now.

I need money first, before I consider quitting the paper to concentrate on my novel, and for that to become my reality in the future, I need to start saving it.

"Absolutely." Poppy nods, eagerly hoping Kayla will leave us alone so we can finish our coffee in peace.

Ugh, this woman... What an inconvenience. We still have ten minutes left.

Kayla studies us both before seeming satisfied and turning on her heel, parading out of the break room and back to her office. I almost let out a sigh of relief.

Poppy lets out a heavy breath, leaning against the counter. "I swear to you, sometimes I wish I could take one of those heels of hers and stab her in the back with it. What a bitch."

I laugh, shaking my head. "You shouldn't say things like that if you want to take her place one day," I tease, sarcastically.

"I hope I do, just so I can be responsible for putting her ass on the street. Why does she have to make our lives so miserable? Why does she have to be so hard on you?" she adds, looking intrigued. "Do you think maybe she has a secret crush on you?"

"Ew, no! Poppy! Inappropriate much?"

"I'm just saying." She throws her free hand in the air in surrender before taking a last sip of her now cold coffee and washing her mug. "I just don't understand why she always tries to belittle you and underestimate your abilities. You'd make a much better editor-in-chief than she's ever been."

"I appreciate you defending me, but Kayla is not a bad editor-in-chief. She's just..."

"A bitch," Poppy completes with a shrug, heading back to her desk. I follow her, still holding onto my coffee since I didn't have the chance to drink all of it. "Anyway, let's talk about the good stuff. Aren't you excited about the school celebration? I mean, we're going to see some old faces we haven't seen since graduation. I am so curious to know how everyone's lives turned out."

"As if you don't have social media for that," I point out with a chuckle. "But I guess you're right. It will be fun. Although, I'm not so excited about seeing some of the people who picked on us back then. We were kind of bookworms, remember?"

"Whatever. Who's laughing now, huh?" Poppy leans back in her chair, suddenly looking pensive. "I mean, we weren't that bad. If I remember correctly, you dated the captain of the football team, didn't you?"

"That doesn't count. He was just being a good friend to my brother," I counter with a smile.

"Right. Spencer dated you to do your brother a favor." Poppy rolls her eyes.

"What about you?" I press, desperate to change the subject before she gets hooked up on Spencer again. "By the time we were freshmen, you had quite a list of guys interested in you too."

Poppy scoffs. "That doesn't count either. All jerks, if I remember correctly."

"Right..." I mumble, directing my attention back to the computer screen in front of me where Poppy's article is open and halfway revised. I glance at the clock on the right corner of the screen, realizing I still have thirty minutes to finish this and have it on Kayla's desk.

"Do you think it's good enough to get Witch Baldwin off my tail for a while? I honestly can't work with her breathing down my neck all the time," Poppy asks, leaning forward and looking at me expectantly.

"I still have to finish it, but it looks amazing so far. Like everything you write, girl. Don't worry," I tell her, turning my attention back to her written words.

"Don't you miss being a reporter? I mean, I know you never really liked that part of the job, but I know you love writing and, well... you're not really working on your book right now, are you?" Poppy pries, folding her arms in front of her chest and studying me with curiosity.

I take a deep breath, trying not to get distracted from her paragraph about the benefits of cardio, specifically running. I should, in fact, take something from this article, given I'm not really concerned about working out much lately. I've been so tired after work that my evening jogs probably shouldn't even be considered cardio. And on the weekends, I have so much stuff to get done at the ranch with Dad that I just pretend that's enough of a workout for me.

"I'm just not sure what to write about. I'm not inspired," I explain. "It's been years since I tried it, to be honest."

"Well, maybe all you have to do is try again. You need to take the first step. Otherwise, you won't get anywhere, Hays."

'Yeah, I guess you're right."

The weekend of the high school celebration arrives, and I'm suddenly dreading it–for no apparent reason at all. I don't know why I feel so anxious about it. It's just me meeting people who I used to go to school with—what's the harm in that?

There's this little voice deep down inside my head whispering Spencer's name, but I shake it off, knowing it makes no sense whatsoever. Why would I dread something just because Spencer will be there? I went to Ryan's wedding, didn't I? This event should be considered a piece of cake next to that.

Maybe I just don't feel like taking a trip down memory lane. Seeing all those faces might remind me of things I tried hard to bury.

But I guess I *could* have fun tonight. High school wasn't as bad as I sometimes make it sound like it was. I had nice friends—although few —cool memories or life altering experiences. I've learned a lot since then, and it's helped me shape the person I am today.

"Are you ready?" Lauren asks, straightening her navy dress. It's a casual chic night, but considering this is a small town, and people love an opportunity to get dressed up, we're all wearing something fancy.

"I guess so. You look amazing by the way," I say, applying some lipstick and making sure everything is in place.

Lauren stares at me with widen hazel eyes. "Are you kidding me? You look absolutely stunning, sis. You're rocking that dress."

I analyze myself in the mirror once more, noticing what she means. I don't normally gloat about my looks or anything—I don't even see myself as a beautiful woman though people normally tell me I am—but this burgundy dress really compliments my fair skin, chestnut-brown hair, and it even accentuates my brown eyes and the freckles on my nose and cheeks.

I tried not to apply too much makeup, going for a more natural look, but I did put on some lipstick to give me that healthy glow.

"Thank you, pony. Poppy picked it out for me."

"Of course she did. If it were up to you, you'd be wearing jeans and that horrendous pair of caramel boots of yours." Lauren grimaces, tossing her hair over her shoulder.

I flip her off, narrowing my eyes at her. "Watch it, or I'll give you a new hairstyle and a new design for your dress," I threaten, hearing her laugh at my stupid attempt to intimidate her. Truth be told, Lauren has always been way stronger than me, and after she became a fire-fighter and had some training, I was officially lowered to the spot of the weakest Jenkins.

"Are you girls getting ready for a party or your wedding?" Chad complains, knocking on my bedroom door and opening it before I tell him to come inside. "Wow, are you trying to give the male population of this town a heart attack?" he adds, scanning us both with creased brows. "Or maybe you're trying to give ME a heart attack by having to deal with those stupid vultures from Sentinel."

I laugh while Lauren rolls her eyes at him. Chad has always been a bit overprotective of us—sometimes too much for his own good. I never cared much, but Lauren always seemed to have a problem with it.

"You will mind your own business tonight, sir. Don't come raining on my parade," she warns darkly, pointing a finger at him. "I've been single for only God knows how long and—"

"Three years," I cut her off with a smirk on my face.

"Shut up," she hisses, looking at me but immediately turning her attention back to our brother. "And you were the one to blame for that."

"What did I do? It wasn't my fault that the guy was a piece of shit and cheated on you," Chad counters, sounding offended. "The black eye and the broken tooth was my fist's fault though, I'll give you that."

I bite my lower lip to prevent a laugh from coming out as I watch Lauren's nostrils flare.

"Come on, you thanked me for that back then," he adds.

"Whatever. I don't need your fists tonight. I can handle myself just fine now."

"Oh, that's true. I'd hate to be the one on the other side of your fist, sis," I mumble, taking my purse from the bed and heading toward the door.

"Um, Hays?" Chad calls to me as I pass by him.

"Yeah?" I turn to look at him, and I notice how good looking he is tonight. He's wearing black tie. His light-brown hair looks a bit shorter—which makes me think he just got a haircut. His hazel eyes inspect me as if he's trying to study my mood before he says anything else. He suddenly looks a bit uneasy, glancing anywhere but my eyes.

Chad clears his throat, shoving his hands in his pocket. "So, since we're all going to the same event, I thought it'd be okay that we went with Spencer. He offered to drive me, and since I had agreed to pick you two up, well..."

I'm not surprised. We used to do this all the time when we were younger. All of us going together to parties and stuff. I guess I should feel uncomfortable arriving at the celebration with Spencer, but surprisingly, I don't give a damn about what other people will say. It shouldn't matter. They will always talk about it, whether I like it or not, so I might as well just play deaf and enjoy myself tonight.

"It's fine, Chad. I don't mind," I tell him, putting him out of his misery.

His eyes widen in shock at the same time Lauren squeaks next to me.

"What?" she breathes.

"Are you sure?" Chad presses, frowning at me.

"Yeah, we talked, and, since he's back now, we don't want to make things awkward whenever we meet, so you can relax," I explain, shrugging.

I head downstairs, ignoring the hushed conversation behind me between Chad and Lauren who are trying to understand when I could have had that conversation with Spencer. It is actually funny to see them this confused, so I don't try to explain anything else to them.

But when I arrive on the porch, I halt in my step, finding Spencer cheerfully talking to my mom and dad.

And seeing how great he looks, my brain blanks for a moment, and I have to convince myself that this really will be as good an idea as I told Chad it was.

CHAPTER SEVEN

A lot has changed in the school since the last time I came here. I guess it should be expected. Now, everything seems... different. There have been some rebuilds and improvements to the classrooms and the common areas. Even the football field is not what I remember. It's much more imposing now, with the Spartans logo painted on a sign by the bleachers, and even the field looks greener.

But when I see the faces I used to spend my everyday life with, I remember it was never about the place, but rather about who we shared it with. Lots of the students who graduated with me moved out of town, so I've barely kept up with their lives through social media. And even so, not everyone likes to share personal stuff online, so I never knew what lots of them ended up doing or how their lives were.

For those who stayed here like I did, I still keep in touch with them, so it's not like I haven't known about them for all these years.

It's exciting to hear their stories, though. Even the ones I see frequently. We don't normally stop to talk and hang out, so tonight is a great moment for that.

"Girl, did you see Bethany?" Poppy whispers by my side when we head to the refreshment station close to the auditorium door. I was expecting her comments as soon as I told her I was going to grab something to drink, and she offered to come with me with more enthusiasm than necessary. "I knew I always hated her for being a bully and an insufferable bitch, but she actually managed to get worse with time."

Bethany Nicholson was my nightmare in high school. She was the popular, mean cheerleader who just liked to think she was better than everyone else. And she was also into Spencer. I guess it was every cheerleader's dream to date the star of the football team, and well, I stole that chance from her when I started dating him instead.

That was the nail in my coffin.

After that, she made sure to make my life hell whenever she had a chance. It didn't help that I was kind of a nerd, preferring to stay inside reading books and watching movies rather than attending parties and doing shit that would probably eventually put me in jail.

"I heard she's modeling in New York," I comment, accepting a glass of soda from a server.

"There's one for every taste. She's not that pretty anyway," Poppy grumbles next to me. She takes her glass, and we head back to the center of the auditorium where they improvised a sort-of dance floor.

"Come on, Pops. She may be awful, but ugly is not something we can say about her," I say begrudgingly. Bethany is definitely a super-model-type of woman.

"Whatever."

"Here they are!" A guy named Nathan who graduated in Chad's class waves at us as we approach a group of people gathered close to the DJ. He's one of the few people who stayed in town, and he works at his family's auto repair shop downtown. He's always been nice to everyone, and Chad and him are still good friends.

"What's up, Nathan?" I greet, glancing around and noticing the other faces in the circle.

This has to be one of the most random groups I've ever seen inside these walls—Chad, Spencer, Bethany, two girls I remember being Bethany's shadows back then who I can't recall the names of, Mitchie and Lila, who were part of the book club alongside me, Brian Fetherston and… Jake Monroe?

Jake was one of Chad and Spencer's enemies while they were in high school. He frequently picked on them, trying to steal Spencer's position as quarterback. They got into fights a few times that led to suspension for both of them—Chad, too, because he decided to play the hero and help his friend.

Jake is an asshole. He isn't a nice guy, but he always had this charm, knowing how to win people over and make them do what he wanted. It helps that he's cute, of course. He is a typical American guy, with blond curly hair and blue eyes, but I guess it's his bad boy vibe that gets to people. He's always carried himself with a nonchalant attitude, as if nothing in the world could affect him.

It feels odd to see him around these people, though. I don't think I ever saw them together before.

"Well," Nathan replies, smirking at Jake. "Jake here was telling us what he's been up to lately. Imagine our surprise to find out you guys went to the same college."

Uh-oh. That's not good.

I chuckle, shrugging at his remark. "Well, what are the odds, right? It's not like we have lots of college options here. Mitchie and Lila went there too, right?"

Mitchie, who's always been a shy girl, nods silently, but Lila laughs as if I've said something funny.

"Yeah, sure." Nathan nods, not giving me his attention. "But none of them hooked up with Jake."

Oh shit!

I knew this would come back to bite me in the ass someday. No matter how much you regret doing something, there's no way you can ever forget it. Especially if you live in a small town.

Hooking up with Jake Monroe is one of the biggest stains on my dating record—if you can even call that 'dating.' After Spencer and I broke up, I went down this whirlwind of bad choices, including attending several frat parties. It's not something I am proud of. But I was so heartbroken, trying to forget about him and move on with my life, that I ended up doing stuff without thinking clearly.

Jake is one of those dark moments in my past. I knew Spencer hated him. I also knew that he would never know what was going on with me in college. If I dated someone, or even slept with them, what were the odds that Spencer would find out while living miles away from me? And until now, that was buried in the past, safely hidden from him.

Chad heard about it back then, and that was a whole other story that I'm not willing to relive. Let's just say there was a huge lecture involved, an even bigger argument, and we stopped talking to each other for two weeks.

I can tell by Chad's face now that he's recalling that time in our lives, and by the grimace on his face, I can tell he's not happy to have to be reminded of it either. But it's Spencer's frown that catches me off guard. Our gazes meet, and, for a moment, I'm not sure how to react. I can feel my cheeks flushing, and I'm suddenly feeling speechless, unsure of what to say to break the ice that's emerged within our group.

"Come on, man. That was ages ago," Jake chimes in, smiling at Nathan and clearly trying to minimize the impact of the news. "I'm sure Hayden doesn't even remember it. It wasn't that remarkable, right, Hayden?"

Hearing my name catapults me back to reality. I clear my throat, laughing nervously. "Yeah, right. It wasn't a big deal, really. We were really young and drunk at a party."

"Exactly," Jake adds, taking a sip from his drink. He seems unbothered, even though I'm sure he can feel the burning gazes Chad and Spencer are throwing at him.

Truth is, hanging out with Jake wasn't as bad as I thought it'd be. It was about sex, since I was too depressed to even consider getting into another relationship. But somehow, he did help me take my mind off things for a bit. At least, when we were together. The sex was nice, so there's no way I could've forgotten that like he said I did, but it didn't even come close to what Spencer and I had.

That, and also the fact that Jake is an asshole, as I mentioned already. Two weeks later, he was sucking another girl's mouth after a game, which was my wake up call to move on and find another guy to drown my sorrows with.

A high-pitched laugh makes me snap my head to the right. Bethany has her head dropped back in complete delight, as if she just heard the most exciting news in the entire world. I clench my fists, my knuckles turning white in a second. Of course, this bitch wouldn't let this go.

"Oh my God! Are you kidding me? Hayden Jenkins, the book-worm, and Jake Monroe? If you told me this ten years ago, I'd have died from laughter," she chirps, her voice giving me the urge to vomit. "This is so much fun."

"What's wrong with that?" Poppy intervenes, coming to my defense. I can almost hear her teeth grinding beside me, and I grab her by the elbow, trying to keep her from jumping down Bethany's throat. "The bookworm dated the quarterback, and it wasn't laugh-able, was it? If I remember correctly, she stole him from you."

Bethany scoffs, too bewildered to reply.

I suddenly feel sick. I can feel Spencer's gaze still on me, and I'm not sure how to behave. It shouldn't matter this much, given I wasn't with him when I slept with Jake, but why does it feel like I betrayed him somehow? Back then, it was my initial intention to get back at him for breaking my heart. So, I thought, what better way to make him suffer than to hook up with his enemy?

Of course, that was a dramatic way of thinking, but I honestly never believed this would get to him. I was just trying to find some comfort, some way to get through the worst time of my life.

"I need to go to the bathroom. Excuse me," I mumble, turning toward the exit without waiting for anyone to say anything else.

I hope no one follows me. Knowing Poppy, she will probably want to talk about it, but I hope she realizes I need some space now. Rushing out of the auditorium, I pass by the bathroom and head outside. What I need is fresh air, to get out of this suddenly suffo-cating building.

The evening breeze is colder than I expected, and I'm immediately hit by it. My entire body shivers, making me regret coming in a strappy dress.

What a rookie mistake.

Glancing around, taking in my surroundings, I walk aimlessly, not really paying attention to where I'm going, but rather noticing the changes the school made over the years and comparing them with how I remember them being when I was last here. The nostalgic feeling is overwhelming. It does make one think about everything we took for granted when we were younger and unaware of what real life had in store for us.

It was such an easier time. Everything seemed simpler, better. True, there was a huge decision on our shoulders, having to decide what we wanted to be in the future, but compared to real life problems, that seems so irrelevant now. It's not like we had to sign a contract for life that prevented us from changing our minds in the future. Lots of people change their careers after they graduate. And that's okay.

I know my mom did, Ryan did, and I'm currently thinking of doing the same. And that's fine.

I only realize where I am once I see the enormous, green football field in front of me. I don't know why I came here, but subconsciously, I think this place means more to me than I ever gave it credit for. Before I started dating Spencer, I used to come here to watch the games like every other student did, of course. I liked to watch the team practicing, too, especially Chad. I was so proud of him when he made the team that whenever I had some free time, I'd come to watch him.

Or I'd study in the bleachers, finding it to be the most peaceful spot around the entire school.

And then, when I started hanging out with Spencer, I'd come here to watch him practice or to wait for him so we could go home together.

Those were definitely good times.

"Monroe, huh?" a deep, hoarse voice says behind me, making me jump out of my skin. I turn on my heel, my hand darting to my heart to make sure it doesn't stop beating after the scare I just received.

"Holy shit!" I hiss, taking a second to compose myself. And that's when I realize who came to disturb my peace. "Spencer?"

He's standing there, both hands deep in his pants pockets, his tie loosened up around his neck, his dark hair perfectly combed—although I can see it has grown a bit over the ears, giving him that playboy look I love so much—and his piercing blue eyes studying my face from under his frown.

"I'm trying hard not to judge you, but Monroe was a low blow," he carries on, his tone bitter and serious. "Did you really sleep with him?"

I gulp and divert my gaze, buying myself some time to think about the right answer. What should I even say to that? It's not like I owe Spencer any explanation, but why do I feel like I need to defend myself to him? Sure, I'm not proud of my actions back then, nor of who I was, but it doesn't mean I need to indulge him either.

"What if I did?" I reply, a bit on the defensive. "I wasn't with you at the time, if that's what you're wondering."

Spencer huffs, looking uncomfortable. "I know that. Unlike you, I'm not accusing you of cheating on me. I'm just saying I was surprised to know you got involved with someone like Jake Monroe, that's all."

My jaw drops at his audacity. He's referring to the several times that I childishly accused him of cheating on me when he left for Los Angeles. But all the times I said those things it was just to vent my anger. It wasn't that I truly believed Spencer was cheating on me. He never once made me doubt him. I knew he'd never cheat on me, but at the time, that was the only thing I could do to try and hurt him somehow.

It's pretty hard to find flaws to accuse someone when they are perfect. Trust me.

"Why? I'm sure you got involved with a lot worse in *Los Angeles*," I counter, adding a layer of sarcasm on the two last words.

He takes a deep breath, his gaze darting away from mine. "Yeah, well, I was not as perfect as you seemed to believe I was."

"Neither am I," I fire back. "Why the hell do you care anyway, huh? You came all the way here to shove it on my face that I made some bad choices in my life? That's hardly news around here."

Spencer shifts his eyes back to my face, studying me carefully. I have no idea what's going on inside his mind, but I can't help but wonder if he's seeing me in a different light now. I shouldn't care, but I don't like to think that Spencer sees me as someone unworthy. I always rejoiced in the fact that Spencer thought I was a great woman.

"Of course not. And regardless of what you may think, Hayden, I do care about you. Just because we broke up, that doesn't mean I stopped caring about you," he says.

Why does he have to make my life so much harder? Why does he keep saying these things to me?

"But you should!" I snap, anger boiling up inside me. "You broke up with me. You have no right to come back and tell me you still care about me."

"I'm pretty sure you're the one who broke up with me." Spencer's eyes focus hard on my face, and I shift on my feet, feeling mad and confused. Our breakup was so messy that it's hard to remember all the details. I can't exactly remember who broke up with who. It might have been my idea—in a moment of rage—but he didn't fight me on it. That, I am certain of.

"You agreed. And honestly, why does it matter, Spencer? You have no right to confuse me like this."

In a blink of an eye, and in less than three steps, Spencer is standing in front of me. He's so close that his cologne makes me momentarily numb and spaced out.

Did he get taller with time? And did his eyes turn bluer too? Why are his lips so full and inviting?

Fuck!

Earth to Hayden!

"Why am I confusing you?" Spencer asks with his low and sexy voice.

I take a step back promptly, realizing how close he is. But Spencer is faster than me, and his arm is on my waist before I manage to get away. This simple touch, even though it has layers of fabric separating our skin, makes my entire body shiver. I want to blame the cold breeze, but I know damn well that's not the reason why I feel like my knees have turned into jelly.

"What are you doing?" I whisper, unable to form another sentence that would make sense.

Spencer's eyes still study me, roaming over my entire face as if he's taking in every single detail he's forgotten with time.

"Is this what's making you confused?"

"No! I mean, yes! That too," I counter, trying to shove him by pushing his chest. But his arm doesn't loosen up around my waist. Spencer doesn't even budge. "What do you think you're doing?"

Am I insane, or is he leaning forward? His lips are so close to mine that I can feel his breath brushing against them.

"I told you I missed you, Hays," he confesses in a whisper, his eyes darting from my eyes to my lips and back again. "And to be honest, I thought I could do it, but I don't think the whole friend thing will work for me."

I want to tell him that it doesn't work for me either, even though this is the only option for us. There's no way we can be together again. We've hurt each other too much.

But before I have the chance to say anything, before the words even come to my brain, before I have the chance to gasp for air, Spencer closes the distance between us, his lips finding mine as if they were two matching puzzle pieces finally coming together.

CHAPTER EIGHT

It amazes me how a kiss can feel so familiar, and yet, so new and exciting after so long. For years, I wondered what it'd be like to kiss Spencer again, to feel his lips on mine, his electrifying touch on my skin… And now that I am experiencing it again, it's nothing like I imagined it would be.

It's so much better that it's hard to put into words. It's hard to even understand what I'm feeling.

It's like he was molded just for me. Our mouths, our bodies, they complement each other so well.

The kiss is not as desperate as I remember us being back in high school, but I can still feel the passion behind it, even though it's a soft, almost hesitant, kiss.

I can feel Spencer is holding back. I know I am. My entire body is on fire right now. If I could simply shut off my brain, I know I'd be encouraging him to go further. But there is this distant, tiny string being pulled in the back of my head, reminding me of why this is so wrong.

Utterly, seriously, terribly wrong.

But for a moment, I allow myself to ignore that nagging voice and relish in his kiss and the feelings it's causing me.

Spencer has one arm wrapped around my waist, keeping me close and tight against him, while his other hand cups my face, gently guiding me as he tilts his head to have more access to me. He licks my lower lip, and I hold back a moan, giving him full access to my mouth. It's a dance I could never forget.

Kissing him has always been so thrilling. He's always had the ability to make me daydream, to forget about anything and anyone—it was always just the two of us whenever we kissed.

I sprawl my hands on his strong, muscled chest, melting under his touch and into his embrace. He's somehow even stronger than I remember. Back in high school, Spencer used to work out every single day for football—sometimes more than once—and he had this 'to-die-for' physique that had every man envying him and every woman desiring him.

But now, even though Spencer doesn't play anymore—if only occasionally and as a hobby—he looks more built and in-shape than ever before.

This is so not fair. How can he get better with time? He's aging like fine wine, I'll give him that.

I should give myself some credit, too, because, even though I remain a skinny little thing, I'm stronger than when I was seventeen. Helping Dad around the ranch has gained me some muscles—and fine legs from walking back and forth between the house, the horse barn, and pastures to do the chores.

I have a fine ass too—or so I've been told.

By the way Spencer is holding me—as if he's afraid I'll vanish from his sight if he lets go of me—I can only assume he's still attracted to me too. And if the way his body is reacting to our kiss is any indication of his desire for me, I can't say I'm alone in this.

I was never the horny type of woman, even though I had experienced dark times during college when I tried to bury myself in meaningless sex, but being with Spencer has always felt different. He has this effect on me that I can't put my finger on. It's like my whole being is drawn to him whenever he's in my orbit.

I'm starting to feel breathless, and I know Spencer is, too, but I'm too afraid to break this kiss. I don't know what will become of us once I do that. But the voice of reason inside my head cuts through the defenses I raised, getting to the front of my brain and making me snap back to reality.

This can't be happening. I can't kiss Spencer. This is wrong. This will only cause us another heartbreak.

Why did he even kiss me? What were we talking about anyway? I can't remember a thing.

He said the friend thing didn't work for him. He said he missed me.

What is he thinking? That he can come back after all these years and have his way with me as if nothing ever happened?

He wishes!

With a renewed determination—and my subconscious whining inside—I step back from Spencer, pushing him away from me and releasing myself from his grasp.

"What the hell do you think you're doing?" I bark at him, trying to compose myself as I straighten my dress and make sure everything is in place, even though my insides feel like they are about to be torn apart from the distance I just created between us.

There's this annoying, inconvenient longing between my legs reminding me that I haven't had sex in a long time and that Spencer has just given me a little sample of what it would be like to have him claim me, but I can't indulge those thoughts.

Not tonight.

Not ever.

Spencer looks just as distraught as I'm feeling. Well, that makes me feel less remorseful that I allowed myself to be this weak. If anything, he started it. I just...let him.

No, I kissed him back, too, but that's not the point.

I shove aside the image of what he could do to me if I allowed him to carry on with whatever we were doing and take another step back, just to make sure he won't try anything again. I won't have the strength to push him away another time.

He runs his hands through his hair in frustration, messing it up even more. I haven't even realized I did that much damage to his perfect hairstyle until now.

"I'm sorry, Hayden. I got carried away," he says in a sorrowful, almost hurt tone.

"What's that supposed to mean? You can't show up after years, Spencer, and tell me you want to be friends, and then all of a sudden, tell me you can't do it and kiss me like that. You can't—" I cut myself short, taking a deep breath and closing my eyes so I can put my thoughts in order. "You can't say you missed me. You can't do that to me," I add in a pleading tone.

"Why not? It's the truth," he simply adds with a shrug. His eyes are dark and narrowed at me, as if he's trying to read between the lines I'm speaking.

"It doesn't matter!" I yell angrily. "Can't you see how wrong this is?" I insist, staring at him. But he doesn't seem as bothered as I do. Does he need me to explain to him how bad this seems? Does he need a reminder? Because I sure as hell can do that. "We hurt each other, Spencer. A lot. What good do you think this will do, huh? I don't know about you, but I don't want to live that hell again, okay? It was the worst time of my life."

Spencer looks at me, his beautiful blue eyes piercing my soul as he considers what I've said. Then, he nods slightly at me, his lips turning into a thin line.

"It wasn't easy for me either, Hayden. I don't know what makes you think it was, but it wasn't. The only other time I felt this lonely and sad in my life was when I lost my parents. You know how that fucked me up big time. You were there."

That's definitely a memory I wish I could forget. His parents' death was one of the saddest moments in my life—one that I can't think about to this day without feeling my eyes fill with tears.

Emilia and Ben Bailey died in a tragic accident when they went on a snowboarding trip to Sierra Nevada when Spencer was seventeen. There was a terrible avalanche, and they didn't manage to save themselves or get rescued in time. They always went on those trips, but for some reason, they didn't predict the bad weather and how dangerous it could be to go snowboarding in such conditions.

Or maybe they did, and Emilia and Ben went anyway—no one will ever know.

What I do know is that Spencer and his sister Aubrie looked like zombies for months, having become orphaned overnight. That was a moment when I thought it was possible that a heart could physically —and literally—break into pieces. I couldn't stand the sight of Spencer crying and suffering so much. But my mom said having me by his side to support him and just be there for him was the best thing he could have at that moment, so I took comfort in that, even though it hurt me to see him so distraught.

It took them a while to overcome this—as much as that's possible, given the fact no one can ever move on from losing the ones they love —but eventually, I saw that sparkle in his eyes again, and I knew everything would be okay.

"I know it doesn't compare, but losing you hit close to home. Too close. It stirred feelings inside me that I thought I had buried and wouldn't have to face again any time soon," Spencer carries on, glancing away beyond the bleachers and the football field. I know he's reliving those memories, and I wish I could make him stop. I can't stand the way he looks so hurt, so...vulnerable.

His jaw is so tense and sharp that I'm afraid he might break his teeth with this much pressure. His knuckles are white as he clenches his fists beside him, and his eyes are so narrowed and dark that, for a moment, I even forget they are the brightest blue I've ever seen.

My throat is dry and burning as I feel tears pooling at the corner of my eyes. I want to cry so bad, but I can't do this right now. I don't want him to see how weak and vulnerable he makes me too. I know it's only fair, given the fact he's opening himself up to me, but I'm afraid to do it. Not again anyway.

I've done that before, and look where it got me.

I was never the same Hayden again. When Spencer and I broke up, it was like he took a part of me with him. And now he's here, wanting to...what? Try again? What is it that he wants anyway?

"I'm sorry," I choke, swallowing down the lump forming in my throat. "I didn't mean to make you relive that moment. I know it was hard, and it doesn't even compare to what you've been through, but… you've always been stronger than me. I can't go through any of that again, Spencer. I just…can't."

"I get it," he mumbles in a low voice, his eyes turning to me again. "I—"

"Hayden!" I hear Chad calling me, but it doesn't even sound like him. I dart my head to the side, spotting him a few yards away from us, his eyes heavy on Spencer. His voice is raspy and serious, nothing like the cheerful Chad I know. "Time to go."

"Hm, yeah, sure. Spencer and I were just—"

"Lauren is waiting for you. You can go ahead, I'll see you tomorrow." Chad takes a few steps forward, and I don't know what it is, but by the way he's behaving and portraying himself, I can tell he's pissed, although I have no idea why. Also, he's talking to me, but his eyes never leave Spencer's face, so I wonder what the hell is that about.

"What do you mean?" I frown. "I thought we were leaving together. Spencer will drive us home."

"No, he's not. I need to have a word with him, so can you please just go?" Chad insists through clenched teeth.

I open my mouth to retort, to ask him why he's acting like a son of a bitch all of a sudden, and why he seems about to beat the hell out of Spencer, but the words never come out. I was never afraid of Chad before, but right now, I don't feel comfortable with the dark aura coming off him.

I glance at Spencer who looks just as tense and serious as Chad. It's like they can communicate through their eyes, and I'm the only one left in the dark having no idea of what's going on between them.

"All right, fine. You don't have to be so rude," I groan, walking in his direction. I stop for a second, turning back to look at Spencer one last time. There's still so much I want to tell him, hear from him, but the moment is gone. But there's still one thing that I want to make sure he understands from our conversation, so I gather the courage to tell him before I go. "Spencer, I'm sorry," I say in a whisper.

He nods slightly at me, his eyes still dark as they divert to Chad again.

I don't look at my brother as I walk away. I just brush past him, bumping my shoulder into his on purpose so he knows I don't like the way he treated me. Or Spencer, for that matter.

My footsteps are hard against the concrete as I walk to the front gate of the school, looking around and trying to find Lauren. When I spot her, she's waving at me from the other side of the street, a car I don't recognize parked behind her.

"Come on, pony. I don't want to get a bad review on Uber," she whines, opening the door for us. I climb inside, too bitter and angry to say anything to her.

No matter how hard I try to find a reason for Chad to have been so stupid with Spencer and I, I can't understand what happened. He was fine when I left the party a few minutes ago.

"Did something happen after I left?" I ask tentatively after a couple of minutes in silence, turning in my seat to stare at my sister.

"What do you mean?" She looks at me with a frown.

"Well, Chad told me to meet you and he seemed…angry? And we came with Spencer, so why are we riding back home in an Uber?" I add bitterly. I see the driver glancing at me through the rearview mirror, and I smile shyly at him. "Sorry, no offense, sir."

If the guy responds, I don't hear it, but honestly, whatever… He isn't supposed to be paying attention to our conversation.

"Really?" Lauren creases her brows, looking out the window contemplatively. "I mean, I don't know. He texted me and told me to call a cab or something. And then he told me to wait for you, that we should go home and not wait for him or Spencer," Lauren explains with a shrug. "He seemed okay, though. Maybe he just wanted to hang out with Spencer and the guys? They're probably planning on going for a beer or something. You know them… men."

I grimace, trying not to think of Spencer spending the rest of the night with another woman other than me. Could that be it? It's not weird to think they would want to have a guys' night out, but Chad seemed different. As if he had something to discuss with Spencer.

As if he wanted to clarify something, as if he...wanted to pick a fight.

Unless...

Shit!

No, no, no. This can't be happening.

"Shit..." I mumble to myself, but Lauren looks at me as if I have grown three heads.

"What is it, Hayden? Why are you acting so weird? What happened?" she presses, turning in her seat to face me once more. "Did Chad say something to you?"

I shake my head, too numb and confused to answer her.

It's the only explanation I can think of. Chad wouldn't be rude to me or Spencer if he didn't think he had a good reason to.

He saw us kissing.

There's no way I'm wrong about this. He saw Spencer and me kissing and didn't like it. He's always been very protective over Lauren and me. He never caused a scene over my relationship with his best friend, but I'm sure they must have had some conversation about bro codes or something in the past.

Knowing Chad, he's probably thinking Spencer is taking advantage of me. He's probably thinking Spencer will make me suffer again.

"Hayden, you're scaring me. What happened?" my sister presses, grabbing my arm and shaking it so I will turn my attention back to her.

I blink, trying to choose the right words to tell her what went on.

"Okay, well, do you want the long version or the short one?" I ask, flashing her a forced smile.

"Just spill it out, Hays. You're making me anxious."

"Okay, short it is then..." I clear my throat, composing myself. "Spencer kissed me. Well, he started, but I kind of...let him. And I think... I THINK... Chad saw us." I wince, trying to erase the thoughts of Chad and Spencer fighting over something as stupid as a kiss from my mind.

But judging by Lauren's shocked face, I can tell my thoughts are not so absurd. Chad has gotten himself into fights over us for less than that.

"What?" she hisses, her voice so raspy and squeaky that I barely recognize it. "Spencer kissed you?" Her hands dart to her mouth so she can hide the huge 'O' her lips are making. Her eyes are wide open, and her brows are pulled up to her forehead as she stares at me.

"It's not a big deal. Chad wouldn't do anything stupid, right?" I urge, afraid to hear the answer.

I'm not happy that Spencer kissed me and confused me even more, but I don't want him to get into a fight with my brother because of it either. And ever since Chad joined the police, he's learned some new fighting skills. I have no idea how well Spencer can fight.

Although, truth be told, I don't think he'd ever hit Chad.

Not even to defend himself.

"It's Chad we're talking about here, sis. And Chad thought I'd be the one giving him a heart attack tonight." Lauren shakes her head, still in disbelief, but I see the corner of her mouth curling slightly up. "I can't believe Spencer kissed you. What is that supposed to mean?"

That's a question I wish she had the answer to because I sure have no idea.

CHAPTER NINE

As much as I try to wait up to see if Chad comes back to the ranch to sleep here, I know it's not likely. He has his apartment downtown, and he looked so pissed at me and Spencer that I don't believe he'll show up tonight.

He did tell me he'd see me tomorrow, so staying on the porch waiting for him is just stupid.

Honestly, I don't know what I'd tell him if he asked me what that was about. He knows I still like Spencer, so it's not like that was a surprise. But I can understand him being overprotective of me.

Maybe I'm just overreacting. Maybe he just wanted to talk to Spencer and ask his friend what was going on. Maybe it was a surprise to Chad that Spencer still has feelings for me.

Is that what it even was? Does that kiss mean that he still has feelings for me?

Or maybe Spencer was just feeling nostalgic after returning to school and seeing those familiar faces that were around us when we dated, so for some reason, he felt like he wanted to take another trip down memory lane. Who knows?

Frustrated, I exhale and head to my bedroom, my brain exhausted from trying to think of reasons and explanations for this stupid kiss.

I don't hear from Chad the next morning. Nor Spencer.

I hear from Poppy though, who's sent me a thousand text messages asking why the hell I left the party without talking to her.

"Shit," I mumble to myself as I read her text, shoving a piece of toast in my mouth and pouring some coffee into my mug. The kitchen is empty, given that I slept in, and Mom and Dad probably had their breakfast earlier. Lauren crashed here last night, but there's still no sign of her anywhere, so I'm assuming she's still sleeping.

"A little too early to be swearing, don't you think?" my sister asks from behind me, as if summoned by my thoughts. I look over my shoulder, watching her drag herself to the chair across from me. She grabs a cup for herself and pours some black coffee into it. "God, I'm so exhausted, and I didn't even do anything drastic last night," she complains, leaning back on her chair.

"Maybe you're working too much. Can't you take a break? When is your vacation, anyway?" I ask, deciding to keep my mind occupied with someone else's life other than mine.

Poppy can wait for my answer. Especially since I'm not sure I want to tell her the reason I left her behind was because Chad saw me kissing Spencer and told me to leave the party as if he was my father. Now that I think about it, it makes my blood boil. He had no right to tell me what to do.

"In two months. And no, I can't take a break. We're short-staffed since Kate is on maternity leave, and James is on vacation," she explains with a shrug.

"That sucks," I say, feeling sympathetic. I can tell she's tired and the dark circles under her eyes are not from partying too hard, even though Lauren does like to do that sometimes. "Are you working today? Or can you stay here so we can watch a movie or something? I miss having sister time with you."

Her shoulders sag as she looks at me. "Sorry, pony. I am on duty tonight."

"It's fine." I shake my head, reassuring her. "I can ask Poppy. Although, I'm not so sure I want to see her right now. From her seventeen messages, I can tell she wants to rip my head off for leaving her behind last night."

Lauren sneers as she blows on her coffee, almost spitting everything on her lap. I narrow my eyes at her, daring her to tell me the reason why she thinks this is so funny.

"What?" She tosses her hands up in surrender. "It just amazes me how you're so good at screwing things up. You should slow down and mess things up one at a time," she teases, jumping to the side and dodging my slap.

"Shut up," I tell her angrily. "In my defense, I didn't have much of a choice. Chad pretty much kicked me out of the school. I forgot to call her. I was a bit out of my mind at the moment."

"Yeah, right," Lauren muses excitedly. "The kiss. What's that all about anyway?"

I take a deep breath, not wanting to dive into that topic again. "I don't know. Can we talk about something else other than Spencer? I'm honestly not in the mood."

"Fine, fine." My sister takes the last muffin from the tray on the table and shoves it in her mouth. I realize I'm really not in the best mood since it doesn't even bother me that she took the last one. "So, I've been meaning to ask you. I remember you talked to me a while ago about this book you were writing, and then I saw it open on your computer the other day. Are you back on it?"

Lauren sounds genuinely interested in this, and it's not that I don't think she supports me, but it takes me by surprise that she is suddenly asking me about...well, me. I don't want to make it sound like my family is not interested in things that concern me, it's just that I prefer when we talk about other people.

I shrug, suddenly feeling vulnerable and naked. "I'm giving it a try. Poppy said I should finish it, and honestly, if I ever want to publish it, I need to write it first."

"That is so nice, pony. I love your writing. I mean," she corrects when she sees my confused expression, "I know it's not the same to read newspaper articles, but I remember how good your stories were, and I believe you'd be an amazing writer."

"Thanks, Lauren. I really appreciate it."

"Of course. That's what I'm here for. Anyway…" She jumps to her feet, swallowing the last piece of the muffin that I am now regretting I didn't eat, and cleans her hands on her pants. "I'd love to stay here and chat with you all day, but I need to get home and get some things done before my shift. Talk to you later?"

"Yeah, sure. Have a good day, and take care," I tell her, waving her goodbye as I watch her walk through the back door.

"Always do," she yells back, already out of my sight.

As soon as I'm alone again, I ponder what to do with my day. My phone buzzes once more, and I see another text from Poppy. Since I'm desperate to have a peaceful day, and I know she won't let me be until I reply to her, I grab the device from the table and type an answer. I simply tell her that something came up, but everything's fine, and I'll tell her everything on Monday morning. I don't want to lie to her, but I also don't want her to show up at my doorstep during the day prying.

Poppy tries to convince me to tell her more, but I just say I have to help Dad with the chores, and I'll make it up to her another day.

It isn't a lie. I barely have time to think about something to do with my free time when Dad shows up on the porch, calling me and asking for a helping hand. I honestly consider telling him that I'm too tired to help today, but I can't bring myself to do it. I can't remember a day where I denied him my help.

Yeah, I'm that good of a daughter. It's one of the few things I do with my life that I'm proud of.

We spend the rest of the morning and most of the afternoon cleaning the barn and feeding the horses, and I even have the opportunity to race Dad across the field on the back of my favorite horse. The day is chilly, and I have to wear a few layers of clothing, which makes me stiffer than I like to be when I'm on a horse, but I love this weather.

I can't wait for winter, although I know it's hard to simply go outside, or even get up from bed. But I love the cloudy days, the

Christmas spirit, the snow... It makes everything so magical. It's my favorite time of the year.

By the time Mom calls us to come inside and grab an afternoon coffee, we're all spent and desperately in need of a shower. I have hay all over my boots and under my flannel shirt, and my hair is sweaty and plastered to my forehead. But I enjoy some family time with Mom and Dad, planning to go upstairs and spoil myself with a hot shower in a bit.

"How are things going at the newspaper, sweetheart?" Mom asks me kindly while she cuts Dad a piece of her apple pie.

I'm already drooling just from smelling it from afar.

"Well, you know, it's just...going," I tell her with a shrug, looking beyond the porch, staring at the mountains in the distance.

"You don't sound very enthusiastic," Dad observes, chewing his pie.

"That's because I'm not. I love being a writer, but I don't love my career anymore," I explain. "I'm not as moved by it as I used to be."

Mom studies me in silence for a second before chiming in.

"Do you think this is just a phase or you simply don't like it?" she asks curiously.

"I don't know. I like my routine at the newspaper, even though my boss makes my life harder than it has to be. But I feel like I want to try something different, even though I have no idea what that might be." I take a sip of my coffee, trying to ignore the worried looks they shoot at me. I know they're only concerned about my future and my happiness, but it sucks not to be able to give them a proper answer.

"So why don't you do something else? Why don't you quit?" Dad presses, flashing me an encouraging smile.

Quit? How could he suggest something like that?

I went to college, studied all those years, graduated, and got a job so I could make a living and help around the house. Quitting sounds like giving up. Like I failed somehow. I'm used to earning my own money, to be able to give back—even though in smaller doses—everything they did and still do for me. It's not fair to them to simply quit. And do what?

"Why would I do that? I don't have any idea about what I want to do," I tell them, creasing my brows in confusion.

"You can write your book. Isn't that something you always wanted?" Mom suggests.

"This won't pay my bills, Mom."

"You don't have to pay for anything. That's what we're here for," Dad adds, leaning back in his chair.

I turn to face him in disbelief.

"Of course not! I'd never do something like that. I'm almost thirty, Dad. I can't expect you to provide for me for the rest of your lives," I retort, keeping my voice low even though the idea frustrates me. I should be the one providing for them now, not the other way around. They've done so much for me and my siblings. It's only fair that we reciprocate now. But I can't do that if I decide to quit just because I'm being greedy and selfish.

"Don't be ridiculous, Hayden. We're your parents," my mom says in a scolding tone. "If not us, then who? It's okay to accept help."

"And I already do. I live here with you. Everyone else is out of the house and living by themselves, providing for themselves." I would be lying if I said that doesn't bother me a bit. Don't get me wrong, I love my brothers and sister, and I'm always rooting for their happiness and success, but somehow it makes me feel like a failure because I haven't achieved what they have.

Yes, I know I'm not being fair to myself, but I can't help but think like that.

"Is that how you feel? Hayden, there's nothing wrong with living with your parents when you're almost thirty. If anything, I'm glad we still have you around the house," Dad confesses. "This ranch is a lot to handle, and even though I have employees, they're not members of the Jenkins family. You are. I love that you care for this place as much as I do. And I know you don't do this out of daughterly duty but because you love it here."

He's right. I do love this place. That was one of the reasons why I didn't go to LA with Spencer in the past. I wasn't ready to give up on this place.

This ranch, this city, is a part of me. I could never leave it behind.

"You know what? Why don't you come help me at the bakery? You'd have time to write your book, help your dad with the ranch, and still pay for your bills," Mom offers, a wide smile on her face.

I frown at her unexpected invitation. "You already have Alice."

My sister-in-law has been working with my mother at the bakery for quite some time now. It's true that most of the time, just the two of them is not enough to handle everything, but so far, they have managed to do it just fine.

"The poor thing can't handle everything by herself. And I'm constantly in the kitchen," my mother retorts.

"What about Anna?" I insist, reminding her of her other employee. She's still young and is only working so she can help her parents with her college tuition, so she can't be at the bakery the entire day. And Alice and Mom struggle to keep everything in order, just the two of them. I know she could use the help.

"You already know she's only a part-time worker. You could come in the afternoons and help us. Promise you'll think about it?"

The look in her eyes is hard to ignore. Mom has this amazing ability to make her children do whatever she needs just by looking at us. It doesn't help that Dad seems to have learned how to do that, too, so now I have two puppy-faced parents staring at me expectantly.

"Fine, Mom. I'll think about it. I'm still employed, so don't get your hopes up," I tell her. "Now, if you'll excuse me, I'll take a shower, wash my hair, and maybe try to write a little bit of that book I was supposed to finish."

"Am I in it?" Dad asks playfully, winking at me as I get up from my seat and head to the stairs.

"Only if you're the villain," I shoot back, looking over my shoulder and grinning at him.

"Make me a really bad one," he jokes before I disappear to the second floor.

My shower takes longer than necessary, but only because I allow myself to think about my novel while washing my hair and listening to some old hip hop songs. I always loved to pretend I'm giving a concert while in the shower—something that made Chad freak out whenever he still lived here because he always complained about me occupying the bathroom for too long.

It's a good way to just forget about things and pretend I'm a carefree person, singing her lungs out while listening to my favorite songs.

I'm not sure if I want to continue writing my novel from where I stopped or if I should just start over. It's been so long since I came up with the idea for it that it feels like I'm a completely different person now and have new ideas and stories to tell.

Eventually, I step out of the bathroom, my hair wrapped in a towel, dressed in my flannel pajamas, I sit cross-legged on my bed with my laptop on my lap and stare at the old file for a couple of minutes before deciding to reread everything I have so far so I can update myself with the story and remember what my plans were for it.

I don't even realize the time passing as I start changing most of what I'm reading, altering sentences here and there, and adapting some plots I'm not satisfied with anymore.

It's only when I hear a commotion downstairs that I pull my eyes off the screen, perking my ears up to understand what's going on. Mom and Dad should be asleep by now. It's past midnight already.

Chad and Lauren aren't here, and Ryan came back from his honeymoon yesterday, so he should be at his home now.

No employees would come to the main house unless something urgent has happened, but to be fair, I don't remember that ever happening before.

Frowning, hearing the sounds downstairs rising, I toss my laptop aside, shoving my legs out of the bed, and forcing myself out of the room. My heart is beating rapidly against my chest, and the hair on the back of my neck is standing on edge as I shoot down the stairs, completely unsure of what to expect.

Did someone barge in?

Should I grab a gun or something?

On second thought, I should have grabbed the baseball bat Chad gave me when I was a teenager. He said I should keep it behind my bedroom door just in case. Now is that time, and I don't have it.

By the time I reach the end of the stairs, I see Dad rushing from one side of the living room to the other, his wallet and car key in his hand, while the other holds his phone against his ear.

"We'll be there in a minute. Keep us informed," he says to whoever is on the other end of the line.

I hear Mom sobbing on the couch, and that's when my entire body freezes. I can't make my legs move. I can't open my mouth. I know something bad happened. I can feel it in my bones.

Forcing myself to take a step forward, I walk toward the living room where Dad is helping my mom off the couch. When I get to the doorway, he looks up at me, his eyes watery and his brows creased in concern.

"What happened?" I manage to say.

I don't know if I want to hear the answer, though.

"Sweetheart…" He clears his throat, staring at Mom before glancing at me again. "It's your sister. She's in the hospital."

CHAPTER TEN

I can't believe this is happening.

As Dad drives us to the hospital, my mind is swirling with horrible scenarios of what could have happened to Lauren.

She was supposed to be on her shift. She told me this morning she would be working.

Did she get hurt on duty? How bad is it? Is it a good sign we don't know anything else?

After my father said she was in the hospital, I helped him get Mom off the couch and put her in the truck. I climbed into the back seat, completely mute. I couldn't make myself utter a word, and I still can't.

I don't know what to say. Anything I say will be meaningless until we know more.

Should I comfort my parents?

I shake my head, not allowing myself to go down that road.

Lauren is fine. I know that. She's the toughest, strongest person I know. Whatever happens to her, she will survive it.

There's no way I can accept any other outcome.

The tires of Dad's truck squeal as it comes to a stop in the hospital parking lot a few minutes later. I don't think he's ever driven this fast in his life. Mom is out of the truck before he can even turn it off. I rush after her, making sure to stay by her side as Dad catches up with us. We all rush to the reception desk, which thankfully seems to be calm with the waiting area nearly empty tonight.

The sweet-looking, calm receptionist looks up at my mom, taking in her worried face.

"How can I help you, ma'am?"

"I'm Norah Jenkins. My daughter was taken to this hospital. She works for the fire department. Her name is Lauren Jenkins," Mom blurts out in a rush, her voice quavering.

The woman types a couple of things on her computer and turns to us once more. "She's on the second floor. I'm afraid she can't receive any visitors yet, though, since the doctors are still working on her I'm sorry."

"I need to see my daughter!" Mom yells, drawing the attention of other patients and people around us.

"Mom…" I say in a low voice, hoping to calm her down. The last thing we need is to make a scene. I know she's worried and impatient, but unfortunately, we need to wait.

"Norah?" a loving, sweet voice calls from behind us, and the three of us turn on our heels to see the source of it. Valerie West is standing before us, her eyes red and her always perfectly styled gray hair loose and unruly around her face. She's a kind woman, around her seventies, who's always been a good friend to our family, and a caring and important part of our city.

"Valerie, what is going on?" my father asks hesitantly.

Valerie looks at him, shaking her head and suddenly looking guilty. "Oh, Oscar. Your sweet girl saved Bob's life tonight."

"What do you mean?" Mom chimes in, tears running down her cheeks already.

My throat is so dry, and my hands so sweaty, that all I manage to do is stare at Valerie's face, trying to make sense of what she's saying. We haven't heard from Lauren yet, so I have no idea what's going on, but apparently, Valerie does, so that's something.

"Bob insisted on going to the restaurant, saying he thought he had forgotten to put something into the fridge. I told him not to go, to call one of the boys that work there since it was late, but he ignored me, stubborn as always," she explains. She loses her balance for a second as her tiny frail frame stands across from us. My father notices it and helps her get to a chair in the corner of the room, away from the chaotic routine of the hospital.

"Thank you, Oscar. I told Bob to wait until tomorrow, but he got into his car and drove to the restaurant anyway. Next thing I know, he's calling me, saying there was an explosion in the kitchen. He told me to call the fire department because the smoke was getting too thick and he couldn't find his way out," Valerie carries on, her eyes filled with tears. "I don't know how this happened…"

"What happened to my sister, Mrs. West?" I ask tentatively, desperate to know about her state. I already know Bob is fine, which is great, so for now, I just need to hear the same thing about Lauren.

Valerie stares at me with a sympathetic look on her face. "I don't know. They told me that she barged inside when she realized Bob was still in there. Her colleagues were just here a minute ago. Maybe you can catch them? I think they went to the cafeteria."

"Thank you, Mrs. West. I'm really glad to know Bob is all right," I tell her honestly. I am so proud of Lauren for saving him, I really am. I just hope she managed to save herself too.

"Mrs. Jenkins?" the receptionist who greeted us when we came in calls to my mom, rising from her chair behind her desk. "The doctor will see you now. Your daughter is awake."

Only God knows how I don't collapse on the ground when I feel my knees buckling beneath me.

Lauren is awake. She's fine. I know it.

Completely disoriented, we mumble some words to Valerie, saying we'll catch up with her later, and we head to the second floor where the receptionist tells us to meet the doctor who tended to Lauren in his office. As soon as he sees my mom's condition, he hands her a bottle of water and assures her that her daughter is fine.

He then proceeds to explain to us what happened. As Mrs. West told us, Lauren went inside to save Bob, and apparently, there might have been a malfunction in her protection equipment.

"She inhaled a lot of smoke and had to undergo a few procedures such as X-ray, arterial blood gas analysis, and monitoring of her vital signs," the doctor tells us.

He names a few other procedures that Lauren went through that I don't understand. The only thing I register from what he tells us is that my sister should be fine.

"She just has to be under observation since the amount of smoke she inhaled caused inflammation in her lungs, so it's wiser to keep her under monitoring, at least for the night," he concludes, and I can't express how relieved I am to hear this.

Mom and Dad remain silent, but nod at him.

"One of you can stay with her overnight," the doctor offers.

And, of course, Mom volunteers. Visitor's hours are over, but I think the doctor feels bad for my father and I, so he allows us to see Lauren, only for a few minutes.

She still has a mask on her face when we get to her room, but she's awake, like they said she was, and that's more than I could've asked for. My mom runs to her as soon as she crosses the threshold, gently wrapping her arms around my sister, careful so as not to suffocate her—no pun intended.

"Mom, be careful," I warn her anyway, afraid she might make Lauren's state worse, but my sister doesn't seem bothered. She just chuckles, patting Mom on the back and saying words of reassurance.

When she's finally released from mama bear's hug, Dad and I get to her.

"You scared the hell out of us, pony," I murmur, my eyes burning with unshed tears. Now that the adrenaline is wearing off, I feel all the emotions coming at me like a tidal wave. I don't want to cry in front of my parents, especially now that I see my sister is well, but it's so hard to control it when realization hits me. "What happened?"

I could've lost Lauren tonight.

"I'm sorry I got you all worried. I don't know what happened with the equipment, but when I realized it wasn't working properly, I was so close to get to him… Bob is really old, and he'd never be able to get out of there by himself. I had to get him out," Lauren explains, coughing a bit afterward. I can tell she's struggling to speak. Her lungs and throat are probably very sensitive and hurting from all the smoke she inhaled.

"It's all right. You don't have to say anything else now. Just rest," Dad orders, squeezing her hand gently. "Your mother will stay with you tonight, but I'll be here first thing in the morning, okay?"

"With my favorite chocolate chip cookies?" Lauren smirks at him.

"I'll see if I can sneak in one or two for you, don't worry." Dad winks at her before leaning in and giving her a kiss on the forehead. "Call me if you need anything," he tells Mom before pecking her on the lips.

As soon as we head outside, some guys from Lauren's work spot us and come to talk to my dad and me, but I'm still too distracted and lightheaded to pay attention, so I excuse myself, telling my father that I will go grab a coffee or something.

The elevator door opens on the first floor, and I head out, almost bumping into two huge guys with familiar faces staring back at me.

Chad and Spencer are standing side by side, their eyes widen as they recognize me.

"Hayden, what happened? Is Lauren okay?" Chad spits out as I step out of the elevator. I nod at him as he keeps shooting his questions at me. "I came as soon as Dad texted me. Why didn't you call?"

I shrug, still making sense of everything. It feels like my head is empty and void all of a sudden. "I don't know. He got this call, and we rushed here. But she's fine. I just came back from her room. Mom will stay with her tonight."

"Where is she? I won't be convinced until I see her with my own eyes," Chad presses. I know it won't help to try and convince him that Lauren is okay. I wouldn't calm down either before seeing her myself. So, instead of telling him she can't have visitors, I just give him her room number, saying he'll find Dad in the hallway outside.

Spencer is completely silent by his side, and even though I don't look at him, I can feel his eyes on me.

"Where are you going?" Chad asks with his brows creased as I continue moving in the opposite direction.

"I'm just going to grab some coffee. I'm feeling a bit lighthearted, and Dad is still talking to Lauren's coworkers," I reply slowly.

Chad's eyes move from me to Spencer, and with a silent nod, they come to an agreement on something. I have no idea what it is.

"Spencer will go with you. Leave Dad to me, I'll get him home," Chad says, and before I make sense of what he's saying, he's out of my sight, stepping into the elevator and vanishing.

Only then I turn to look at Spencer, feeling completely confused.

"What the hell just happened?"

Spencer is staring at me, his piercing blue eyes studying my face carefully. He's dressed in black sweatpants and a hoodie, his hands in his pockets. Were he and Chad hanging out before coming here? They didn't seem to be on good terms when my brother told me to leave the school last night, but now they are here together, so it makes me wonder if it means they're okay.

I'm instantly reminded of our kiss, and I feel my cheeks burning with embarrassment, so I try to cover them with my hair, letting it fall over my shoulders and face.

"I'll take you home," Spencer answers matter-of-factly, as if the whole silent exchange with Chad was this obvious.

"Why?" I press stubbornly. "I came with my dad. I can go back with him."

"You heard Chad. He'll take your dad home. Come on, you look like you need some sleep," Spencer insists, taking one hand out of his pocket and laying it on my lower back, guiding me toward the exit. I ignore the way my entire body shivers under his touch and try to fill the awkward silence with another witty remark.

But nothing comes to mind.

Maybe he's right. I do need some rest. My brain feels like it has melted, and I have such a headache that it seems like my skull is about to explode from the inside out.

"Are you feeling okay?" Spencer asks softly as we finally get to his car parked outside, and he opens the door for me. I wonder if Chad came with him, which I'm assuming he did, so at least Dad won't have to drive back home alone.

"Yeah, I'm fine," I whisper, leaning back on the leather passenger seat and closing my eyes, enjoying the comfort it provides me. I suddenly miss my bed.

It's so funny how adrenaline works in our bodies. At one moment, it feels like we can face the world to get to our loved ones, making sure they are well, and once that fear and the scare wears off, our bodies feel so heavy and exhausted that we can barely keep ourselves up on two feet.

I keep my eyes closed as I feel Spencer driving out of the parking lot and onto the street. I allow myself to relish the smooth curves the car makes, almost as if it's lulling me to sleep. But even as I try to ignore my surroundings, Spencer's magnetic presence keeps me on the edge of my seat. I can't ignore him seated right next to me. Nor can I ignore his amazing scent inebriating my senses.

Opening my eyes slowly, I dare to glance to the side, taking in his stoic profile. He looks so focused on the road ahead that I don't think he notices me staring. His sharp jawline, his perfect nose, the dimple on his right cheek, his slightly long hair covering his ears and eyebrows, almost long enough to get in the way of his eyes... All of it is so mesmerizing and breathtaking.

Sometimes, I think Spencer isn't even human. He seems to have climbed off the cover of a magazine.

There's also this masculine charm that exudes from him, as if he carries this aura that immediately draws everyone to him.

And then there are his lips. So soft, so inviting, so irresistible, so... swollen?

Is that dry blood on the corner of his lower lip?

Now that I'm paying attention to it, I do notice his lips look puffier than I remember them being last night.

Did I do that? No, that's not something I'd do. I'm not that...savage. Am I?

"What happened to your lips? Did I do that to you?" I hear myself asking, my voice coated with disbelief.

To my surprise, Spencer smirks to himself, a breathy chuckle coming out of his throat.

"I wish I could say it was because of something as good as your kiss," he answers without looking at me. My entire core bursts into flames just by his mere flirtatious sentence.

Stop being such a softie, Hayden. Grow up!

"Although, I must confess the kiss was indirectly responsible for it," Spencer adds, darting me a side glance and winking at me.

Shit, is it possible to combust from passion and lust? How can he do this to me?

I cross my legs, feeling slightly uncomfortable in-between them, deciding to look at the road ahead instead of his pretty, stupid face.

"What is that supposed to mean?" I act nonchalant, ignoring the way my insides are twisting and screaming because of him. "Are you saying you got your fun somewhere else after I turned you on and left?" I blurt out, hating the fact that this idea makes me bitter with jealousy. I don't know if I want to hear him say he had to find someone else to take care of him after I interrupted our make out session and left him hanging.

A hoarse, throaty laugh comes out of him this time. Spencer shakes his head, leaning his head against the headrest.

"What?" I squeak, frustrated.

"You were always so creative," Spencer tells me in response. "How do you come up with these things anyway?"

"I don't see what's so unbelievable about that. It's not like a slut couldn't do that to your lip," I bark back.

"No, it's not, but that's not what happened," he counters.

"So, what do you mean my kiss was indirectly responsible for you ending up with a split-lip?" I press.

Spencer takes a deep breath, suddenly turning serious again. Any glimpse of entertainment he was getting from this conversation is long gone now.

"Chad punched me because of our kiss," he simply says, shrugging as if it's nothing.

I can't say I didn't see that coming, but now that I'm hearing it, I can't help but let my jaw drop. "He did what?" I don't know why I sound so surprised, given that this was the first thing I feared happening when Chad met us out on the field last night. But since I didn't hear from either of them today, I thought that maybe, just maybe, I had misinterpreted Chad's reaction and was just being over-dramatic.

"I can't hold it against him. He had every right to do it," Spencer points out, unbothered.

"What are you saying? He had no right to hit you. Are you animals now? Why did he have to hit you?"

I don't know why I'm so annoyed, but I am. Why would Chad punch Spencer for kissing me? I get that he might be trying to protect me and all, but Spencer is his best friend, not some moron that took advantage of his sister.

"He was looking out for you," Spencer explains calmly. "He's your brother, and I don't blame him for doing it. I shouldn't have kissed you."

"You're saying you regret it?" I breathe, too offended with his implication.

"I didn't say that."

"But you thought it. That's how you feel?" I ask him, turning in my seat to face him. He doesn't answer me right away, but after a minute, the car comes to a stop in front of a house I don't recognize.

This is definitely not the ranch.

"Where are we?" I look around, trying to recognize the street and the houses on it. It's not like I've never been to this side of town before, but I don't remember knowing anyone that lives here.

"This is my house," Spencer answers, his voice less restrained now. His eyes are on my face, although his hands remain gripping the wheel in front of him. He doesn't look as calm and composed now, his jaw clenched and his shoulders tense. "And answering your other question, no, I don't regret it. I would never regret kissing you, Hayden. Even if I had to get punched every time I did it."

CHAPTER ELEVEN

’m not sure how to react to Spencer’s words, so I clear my throat, looking out the window, pretending to analyze his new house’s exterior.

I don’t understand what’s going on with him—with us—lately.

Why is Spencer trying so hard to get back into my life, kissing me and willing to be punched for it? What is all of this supposed to mean?

I know how I feel about him, and I know I shouldn’t feel like this anymore, not after so long. But does that mean Spencer feels the same way? Does he still have feelings for me?

It can’t be…

Seven years is a lot of time. Too much for someone to hold onto feelings that are supposed to be long gone.

I’m one to talk, but I’m different from Spencer. I never thought he could still nourish feelings for me after we broke up in such an ugly way. For all I knew, he was supposed to hate me.

My skin is itching from the weight of his eyes on me. I can’t see him since I’m staring out the window still, but I just know he’s looking at me and waiting for a reply. So, to break the ice and give him something—probably not what he wants—I decide to say something else instead.

"Did you buy this house? What about your old one?" I'm genuinely intrigued and curious. It's true that his family house is now his sister's, so I don't think he'd want to live with her and her family, no matter how much he loves them.

I guess what I really want to know is why he returned. Why he left his life in LA to come back home after so long. But I don't want to be that obvious, so it's better to start with a stupid question. One I already know the answer to.

"I'm used to living by myself. As much as I love Aubrie, Caitlin and Tom, I appreciate having my own space," he explains, opening the driver's door and climbing out of the car.

I don't know what to do, and I have no idea what we're doing here, but I follow him anyway.

"Where are you going?" I ask, jogging to keep up with him.

Spencer crosses the front yard, heading for the porch, the key already in his hand. He opens the front door and steps inside, holding it open for me. I hesitate, wondering why he's taking me to his house, but then I remember this is Spencer. He'd never do anything that I wouldn't want him to. I guess I'm more afraid of myself and my own desires and needs, if I'm being completely honest.

I'm surprised to see his house is more organized and beautiful than I expected. Spencer has always been a man of taste, but he's a man nonetheless, and I'm ashamed to say I never imagined his home would be this neat and...cozy.

The decorations are a mix of contemporary art and antique pieces, but surprisingly, the contrast seems to work perfectly. I love the rustic, wooden furniture, with a heavy oak table in the center of the dining room that reminds me of a forest cottage. It's a one-story house, but it's spacious enough for a small family to live in. And since Spencer lives alone, it's more than enough for a bachelor like him.

He walks inside, heading toward what I think is the kitchen, and I follow behind him, taking in my surroundings as we go deeper into the house. I spot an open door that seems to lead to an office/studio, with several pieces of audio equipment and a computer with at least three monitors on top of a huge desk. I also see one guest room, a bathroom, and a closed door at the end of the hallway which I assume is the master suite, a.k.a his bedroom.

Ignoring this nagging desire to go ahead and peep into his bedroom, wondering what it looks like, I shake my head and meet him in the kitchen where he is now opening a cabinet and taking something out of it. When he turns to me, I notice there are two crystal glasses in his hands.

"Do you want some wine?" he offers, raising one eyebrow at me. "Or are you still into that shitty vodka you used to drink in high school?"

I suppress a chuckle, not wanting him to see me blushing from his good memory about my poor taste in drinks. I'm slightly embarrassed that he still manages to make me swoon with everything he says.

"Wine is fine," I finally answer, shifting on my feet, uncertain what to do with myself. "What are we doing here, Spencer? I thought you were taking me home."

I watch him open the bottle of wine, taking his time to pour the liquid into our glasses. His eyes are focused on the task at hand, but I notice the way his face swiftly grimaces as if he had been expecting this question to come at some point.

"I was hoping we could talk. I know we had a conversation by the river the other day, but it didn't go as planned, and well, I think it'd be nice to be mature about this," he explains, handing me my glass. I take a sip from it, observing him as he leans against the sink and faces me. "Especially since last night."

"When you kissed me," I add, leaning against the kitchen counter across from him, keeping a safe distance between us.

"Exactly," he agrees, nodding at me from behind his glass of wine. The intensity in his gaze is so strong that I'm momentarily distracted by his eyes and the way he watches my every move. The way his throat bobs as he drinks the wine also makes me think about things I shouldn't.

You shouldn't have come inside, Hayden. Standing in the same room with Spencer is never a good idea.

"Okay, do you want to start by telling me what happened between you and Chad?" I ask tentatively, setting my glass on the counter and crossing my arms on top of my chest, trying to look intimidating. "You said he punched you, but you seemed to be very friendly with each other at the hospital earlier."

Spencer shrugs, putting his glass of wine aside as well. "We came to an agreement."

I crease my brows at him. "What was that?"

"Chad saw us kissing last night, like I told you. We argued, and he told me I should stay away from you because you were really hurt when we broke up, and he didn't want you to go through that again," he explains, narrating the story with a firm voice.

"Chad punched you just because of that?" Something isn't adding up for me. Even though my brother is a bit hot-headed when it comes to his sisters, a kiss wouldn't make him be aggressive with his best friend.

Spencer lets out a throaty laugh, holding my gaze. "I might have told him this wasn't his business. And that I wouldn't stay away from you."

I gulp, unsure how to take his answer. Should I indulge the crazy thoughts swirling around in my head, telling me to feed these feelings that Spencer is quickly and alarmingly digging up? Is that even his goal? What if I end up getting hurt again?

"Why not?" I press.

"Because I don't want to. I told you I missed having you in my life, Hayden, and I mean it." Spencer takes a few steps forward, stopping in front of me. Our eyes are locked, unable to focus on anything other than each other. At this point, my entire body is frozen, unable to move, shivering from head to toe as I take in his closeness, his scent, his presence... It's almost too much to bear.

"What are you doing, Spencer? What are WE doing?" I let out in a low voice. "This is wrong. We hurt each other. This can only end badly, so why are you doing this?"

"Why do you think, Hayden? I never forgot you. I couldn't," he tells me softly. "In all these seven years away from you, there wasn't one single person that ever made me feel the way you did. Don't you feel the same? Don't you feel the same things I do whenever I'm close to you?" Spencer takes another step forward, and his arms wrap around my waist, pulling me gently against him.

His eyes search my face, looking for any sign of resistance, anything that will tell him that I don't want this. Spencer will respect whatever I say. He's noble that way.

But no matter how hard I try to convince myself that telling him no is the right thing to do, I can't voice it. I can't push him away. I can't make him see reason. Because, at this moment, all I want is for him to take me in his arms and say he loves me.

"Why now? I mean, we haven't seen each other in seven years. How is it even possible that we still harbor feelings for each other?" I sound frustrated, but the frustration is entirely directed at myself. I wish I could control these feelings, to tell my heart who to love and who to hate, but whenever Spencer is concerned, I don't seem to have the reins over my life anymore.

"I admit I've been afraid to see you. I was thankful that all the times I came home in the past, you managed to find a way to stay away," Spencer confesses, his eyes crinkling as he smiles softly at me, noticing my surprised reaction. He knew I was running away from him this entire time? "I know that's what you've been doing. I wasn't sure how I'd feel seeing you again either. I was afraid that whatever I felt for you back then would come back and sweep me off my feet again. I wasn't ready for that."

"And what changed?" I pry, feeling my insides tighten with desire and love for this man. He always knew how to be romantic and say the right things to win me over.

"I couldn't escape you at your brother's wedding, could I? I wasn't planning on staying here, I didn't expect to be so affected by you after so long, but I guess I was wrong."

"You didn't seem affected when you were waltzing around with that supermodel dangling on your arm," I tease, biting down the jealousy I feel just by remembering the sight of Spencer's arms around that woman.

He chuckles, his eyes narrowing on my lips. "Millie stood no chance against you. From the moment I set eyes on you again, I knew I was doomed."

At this point, my entire being is melted by his words. My core is on fire, and I feel my knees buckling under me. Good thing Spencer is holding me. In fact, he's slowly but surely pushing me backward, pinning me against the counter. I can feel he's just as eager to get through my clothes as I am to get through his, but he's always been gentle and respectful with me.

However, there's a fire in his eyes, a hunger in his touch, that tells me that he's struggling to keep himself composed.

I chew on my bottom lip, waiting to see what he's going to do. His eyes dart to my lips and instantly darken, a flash of longing rushing through them.

"Don't do that," Spencer orders in a warning tone, his gaze still stuck on my mouth.

"Do what?" I play dumb, slightly darting my tongue out and licking my lips.

I can't think of anything else at this moment. I have so much to worry about. There's so much happening in my life—my sister is in a hospital bed, for heaven's sake—but all I can focus on is Spencer's strong arms around me, his eyes eating me whole, and his inviting lips curling up in a smirk as he presses himself against me.

"You should know better than to provoke me, Jenkins."

I used to love it when he called me that. That has always been Spencer's way to flirt with me, and God, does it feel good to hear him call me that again. I don't know where I'm gathering all this courage from, but the way he's looking at me makes me feel empowered, desired, like I haven't felt in a long time.

Sure, I have men looking at me like I'm a piece of meat all the time, but with Spencer, it's different. It's like he desires and worships me at the same time. It's like there's no one else in the world other than me for him.

"I'm not doing anything, Bailey," I retort jokingly, lifting my chin in defiance. "You're the one trying to seduce me with wine and all this sweet talking."

Spencer lifts his brows, amused, his grin widening. "Is it working?"

"Yeah, you've always been very good at that," I whisper, tossing my arms around his neck and pulling him down toward me. Our lips meet, and if there was any restraint around Spencer before, that is forgotten as soon as our lips touch. His entire body relaxes, and he suddenly feels more confident and sure of what to do. He grips my waist as if he's afraid I'll disappear into thin air if he lets go of me.

His hands find the hem of my shirt and sneak under it, caressing my stomach with feather touches. It's only at this moment, when I feel the cold touch of his fingers on my skin, that I realize I'm wearing my flannel pajamas. My self-consciousness is immediately on alert, reminding me that I must look terrible. I fled from the house with my parents when I heard the news about Lauren, and I didn't even have the time to brush my wet hair.

I pull it into a messy bun, in an attempt to make it look slightly better, but also unable to do anything else without a brush and a mirror.

It might not make any difference though. The flannel set I'm wearing is not sexy at all. If anything, Spencer should be unstimulated by the sight of me in long pajamas. But he definitely doesn't look or act like it. The way he's kissing me so passionately and hungrily makes me forget all my concerns about how I look or what I'm wearing.

While one hand grips my waist, making sure I'm exactly where he wants me to be, his other hand continues to travel up my stomach, across my ribs, reaching the lower part of my breast. My body instantly stiffen, my nipple going hard as I feel his hand getting close to it. A soft moan escapes my throat when Spencer cups my breast, squeezing it between his strong fingers, his thumb brushing against my aroused nipple.

It's been so long since I've been with a man, but I don't remember ever feeling this sensitive, this turned on, this pleased before. Even when Spencer and I dated, it was amazing, but still different than this. We weren't as experienced and mature as we are now. But he's always known how to make me feel good.

And he's barely even started.

Without breaking our passionate kiss, Spencer effortlessly grabs me and sits me on top of the counter. I spread my legs slightly to accommodate his figure between them, but that only makes me realize how wet and ready I am for some release. I scoot forward a bit, trying to get some friction, anything to satiate my need for him, and that proves to be enough of a signal for Spencer to speed things up a bit.

A raspy growl escapes his throat as his hands dart to my ass and pull me even closer to him. This is not the ideal position for me to get what I want, but it'll do for now. I can't even consider the idea of pulling away from him for a second. My entire body is in a frenzy to get more of him and his touch. He lowers his lips to my jaw, and then down my neck, and I hum in pleasure.

He does get a bit farther away from me while doing that though, so I lock my ankles behind him and bring Spencer closer against me again.

"As much as I love a good make-out in the kitchen, don't you think we should move to the couch or maybe your bed?" I suggest, searching his eyes.

Spencer looks at me, his gaze still darkened and lustful, but as he considers my question, I see a flicker of reason in his features, as if he's just now realizing what we're about to do. His face hardens a bit, a serious facade taking over as he removes his hands from my butt. My insides twist in protest, the absence of his warm touch momentarily leaving me on edge.

"Are you sure about this, Hayden? I didn't mean to force you, I—"

"Don't you dare leave me hanging like this, Spencer," I scold, wrapping my hands around his neck again, trapping him there. "It's not fair," I whine, climbing off the counter and gluing our bodies together. I can feel his hardness against my stomach, and it only makes my brain more numb and hazy than it should be right now.

"I don't want you to regret it," he counters, his voice hoarse with lust, but determined. It's clear to me that he'll back down in a second if this means me regretting sleeping with him tomorrow.

But I don't want to regret it. I don't want to think about tomorrow. I don't want to think about anything other than us right now. I just want him to make me feel the way he used to in the past. Those were the happiest days of my life, and I'm in desperate need to feel like a teenager again. If only for tonight.

"I won't," I tell him firmly, staring deep into the deep pools of blue that are his eyes. "No regrets. I promise."

CHAPTER TWELVE

Spencer doesn't need to hear anything else from me after that. His hands easily grab the back of my thighs, lifting me from the floor and carrying me to the end of the hallway, to a room I'm sure now is his bedroom. I wrap my legs around his waist, nibbling his ear and neck as he walks us through the house.

His grip around me tightens as I reach his earlobe, and I feel his chest reverberate as he groans.

"Hayden," he warns.

I chuckle to myself, not caring to stop what I'm doing. I know exactly where his weak spots are, and I sure as hell don't intend to stop now.

"I'm glad to know I still know some things about you," I whisper against his ear before tugging my hand into his hair and pulling him toward me, claiming his lips once more. He reciprocates my kiss while blindingly kicking the door open, not caring to close it behind him once he steps inside.

Before I know it, Spencer tosses me on my back onto his soft mattress, climbing on top of me. He holds his weight with both his hands placed on either side of my head, watching me from above.

"I can't believe you're here," he mutters, and I can definitely hear the emotion behind his voice. But if I allow myself to be sentimental about this, this will soon become a teary encounter instead of a steamy one.

"Me neither," I concede.

But who am I kidding?

There's no way things between us can ever be something else other than sentimental. Even when we were together like this, it was never just physical. There was always something else there. Call it love, soulmates, companionship, whatever... It's just always been more powerful and meaningful than anything else I've experienced in my life. And by the way Spencer's looking at me now, I assume he feels the same way.

His fingers find the hem of my shirt again, darting to the last button as he slowly starts to open it. My eyes follow his every move, enjoying the sensations he causes in me. Soon enough, Spencer removes my shirt, which flies above his head and lands somewhere on the floor. He takes in the sight before him before burying his head in the nape of my neck, lowering himself until he's between my breasts. With soft kisses, he caresses my skin, moving from one nipple to the other before grabbing one between his teeth, nibbling at it before savoring it in his mouth.

I gasp with pleasure, arching my back and hips involuntarily, needing more contact, more of him. Spencer chuckles against my skin, and with his free hand, he reaches between us, finding the hem of my panties under my flannel pants. I brace myself for what's to come, closing my eyes in ecstasy as Spencer's fingers find my most sensitive spot. They easily slide through my already wet folds, and I can't help but relish how he moves so skillfully, knowing exactly where I need and like him the most.

"Holy shit," I hiss, unable to think of anything else to say.

Spencer pulls his head from my breast, looking me in the eyes with the largest smirk on his face. "I'm glad to know I still know some things about you," he repeats my exact words, teasing me.

So, this is how he's playing, huh?

With a sarcastic smile—or the closest to it I can pull off while he plays with his fingers inside me—I reach for the bulge in his sweatpants, noticing his eyes close as I squeeze his manhood in my hands.

"Shit, Hayden…" he curses under his breath, savoring the way I'm teasing him.

But with a swift movement, Spencer is out of the bed. Before I can complain or utter a single word, he pulls his hoodie over his head, revealing his toned abs, his six pack so defined that it's ridiculous. I remember Spencer being sculptured when he was younger, but this… this is something completely different. He's a grown man, bulkier and hotter than ever. I'm sure I'm drooling, my mouth agape, as I watch him undress, but I don't give a damn.

He drops his pants and boxers to the floor, standing completely naked in front of me. I'm squirming on his bed, eager for him to return and cover me with his weight and warmth, but Spencer seems to suddenly want to take his time and torture me. From under his hooded gaze, he looks up, flashing his grin at me as his hands excruciatingly slowly remove my pants, sliding them down my legs, doing the same with my underwear next.

I spread my legs open to accommodate his full frame when Spencer lowers himself on top of me again, no layers of clothing in the way preventing us from feeling each other's skin completely now. I'm taken aback for a second at how right it feels to have him here. It's like we're molded for each other. The way we move, the way we connect, the way our bodies fit together—it's all so…familiar.

"God, I missed you like crazy," Spencer murmurs as he gently caresses my cheeks, cupping my face and holding me still under his stare. He leans down, grabbing my lips with his once more. Without breaking our kiss, I feel Spencer adjusting his hips, and with a gasp, I feel him sliding himself inside of me.

My body is sore and stiff as I yawn and stretch on the softest, most comfortable mattress I've ever laid on. The smell of fresh coffee fills my nostrils, and I smile to myself, the first seconds of my day already giving me so much pleasure that it's hard to force my eyes open. But when I do, reality comes crashing down on me.

I don't know this room.

I snap my head from one side to the other, taking in the expensive wooden furniture around, the luxurious and plush bed, and my flannel pajamas and panties spread out on the floor.

"Shit!" I hiss, sitting straight up and burying my face in my hands.

I slept with Spencer.

I barely took a sip of the wine he offered me last night, so I can't put the blame on alcohol this time.

And I also told him I wouldn't regret it.

Which I don't.

But now that the passion has dissipated, I'm not sure how to feel—or think—about it. What did it mean for him? For us? Does this change anything? Where is he anyway?

His side of the bed is empty and cold, so he hasn't been here for a while now. But the smell of coffee is still strong, so does that mean he's preparing breakfast for us? Or is this a clear sign of a one-night-stand? Is he trying to tell me this was just a reconnecting kind of thing and that I shouldn't expect anything else?

I wasn't planning on sleeping with him last night. It just sort of happened. I guess it is a good thing I'm on birth control pills, though, because the last thing I need right now is having to worry about a baby.

You're overthinking again, Hayden!

Spencer said such nice things to me last night, I don't doubt for a second that he meant them. But we should discuss this. There's no way we can just keep doing…whatever this is. He told me he wanted to talk—to be mature about this—but we barely exchanged a couple of words before going to this room.

Swinging my legs out of his bed, I collect my pajamas from the floor and head to the ensuite bathroom, hoping to make myself some-what presentable before facing him. Not that he hasn't seen my morning face before, but still, things are different now. Luckily, there's a spare towel hanging close to his, and I decide to take a quick shower.

Memories of what happened last night come back to me, and I'm reminded of Lauren. I left the hospital with Spencer and didn't tell anyone about where I'd be. Dad must have freaked out when he didn't see me at home. Or maybe Chad told him I was with Spencer?

Rushing out of the bathroom, I head to the kitchen, hoping to find Spencer and ask him to take me home. I don't have my phone with me, so I don't even know if anyone tried to contact me during the night.

As soon as I get to the door, I spot Spencer with his back turned to me, cooking something on the stove. His back muscles stretch under a plain white T-shirt as he stirs something in a pan, and for a second, I'm distracted by the sight. But I'm quickly pulled back to my senses.

"Spencer," I call, entering the kitchen and heading for the kitchen island behind him.

He looks at me over his shoulder, flashing me his cute dimpled smile. "Good morning, Jenkins."

I feel my cheeks heating up but ignore it. "I have to go home. I don't have my phone, and I didn't let them know that I—"

He shakes his head, cutting me off. Turning off the heat, he turns to face me, crossing his arms across his chest nonchalantly.

"Your family knows you're with me, so don't worry. And Chad said Lauren will be released later today, and that she's fine."

I exhale, letting out a sigh of relief, plopping myself in one of the stools. "Thank God. Wait…" I narrow my eyes at him, only now realizing what he said. "Did you tell them I slept here?" Panic claws at my chest, and I rise from the stool again, too freaked out to stay still.

"Yes? To be fair, though, Chad told them first, so it's not on me this time." Spencer tosses his arms up in the air, turning to the cabinet to grab two plates.

"Chad… knew about it?" I'm astonished, too perplexed to form coherent sentences.

"Of course he did," Spencer replies with a shrug. "I wouldn't risk having a black eye, or my lips ripped open by another punch, Hayden.

No matter how worth it it was, I'm all for transparency, you know?" he jokes, setting a plate filled with pancakes, butter, and maple syrup in front of me. Exactly how I've always loved it.

He remembered.

I feel my heart beat rapidly in my chest with this small, but kind, gesture. Spencer fills a cup of black coffee for me and places it beside my plate before sitting on the other side of the kitchen island, across from me. He still has his dimpled smile stamped on his face as he grabs a first bite of his eggs, bacon, and toast.

"So, let me see if I've got this straight. Chad punched you for kissing me, then you two talked, and now he's helping you fuck his sister?" I raise my brows at him, amused.

I watch Spencer frown, considering my words, his mouth full as he chews his breakfast.

"Well, I haven't thought of it that way, but... I guess that's exactly what happened," he agrees with a nod. "And let's be honest, Hays, I didn't fuck you. We made love. But we can definitely do that before you leave–if you want." Spencer winks at me, and his implication makes me forget to chew my food before swallowing it down, and I choke on it.

I cough, chugging a sip of coffee, my eyes watery from the effort. Spencer looks slightly alarmed for a moment, but soon realizes I'm all right.

But I'm sure my cheeks are fucking red because of his bold suggestion, and I don't know what to do to hide it from him.

"You don't have to be so...direct about things, you know?" I reprimand him, cursing myself inwardly for not being able to come up with something wittier.

"Why not? You look so cute when you're flustered."

He grins at me from across the counter, and I have to focus on my plate so I don't lose control of myself again. Spencer looks so fucking handsome this morning, the rays of sunshine reflecting off his beautiful, sparkling blue eyes. His hair is unruly and covering his eyebrows, and the way he keeps shaking his head to move them away from his eyes is endearing...not to mention hot as hell.

I clear my throat, trying to break the uncomfortable silence that suddenly erupts between us. Spencer doesn't look bothered, though, as he keeps chewing his breakfast peacefully. I guess I'm the only one behaving like a fucking teenager after she finally got to sleep with her high school crush.

"I really need to go. I want to be at home when Lauren gets there," I tell him honestly. I'd love to stay here and spend the day with Spencer, but real life is calling me. "I also need to stop by the newspaper and see if I can have the rest of the day off so I can help with things at the ranch. Since Mom had to stay in the hospital, I bet the place needs a woman's touch. She will be too tired to get it all done," I explain.

"Of course." Spencer nods. "I could offer my help, but I'm sure you probably want to spend some time with your family. Let me know if you need anything, though," he offers kindly, and I feel my heart swelling with even more pride and joy.

I just love how Spencer knows me so well, and most of all, respects my wishes and personal space. I do want to have him there with me, but since all of this is so new, and I still don't know what this means for us, bringing him back to the ranch would only raise more questions.

"Thank you," I say in a low voice. "Do you think we can reschedule our talk for tomorrow, maybe? Since we didn't accomplish much of that last night?"

Spencer scoffs, pointing his fork at me. "I wouldn't put it that way, Hays. You looked accomplished all right after I was done with you."

I rise from my stool, just enough so I can reach him across the counter and punch him in the arm. I manage to do that, but Spencer grabs my wrist before I can return to my seat. Tugging me toward him, he lifts his chin, our noses almost touching.

"Careful, Jenkins, or I won't let you leave this house. I'm trying to be very understanding, but don't push it," he adds in a warning, but seductive tone.

He pecks me on the lips and releases me from his grasp, returning his attention to his almost finished meal.

I slowly return to my stool, shaking my head at his audacity.

"I'd love to reschedule our conversation," he finally adds, leaning back on his stool. His face is serious this time as he stares back at me. "Just let me know where, and I'll be there. Or you can come over if you want," he offers.

"Thank you. What about you? What are you going to do with your day?" I ask, realizing I haven't asked him about his career, his job, or what he's going to do now that he gave up his life in LA. "What are you doing exactly? Did you quit your job?"

Spencer clears his throat, looking shy, his cheeks reddening slightly as he nods at me. "Yes, well… sort of. I decided to open a record label of my own."

"What?" I squeak, too surprised and shocked to suppress my excitement. "That's amazing, Spencer."

"Yeah, I guess so." He shrugs, but I can tell by his face that he's proud of himself but doesn't want to flex much.

"Are you kidding? I mean, I've always known you were great, but this is huge."

Spencer was a big deal in LA, I know that much. Chad mentioned it a couple of times back at the ranch, and I couldn't help but hear it when he'd tell Mom and Dad what he knew. When Spencer dropped his football career to make it a hobby and focused on his musical career back in college, we all knew he'd be big one day.

He ended up becoming an executive for a very important record label and responsible for the career of a lot of big shots in the music industry.

I'm sure he'll be just as successful here as he was back in the City of Angels.

"Do you have clients already?" I lean forward to hear more about it. I have to go home, but I just need to hear more about him and his life. Seven years apart is a lot, and I suddenly feel like I have to know everything that happened to him during our time apart.

"I do. Well, I still have some of my clients who wanted to follow me no matter what, and I have a lot of samples from new people who are looking for a label, so… I have a lot on my plate now, thank God," he answers, and I can hear a note of happiness in his voice.

But what surprises me the most is how proud and happy I feel for him. I mean, I always rooted for him and his dreams, don't get me wrong. I was just too young and stupid to allow myself to put his dreams before mine back then. It was one of the many reasons why it didn't work out between us.

"I am truly happy for you, Spencer," I mutter, looking down for a second before gathering the courage to look him in the eyes. "I'm sorry I was too selfish to express that in the past."

His stare is almost too much for me to hold. I can feel my soul being ripped open under his gaze, as if it's a book being read from beginning to end. "It's okay, Hays. The past is the past, right? Let's not allow that to hurt us anymore. Or stand in our way. We're different people now."

I nod slowly, but deep down, I'm fighting the biggest battle I've ever had to fight.

Are we that different though? Or are we just more composed versions of our past selves?

Can I forget everything that happened and try again?

What if I ruin all of it once more?

CHAPTER THIRTEEN

I call the newspaper, and after begging for Kayla to let me take the day off so I can help at home—which she only allows because I offer to work an extra day to pay for the missing hours—Spencer takes me to the ranch.

When he drops me with the promise that we'll meet again tomorrow to solve things, I rush inside to change my clothes for the day and start with the house chores.

The place is empty, and I assume Dad returned to the hospital early in the morning to take something for Mom to eat and wait for Lauren to be discharged. I blast my playlist on the speaker while I clean the kitchen and decide to prepare a meal for when my sister comes home later today.

That's when I have the coolest idea to welcome her back. Grabbing my phone from the kitchen table, I dial Chad's number, waiting a couple of seconds until he picks up.

"Hays, what's up?" he greets me from the other side of the line. His voice is cheerful and light, which makes me believe he isn't slightly mad at me for sleeping over at Spencer's.

"Are you working now?" I ask bluntly, afraid to be disturbing him during work hours. I could've texted him, but I'm way too anxious to wait for him to text me back.

"Yep, but things are slow this morning, so don't worry. Did something happen?"

"No, not really. I was just calling to ask if you'll be free tonight. I was thinking about throwing a sleepover party for Lauren," I say, stirring the cookie dough I'm starting to prepare. "As a way to welcome her back."

"Oh, that's a nice idea, Hays. She loves sleepovers. I will definitely be there. Ryan is back in town, so maybe we should invite him too? Have a sibling sleepover?" he suggests with amusement in his voice.

"A sibling sleepover? That actually sounds great. What about Mom and Dad? Won't it be rude to not have them join us in their own house?" I chuckle.

"I'm sure they'll be asleep before nine. Mom barely slept last night from what Dad told me earlier," Chad points out.

"Oh, okay…" I feel bad for my mom, but I guess the concern automatically comes with being a mother, even if she knew Lauren was fine. "Do you think Ryan will want to come? He must be tired from his trip."

"Of course he will. He stopped by the hospital this morning to check up on Lauren. And it's not like he really has a choice. It's not just because he's married now that he can skip family time. He's still a Jenkins," Chad muses. "I'll have him bring the wine."

"That's great. I'll make us popcorn with M&M's. What will you bring?" I ask, spreading the dough on the counter so I can cut the cookies round before putting them in the oven.

"I'm bringing myself. What else could you want?" he snorts, and I can hear him muffling a chuckle.

"Very funny, Chad. You won't get inside if you don't bring something tasty. I have to go finish cleaning the house before they come home. Call Ryan and tell him not to be late," I order, hanging up and dirtying my phone with cookie dough in the process.

By the time I hear Dad's truck in the backyard, the sun is already setting behind the mountains, the house is sparkling and smelling of lavender, the cookies are safe inside an airtight container hidden on top of the fridge so Chad doesn't finish them before anyone else has the chance to eat them, and I'm freshly showered, wearing a new set of pajamas with my hair washed and blow dried into a ponytail.

My body is sore from all the cleaning—not to mention the previous night that I spent the entire day trying to erase from my mind, or at least hide it away until I have proper time to figure out what I am doing with Spencer—but I rush outside anyway, eager to see my sister.

Lauren is climbing out of the car with Mom and Dad surrounding her like hawks, making sure she can walk without falling. But by the look on her face, her eyes rolling so dramatically that for a moment I think they won't return to normal, I can tell she's already tired of their overprotectiveness.

"Mom, for the hundredth time, I'm fine. My legs are working just as good as they were yesterday, so can you please chill out?" she asks as kindly as possible, but when she sees me, she can't help but let out a heavy breath. "Good Lord, pony, just tell them to let me walk by myself."

I chuckle, walking toward her and throwing my arms around her. Our parents take a step back, which seems to be enough space for Lauren to feel less stressed out.

"I'm so glad you're home," I whisper in her ear while still holding her. "Are you really fine?" I ask, pulling away from her to study her face. She does look well. Her cheeks and lips are back to their normal pinky color, although the dark circles under her eyes tell me she hasn't rested well enough.

Lauren hates hospitals, so I know, like Mom, that she barely slept last night.

She nods at me, and I smile, feeling so grateful that she's safe and back at home. "We're having a sibling sleepover, so take a long shower, and wear something comfortable," I tell her, hooking my arm through hers and guiding her toward the house. "I doubt Mom will let you go back to your apartment anytime soon, so we might as well make this time entertaining for you."

"A sibling sleepover? Oh my God, it's been ages since we had one," Lauren muses excitedly, her hazel eyes sparkling as if she's a little kid.

Mom and Dad smile at us, and I can see the dark circles under Mom's eyes, too, as Dad helps her get inside with his arms around her shoulders.

"You should rest, sweetheart," he suggests to her. Mom sighs, and I know she's exhausted. It was a very emotional and difficult time for all of us last night. I'm just glad it's over.

"I made some cookies and cooked soup for dinner. Eat something before you go to bed. Both of you," I order, pointing an accusatory finger at my parents before they disappear inside the house.

"How are you really feeling?" I turn to look at Lauren once more, narrowing my eyes at her so she knows I need the full truth now that our parents are out of earshot.

"I feel fine. I'm not even that sore, so don't worry, okay? I promise you, I'm fine. I just have a little cough, but the doctor said it should pass in the next few hours," my sister explains as I close the front door behind us.

I study her for a few seconds before I feel convinced enough. "Okay, I believe you. But if anything feels wrong, just tell me. Go rest for now. I'll call you when Chad and Ryan arrive," I offer, ushering her upstairs.

When our brothers finally show up, Lauren is still napping in her room, and Mom and Dad have just finished their dinner and called it a night. Just like when we were kids, I used my spare time to build a blanket fort in the living room so we can watch movies and pretend we are all kids again. We used to love when our parents did that for us in the past, so I thought, why not?

Chad walks into the house and immediately spots the fort, widening his eyes in surprise.

"What's that? Did I just walk into a time machine?" he teases, putting the bags he's holding on top of the coffee table and looking at me. Ryan comes right after him, a soft smile on his lips as he takes in the scene before him.

"It feels like we're back in the '90s again," he adds, coming to greet me with a tight hug. "Hi, Hays."

"Hey, brother. How have you been?" I reply, hugging him back. "How did the honeymoon treat you?"

"It was amazing. Alice says hi, by the way."

I suddenly realize my mistake. "Is she mad we didn't invite her?" I didn't consider inviting her just because it is supposed to be a sibling's kind of night, so I thought she would feel a bit out of place. But she's part of our family now, so it isn't nice that I didn't consider inviting her too.

"Of course not. She knows it's a bonding moment, so don't worry. She's taking the time to organize the house since she didn't have time to do it after the wedding." Ryan dismisses me with a wave of his hand and heads to the kitchen to open the bottle of wine he brought.

My gaze meets Chad's, who's leaning against the counter now, already getting down the container I hid on top of the fridge, shoving an entire cookie into his mouth, the corner of his lips turning into a grin as he notices me narrowing my eyes at him.

"Those are not all for you. Or for now, for that matter," I hiss, walking over to him and snatching the container from his hand. "Lauren is not even up yet, you glutton."

"I was only grabbing a snack. I just got out of work, Hays. I've been at the police station the entire day. Don't you pity your brother?" Chad pouts at me, knowing full well that's my weakness. I do feel bad that he's been working all day and probably hasn't had a chance to eat a proper meal. Especially since Mom wasn't home to prepare some-thing for him.

I sigh, rolling my eyes and shoving the container back into his hands. "Fine, but leave some for Lauren. There's soup on the stove, too, so you might as well eat something healthy for once."

"Awesome, I'm starving," he chirps, tossing another cookie into his mouth and walking toward the stove to peek at the soup pot. "I asked Ryan to buy that ice cream you and Lauren love though, so you *should* appreciate me more."

I smile at him.

"Where's Lauren anyway?" Ryan asks, handing me a glass of wine and pouring one for him and one for Chad.

"She's taking a nap. I promised to wake her when you arrived," I tell him. "Do you want to go up and do that yourself?"

Ryan nods, putting the cork back in the bottle and handing it to me so I can put it in the fridge. "Sure, she wasn't awake when I visited this morning, so I want to check on her before we start this wild night of sugar overdose and bad movie choices."

"Hey," I complain, slapping him slightly on the shoulder and frowning at him.

"What? It's you and Lauren we're talking about. None of us expect to watch anything impressive tonight. Do we, brother?"

Chad simply shakes his head, grabbing his glass of wine and heading toward the living room to flop himself on the couch.

"Very funny," I mumble to myself, starting to prepare the popcorn since Ryan is going to wake Lauren up. By the time she gets downstairs, overly excited about the blanket fort, the popcorn is ready, Chad and Ryan are entertained with whatever story Ryan is sharing about his honeymoon, and I'm scrolling through the TV to pick a good movie, one that won't have our brothers rolling their eyes at us and saying they hate girly movies.

"What are you in the mood for?" I ask them, hoping we don't spend two hours picking the film and getting nowhere close to half of it watched before feeling sleepy and giving up on it completely.

"No cheesy romances," Chad mumbles immediately.

"We already know that, Chad," Lauren complains, sitting beside me and crossing her arms across her chest. "You say that every single time."

He shrugs and tosses his hands up in the air. "Just making sure we're on the same page, sis."

Lauren huffs, and I turn my attention back to the screen. Action movies are something we all agree on every time, so I go for that list instead, not wanting to waste any more time. We all settle for one that was just released, and for a couple of hours, we manage to entertain ourselves with it.

By the time it's over, the popcorn is long gone, the second bottle of wine is almost empty, Lauren is pissed off because she can't drink due to the medicines the doctor prescribed, and I'm feeling slightly lightheaded.

Chad then suggests we play a board game, which actually sounds like a good idea. I'm not ready to go to bed yet. I want to enjoy this night as long as I can. I don't know when we'll manage to have another one, so I might as well enjoy it while it lasts.

But what I didn't know is that this was an excuse for the prying to start.

"So, Lauren, I know you were in the hospital last night, but I feel like you'd want to be updated on the latest events for the rest of the family," Chad starts with fake seriousness, shooting me a side-eyed glance that makes my stomach churn. "Isn't that right, Hays? In fact, I'd like to be updated as well. I feel like I'm missing some information."

I fight the urge to curse at him. What is he trying to do? Mess with me in front of Lauren and Ryan? Tease me for sleeping with Spencer?

"I have no idea what you're talking about, brother," I hiss, failing to hide the annoyance in my voice.

Chad seems way too amused for my taste as he leans back on the couch, bringing the wine glass to his mouth, and taking a sip from it.

"Come on, Hays. We're all family here. And I can get that information somewhere else if I want. Is that how you want me to know what's going on with you?" he presses, a teasing tone to his voice that makes me want to jump down his throat.

"What is he talking about, pony?" Lauren asks from beside me, and I tense.

I don't want to have this conversation with her in front of my brothers. Not that I don't trust them or don't want them to know about my life, but I know she likes details, and I will definitely not tell her I slept with Spencer while Ryan and Chad are around to hear it.

"It's nothing. We can talk later," I tell her begrudgingly, taking my eyes away from Chad and looking at her. But before I can quietly send her a signal that I'll share it with her at some other time, Chad chuckles from his seat, catching my attention again.

"I'll save you the trouble then, since you seem too shy to share things with your siblings," he sings with a grin plastered on his face.

"What the hell are you talking about, man?" Ryan chimes in, frustrated with the encrypted conversation that only Chad and I seem to be following. "What's going on, Hayden?" He turns to me, concern etched on his features. "Did something happen?"

"Not really. Chad is just being a jerk," I snarl through gritted teeth.

"I'm not," he argues, his smile almost ripping his face from ear to ear.

"You didn't seem so happy about it a couple of days ago. Why are you picking on me because of it now?"

"I'm not picking on you. I just want to know what's going on with you, that's all," Chad retorts, his amusement wavering ever so slightly as he looks at me.

I'm not completely mad at him for doing this. I guess I just wasn't expecting to be backed against a wall tonight. Especially since I haven't had a chance to analyze everything properly yet. I have nothing to tell them. I don't even know what's going on myself.

"Can someone please just tell me what the hell is going on? Why are you talking in code?" Lauren complains, evidently irritated now.

"She's right. It's fucking annoying," Ryan adds, leaning back in the armchair and staring at both Chad and me. "It's not like we're strangers, for God's sake. What in the world is going on?"

"Fine, whatever," I blurt, closing my eyes and taking a deep breath. "I had sex with Spencer. There you go. Happy?"

I open my eyes to find three pairs of saucer eyes staring back at me. I only realize I've been holding my breath for too long when Lauren squeals by my side, almost deafening me in the process. I have to cover my ear with my hand and scoot away from her on the couch to save my precious hearing.

"Oh my God! You did what?" she presses, approaching me once more, closing the distance I've created between us.

"Okay, you didn't need to be so detailed," Chad groans, looking as regretful as one can be. His face is twisted into a grimace, and that's the only thing that gives me satisfaction for being so straightforward about what happened last night.

"You insisted, brother." I shoot him a sarcastic smile, ignoring the way Lauren is tugging on my pajama sleeve to look at her.

"You did have it coming, bro," Ryan muses to our brother, and I flash him a smile too—an honest one this time.

Ryan is much more mature than us, which I'm grateful for. I can tell he's concerned, his brows slightly creased as he watches me, but I know he respects my personal space too much to pry without me giving him the space to do it. I really appreciate him for it.

Not that I think Chad doesn't respect me. It's just that I know they have different ways of showing their love and concern—and this is Ryan's.

"Girl, why did you keep this from me? When were you planning on telling me? How did it happen?" Lauren blurts, vomiting the questions without taking a single breath.

"You were in the hospital. I was going to tell you eventually, when I figured out what's going on," I tell her with honesty, suddenly feeling self-conscious.

It's one thing to feel confused and lost inside my own mind. It's another way to share my doubts and fears with others. Even if they are my family.

Especially if they are my family.

"But, apparently, Chad can't hold his tongue," I add in a snarl, shooting fire from my eyes as I look at him again.

He seems unbothered by it, though, leaning back on the other side of the couch, sipping from his wine as if he's just enjoying a day at the beach, getting tanned and sipping margaritas while watching the sea.

"All right…" Ryan clears his throat, suddenly looking uncomfortable and awkward in his seat. I can tell he wants to ask something, but I know he's being careful with how he does it. It makes my heart warm, and I almost feel bad for snapping at them because of it. "I don't mean to pry in your personal life, sis, but can I ask what's going on with you two? Are you back together or what?"

Ha, the million dollar question.

CHAPTER FOURTEEN

$\mathcal{A}$s predicted, I don't know how to answer my brother's question..

I mean, I do know the answer to that. We're not back together. Not officially, anyway.

Spencer and I haven't talked about it. And even though last night was supposed to mean something, I don't know if it means *that*.

"I honestly don't know," I finally say, letting my guard down and deciding to open up to my siblings. If there's anyone in this world who wants me to be happy, and will do anything for me to achieve it, these three people around me at this very moment are them. I can say that without a doubt.

Even with all the teasing, I just know they want the best for me, just as I want for them.

"What do you mean? How do you not know?" Lauren asks with a frown, leaning forward to look at me, her big hazel eyes scanning my face.

I simply shrug. "We haven't talked about it. I came home to clean the house and get ready for your return. We didn't have that conversation."

"Guess you were occupied with something more important, huh?"

Chad jokes, receiving a slap on the back of his head by our eldest brother.

"She's your sister. Show some respect," Ryan scolds, and I bite down on my lower lip trying not to laugh. "And don't sulk later if she starts giving details you don't want to hear either."

"I was just breaking the ice, man." Chad rubs the back of his head, wincing in pain.

"I guess your conversation with Spencer went fine, right? After you punched your best friend and told him to stay away from me?" I accuse him in a teasing tone. I wasn't going to bring this up, but since Chad seems to want to put all the cards on the table, so be it.

"You punched Spencer?" Lauren squeaks again, her hand darting to her mouth in full shock. "And you were afraid he would do something stupid." She points at me, her sweet, bright eyes widening even more. "It turns out he did."

"I didn't do anything stupid." Chad stares at me with a serious expression on his face, suddenly straightening up in his spot. "Spencer has such a big mouth. I was just protecting you. Am I a dick for defending my sister's honor?"

Lauren sneers by my side. "Defending her honor? Where are we? In the 1820s?" She teases Chad, receiving a deathly glare in return.

"You stay out of this, little sister. Unless you want this to become your problem too," he warns her. He's clearly not in the mood to tease me or joke about the situation anymore, but even though I feel more like it now, I can feel that the atmosphere has become slightly more serious than before.

"I appreciate you protecting me and taking care of me," I say, not wanting him to misinterpret my words or take this as an accusation. I said that to get to him, true, but I never had the intention to hold this against him. Chad always has the best intention at heart when it comes to me and Lauren, and I'd never blame him for doing what he thought was best. "I was just surprised, that's all."

"You really punched Spencer?" Ryan asks, suddenly intrigued and curious, turning in his seat to get a better look at our brother.

Chad shrugs, not as amused as Ryan, though. "It was just a reaction. Spencer was being a bit of a dick too… but we solved it, and everything is fine now. He told me he wasn't going to play with Hayden's feelings, and that's all I needed to hear."

These words make my heart skip a beat, even though I never doubted that Spencer wouldn't play with my feelings. It's not who he is. Even if he hated me, I don't think for a moment he'd want to get back at me by doing something so low.

"Did he say anything else?" Lauren pries, her voice pitched as she fails to hide her excitement. It's like she's watching a fucking romance movie and can't keep her emotions at bay. "Did he say he still loves her and that he came back to be with her?"

My jaw drops as I turn to look at her. "Of course he didn't say that," I retort in disbelief.

"He didn't have to say it, though, did he? It's pretty obvious to everyone who has eyes and can see," Ryan sings, now looking just as enthusiastic as Lauren. I guess everyone can be childish if they want to be.

Spencer did originally say he wasn't planning on staying in town, and he hinted at changing his mind after the wedding, but isn't it bold to assume he did all of this because of me? I mean, he has friends and family here too. I might have been a part of it, but he didn't come back *just for me*.

Right?

"Why do you guys care so much about that anyway? Can we just go back to watching another movie or something? This is so awkward," I whine, grabbing the remote and starting to swipe through the channels again. But I can't focus on anything with them still watching my every move.

"Sorry, pony," Lauren chirps, her voice softer and lower. "We're just happy but also concerned about you. There's no one else in the world that'd love to see you and Spencer finally getting the happy ending you deserve, but we also worry about you. We don't want to see you suffer again."

"She's right, you know? I might not be the best at expressing my feelings, but I love you, and I love my friend, and I don't want either of you to hurt each other again," Chad adds, looking somewhat sorrowful.

I take a deep breath, feeling their love reach me at catastrophic levels. It feels so good to be reminded that I'm loved and that I have people who care for me and will be here no matter what. Tears prick at my eyes, and I have to sniff them back in so I don't turn this sleepover into a crying fit.

"Don't you think it's weird, though? I mean, it's been seven years. I..." I trail off, not knowing how to express my confusion.

Ryan is the one who answers me, shrugging and taking a sip from his now warm wine. "I don't. Love isn't easy. And what's love without a little drama? Alice and I went through a lot before we managed to work things out."

"Really?" I'm happy that Ryan is opening up to me. We never really talk about these things, but I feel grateful that he's willing to let me in.

"One hundred percent. It isn't always easy, but as long as we're both equally committed, everything will be fine. And for what it's worth, I never doubted for a second that you and Spencer were made for each other. You were just really young and inexperienced back then."

My heart swells because of his words. I never knew he felt like this, and from the look on Lauren's and Chad's faces, I can tell they feel the same. I swallow the lump in my throat, looking at the wall so I can compose myself.

"And I can easily say Mom looked delighted earlier today when she heard you were with Spencer," my sister sings with a wide smile.

"Oh, that's true. I think I saw Dad grin too, but he hid it immediately when he saw me staring," Chad says.

I chuckle. I can see my parents doing that. They've always loved Spencer, and even though they tried to hate him when we broke up, I've always known they never really managed to do it.

It is hard to hate someone like Spencer.

"Thanks, guys," I tell them. "It really means a lot that you're saying all this. And I am really glad to have you all by my side. I guess we'll see what the future holds for us."

Lauren wraps her arm around my shoulders, pulling me sideways into an embrace. "Absolutely. We're here for you no matter what. Always."

I nod, enjoying her hug while looking at Ryan, who winks at me, and then Chad, who has a soft smile on his lips and a kind look in his eyes. We don't have to say anything else to each other because I just know things will be fine between us. They already are.

More than anyone in the world, Chad's been the biggest supporter of my relationship with Spencer. I know he has the best intention at heart, and I couldn't be more grateful to have a brother like him.

I smile back at him, finally allowing a tear to roll down my cheek, immediately wiping it with the back of my hand.

Everyone is already sleeping around me, but my eyes are glued to the dark ceiling, the moonbeams the only source of light coming from the windows and illuminating the living room.

For whatever reason, I can't fall asleep. I'm anxious, feeling uneasy and agitated.

My mind is revisiting so many memories that it is hard for me to distinguish them between reality and dreams.

Then I realize I miss Spencer.

I want to talk to him, to see him, to know what the hell we're doing and what I'm supposed to expect.

As an anxious person, trying to be patient is excruciatingly painful.

As if hearing my loud thoughts, my phone buzzes beside me, making Lauren stir by my side, her leg on top of mine since we're sleeping on the same mattress that I brought over from the guest room. Chad is on my other side, sleeping on a twin mattress, but thankfully, he doesn't even move when I grab the phone from almost under his pillow.

I can barely keep it together when I see it is a text message from

Spencer. I feel like a fucking teenager, squeaking at myself as I read his text.

Spencer: Your scent is all over my sheets. You ruined sleeping for me.

He is so cute. I ignore the way my insides burn with images of last night and type down a reply.

Me: I'm glad I'm not the only one unable to sleep tonight. You ruined sleeping for me too.

His reply comes a few seconds later.

Spencer: I wish you were here. I miss you already.

A sigh escapes my lips. How is it possible that I'm falling in love even more than before with the same person I did more than ten years ago?

Me: Me too. I can't help but think this is insane, though. I can't make myself believe this is actually happening.

Spencer: I know. But we'll figure this out, and everything will be fine. I promise.

I want to ask him how, and what he's planning, but before I have the chance to type my questions, he sends another message.

Spencer: Do you think you can take the weekend off? I want to take you on a road trip, away from everyone and everything. We could talk then.

A weekend away with Spencer? That sounds like the best dream ever. We agreed to discuss things tomorrow, but a weekend away from everything and everyone does sound more appealing. I can wait a few more days if that means I'll get to spend three days with no one else but Spencer.

I do have to make up the hours I missed at, though, and I'm pretty sure Kayla will do everything she can to make me pay her back this weekend.

Me: I'll see what I can do at work. My boss is all over me. I'm this close to quitting.

Spencer: Why don't you?

Me: Because even though I live with my parents, I still have bills to pay, things to buy...

After Mom suggested that I work for her at the bakery, my mind has constantly been sending me messages that I probably should quit the newspaper. I don't love it anymore, and for me to start thinking about what I want to do with my professional life, I need to take that next step. And that'd be stepping away from something that's making me unhappy.

I do feel sorry about leaving Poppy behind, though. We've been working together since forever, and I'm not prepared to let go of that yet.

Why is it so hard to make these decisions?

Spencer: I'm sure you'll make lots of money with your books once you start publishing them. I can help you with that. I have some connections in the publishing industry back in LA and New York.

I feel a shiver course through my entire body at his offer. Spencer is a well-connected person, and I have no doubt he can put a word in for me. But I need to become a good writer first. I don't want to be successful without merit just because I know people. I want to deserve it, even if it takes me years to get there.

Me: Thank you. We'll see about that. One thing at a time, I guess.

Spencer: If anyone can do it, it's you.

I find myself smiling like an idiot at my phone screen, and I'm happy everyone is asleep and can't see how stupid I must look now.

Before I think of anything else to say to him, Spencer sends me another message.

Spencer: Try to get some sleep. And let me know about the trip as soon as you can.

Me: Will do. Have a great night.

Spencer: I will now. Goodnight, Jenkins.

At the end of the day, I didn't have to quit my job.

I didn't even have time to consider it.

Because I was fired first.

Yes, Kayla had the guts to fire me.

"That stupid bitch," Poppy curses beside me as I head toward my desk to start packing my things the next afternoon.

I am fuming, barely able to hold myself together. All I want to do is jump on Kayla's neck and grab her by the hair and just... ugh! I don't even know what I want to do to her right now.

"I know," I hiss through clenched teeth, my brain scrambling as I try to process the confrontation that just happened in the meeting room.

I'm not pissed because I was fired. Sure, she saved me from having to make that tough decision, *and* I'll get unemployment pay since the decision wasn't mine. However, I'm out of my mind because of the reason she decided to fire me.

"I can't believe she used this lame excuse to fire you," Poppy carries on rattling on about it. If anyone is angrier than me about this, it's definitely her. I had to literally shut her mouth with my hand so she didn't get fired too.

Long story short, the election for mayor is approaching, and apparently, Kayla is on the side of the current mayor who's running for reelection. The thing is, she wanted me to edit an article that one of the reporters wrote pretending I don't know it's all bullshit.

The guy is involved in some corruption scandal, and basically, what she wanted me to do was cover it up. I didn't even write the story. I was just the editor. But I refused to do it. And then she took that opportunity to do what she's been wanting to do since she met me—get rid of me.

"We all knew it was just a matter of time before she did it," I snarl, tossing my planner and folders into a cardboard box I find beneath my desk. I don't even look up at Poppy, but I know she's still here because I can hear her huffing. "I just wasn't expecting her to be this...filthy. She's such a sellout," I bark.

"Tell me about it," Poppy whispers, flopping herself on my chair, and when I hear her voice softening, I finally look at her. Her eyes are watery, and if I didn't know Poppy any better, I'd swear she's about to cry.

"It's fine, Poppy. I'm fine," I tell her honestly. She knows I've been wanting to step away for a while now, but even so, it's so different when you're forced to do it before you gather the courage you need to do it yourself.

Looking at my best friend now, reality comes crashing down on me.

I was fired. It's what I've wanted, but I wasn't ready. Not yet anyway.

I'm not ready to let go of my mornings with Poppy, of our coffee breaks complaining about our poor jobs and gossiping about our coworkers. I'm not ready to *not* be a part of her daily life, and I just know that's what's going to happen when we no longer work together every day.

My throat suddenly starts to burn, which is a huge sign that I'm about to cry. Not because of my job, but because I'm finally realizing that this is the end of an era. I've been here since I finished college.

My best friend is looking at me with an expression that tells me she doesn't believe a single word I just said.

"Let's please not do this here," I beg, putting a lid on the cardboard box and taking a deep breath, swallowing down my unshed tears. "Everything will be fine. I was going to do it anyway if she didn't, so at least I'll be able to save some money, right?"

Poppy nods eagerly, squinting and letting a single teardrop fall down her cheek. "You're right. I'm sorry. I just don't know how to do this without you here. But you're right. You should go after what makes you happy," she encourages me, reaching for my hand and squeezing it gently.

"Nothing will change. I'm always going to be here for you. It's not like you can get rid of me," I tell her with a smile. "We still live in this hellhole anyway," I joke.

I don't know how to express what I feel right now. There are so many mixed emotions inside of me at this moment that it is hard to put into words.

"I know. You won't get rid of me either," Poppy whines, getting up from my chair and tossing her arms around me. "I love you, girl. And I really hope you can be happy and find what moves you."

"Thank you, Pops. Maybe that's the push I needed," I confess, truly believing it. "It seems like my life decided to turn everything upside down overnight. It's just a bit overwhelming."

Poppy pulls away from me, staring into my eyes, a soft smile spreading on her lips. "I can feel it in my bones that this is your moment, girl. So, just do yourself a favor and embrace this. Don't be afraid of anything. Just do what you want. And I'm not talking just about your career." She winks at me, and I know what she means.

And I think she's right.

Everyone goes through these moments in life where you find yourself at a crossroads.

This is mine.

It is my time.

And I'm finally getting ready to face it.

CHAPTER FIFTEEN

The best thing about being fired was that my weekend getaway with Spencer was possible.

There was nothing else preventing me from going.

Sure, I had to tell my family I'd be spending some days away. And of course they wanted to know exactly where I'd be and with whom.

I also couldn't keep it a secret from them forever that Spencer and I were…trying again? In any case, according to Chad, everyone already knew, so… there was no reason to hide it from them.

Of course, Mom and Dad wanted to know more about this…*trip*… but I had no answers for them. I didn't want to get into details, so I just told them we were going to spend some time together and solve things—whatever that means.

And that's why, a couple of days later, I'm in Spencer's sports car's passenger seat, listening to his '80s rock playlist, feeling the cool wind in my hair as we ride down the highway toward a resort in Hot Springs. He rented this log cabin with its own private hot spring pool, and I was astonished to realize he remembered this being one of our top places we'd like to visit one day on a getaway trip after we graduated.

We never managed to go after everything that happened—his

parents' death, our break up, college… It makes me somewhat emotional and contemplative to be living that dream now.

"Are you all right?" Spencer asks, his hand darting to my thigh and squeezing it lightly to catch my attention.

I look at him with a soft smile, ignoring the way my skin is tingling under his touch. "Yeah, of course. I'm so excited. We planned this for years in the past. It's just overwhelming to actually be doing it."

Spencer nods, his eyes back on the road ahead. "I know what you mean. Not even in my wildest dreams did I think I'd be able to convince you to go on a trip with me." He chuckles, shaking his head, his dimpled smile widening. "Life is full of surprises, isn't it?"

I adjust in my seat, turning to face him, even though he can't look at me. "So, you've dreamed about me, huh?"

He gives me a side glance, his smile faltering for a second. "Is that even a real question? Of course I did. Didn't you?" he shoots back, sounding somewhat offended that I've implied I haven't dreamed about him during our time apart.

Which is an understatement. I was just trying to tease him. But I wasn't planning on him turning this on me. I feel my cheeks blushing just from the mere thought of having to share the amount of times I dreamed about him. Not to mention the content of those dreams.

"By the way your cheeks seem about to burst into flames, I'm assuming your dreams were wilder than mine," he teases, receiving a slap on the shoulder from me as a response.

"Shut up," I scold, folding my legs and crossing my arms in front of my chest. "Don't pretend you're a prude now."

"Oh, I'm definitely not a prude." He laughs. "I just never thought you weren't one either."

"Will you keep teasing me?" I retort bitterly.

"I'd love to keep teasing you because you look really hot when you're angry, but no," Spencer muses. We remain in silence for a few minutes until he breaks it. "What did your family think about you coming on this trip with me?" he pries, but it doesn't go unnoticed by me that he's genuinely curious about it.

"Well, Mom and Dad kept asking me every five minutes if you and I were back together and what this means. Ryan wasn't really that invested in it. He just told me to do what my heart was telling me to do. Chad, on the other hand, kept glancing at me, opening and closing his mouth as if he was trying to gather the courage to say whatever he wanted to say, but in the end, he simply told me to be careful and to let him know if you were ever a jerk to me," I blurt, chuckling as I see Spencer grimacing at the last part. "And Lauren, well… she just squeaked and told me to buy some hot lingerie, even though I told her we're going to a freezing mountain cabin in the middle of nowhere."

"Always knew Lauren was the most clever Jenkins," Spencer finally says with a grin, his eyes still on the road.

I roll my eyes, pretending my insides are not burning with anticipation. "What about you? Does your family know about this?"

"Ah, this has been the only topic we discuss ever since I returned to town. Apparently, my sister's life has been boring enough, to say the least, because she doesn't talk about anything else other than you," Spencer replies. It seems like he's complaining, but it doesn't sound like it. In fact, if I know him like I think I do, he's enjoying all the attention his younger sister is giving to his love life.

"Is that so?" I ask, raising my brows at him.

"Are you kidding? If Aubrie had any say in my life, you and I'd be married and parents of seven by now."

"Seven?" I squeak, my eyes wide with shock. "Jesus, and she only has one," I huff in disbelief.

"That's Aubrie we're talking about. The woman is a hypocrite," Spencer grumbles. I know he doesn't mean it, though. The tone he uses whenever he talks about his sister is endearing to say the least. They were always close back in the day, and when they lost their parents, they became even closer. Aubrie would frequently go out with us because Spencer didn't want to leave her alone at the house.

She has always been a sweetheart to me. Even though we're the same age, we didn't have any of the same classes back in high school, so we were never close, but she's always treated me nicely, and we actually still get along to this day.

Like me, she's a book lover—not to mention the owner of the town's bookstore—so every once in a while, I'd go to the store and talk to her for an entire afternoon about some book I've read that I thought she'd like.

I've always felt bad because I thought we could be closer than we are, but since my breakup with Spencer, it just didn't seem fair—to me, to her, or to Spencer. It was just...too awkward. But we managed to keep an amicable relationship, and it makes me happy to know she still likes me.

"She's just adorable. I'm glad she didn't start hating me after we broke up," I confess. I never knew how much Spencer shared with her about it, but it was only natural that I'd think his family would start hating me. But none of that happened.

Aubrie continued being nice to me. Her husband, Thomas—although he only met me when I wasn't with Spencer anymore, during a business trip where he fell in love and decided to marry Aubrie and move in to Missoula—is always polite and gentle toward me whenever we bump into each other, and their daughter Caitlin is just the sweetest angel on Earth.

"She would never hate you. She's your number one fan," Spencer tells me. "Whenever I told her I was seeing someone else, she'd find a way to mention your name or bring you into the picture just to remind me of what I had lost."

I bark out a laugh, finding it amusing that Aubrie has always advocated in my favor without me even knowing about it. "I guess we both have clever sisters, huh?"

"Guess you're right about that."

By the time Spencer and I reach the resort, the sun is already setting, and a really cold breeze hits me as we park our car outside of the cottage. Spencer heads to the trunk to get our luggage, refusing to let me help him, and I follow him into our private river cabin. We step onto the porch, which has a swing facing the river and the mountains, and I follow Spencer inside.

He sets the bags in the living room, and I take in my surroundings, mesmerized by how luxurious, and yet cozy, this looks. There's a dining area on our right, a bathroom with a jacuzzi and heated floors, and a bedroom with a king sized bed on our left. The whole place seems far-fetched, something I'd never dream of experiencing, but because Spencer wanted to surprise me, I had no idea we were going to stay in such a place.

"Spencer, this is—"

"Incredible?" He completes my sentence with a smile.

"Yes, but also, too much?" I reply. "I mean, I love it, but you didn't need to spend so much. We could've stayed in some place cheaper."

"Come on, Hays. I don't mean to flex, but money is not an issue," he tells me humbly, coming toward me and wrapping his arms around my waist. He pulls me toward him and gives me a peck on the lips. "And even if it was, I'd still want to stay in a place like this with you. You deserve even more."

I smile at him, feeling my cheeks blush with his flirting. "Trying to bribe me?"

His eyebrows shoot up. "To get what exactly?"

"I don't know…" I shrug, trying to get myself out of his arms but feeling him tightening them around me even more so I don't escape.

"Well, unfortunately for you, and fortunately for me, my charm seems to be enough to convince you," he whispers, leaning forward and finding the spot on my neck where I'm most sensitive. He starts kissing me there, making goosebumps spread all over my body. "I won't complain if this gives me some extra points, though," Spencer adds, guiding me backward to the bedroom.

I ponder letting him, but I am hoping to see the sunset, and I'm also starving. As much as it kills me to have to postpone this moment, I pull away from him, slowly. "I think we should get ready to eat something."

As if on cue, my stomach growls. I look at his devastated face, his beautiful puppy eyes staring back at me, and chuckle.

"See? Just a nice cabin won't be enough for you to get me into bed, mister," I joke, finally getting out of his arms and getting away from him and his intoxicating scent. Otherwise, I won't have the strength in me to keep myself at a safe distance until we're out of this cottage.

"Fine. I forgot you need to be fed first." He fakes a dramatic sigh, picking up our luggage and setting it on top of the couch. "What are you in the mood for?"

I turn to look at him and cross my arms across my chest, considering his question. "Hmm… maybe some steak?"

"That's a great choice. There's a restaurant inside the resort, but there's also a very nice bar downtown with some karaoke and cold beer," Spencer says with a suggestive tone. "I'm sure they have steak there too. What do you say?"

"That sounds like the perfect place to go. You know I love karaoke."

In less than ten minutes, we're parking outside of the bar, which seems to be crowded already, even though it's not even dark outside yet. The last remains of the orange-pink shade are disappearing from the sky, giving space for the moon and the stars to make their appearance. It's a really beautiful night, and I feel so happy to be walking hand-in-hand with Spencer that it feels like I'm living someone else's life for a moment.

We get inside, finding ourselves a spot at the bar. I don't feel like getting a table yet, so I tell Spencer we should just do what the locals seem to be doing—staying closer to the drinks.

Spencer orders us both a glass of beer, which truth be told, it's as cold as he previously mentioned. He also orders me the steak I'm so desperately craving, and by the time it's served, I finish it in a blink of an eye.

Spencer laughs at me, finding it amusing how, "Someone with such a pretty face can eat like a mad man." His words, not mine.

By the time I'm on my third glass, and my head is slightly dizzy, the karaoke music is on full blast, making the blood in my ear pulsate stronger than usual.

"I need to go to the bathroom," Spencer whispers in my ear, trying to make himself heard over the loud girls screaming to *I'm Not A Girl,*

Not Yet a Woman on the microphone. "Are you okay staying here by yourself for a moment?" he asks, looking around as if trying to spot anything that might be off.

"Of course," I tell him, taking another sip from my beer, too entertained by the duo on the stage. They look like college girls—way drunker than they should be, but having the time of their lives—and I can't seem to take my eyes off them. "Just go!" I press, nudging him in the shoulder as I glance at him and notice his hesitation.

Spencer finally turns and leaves, and I drag my attention back to the karaoke. The song has ended, and they are picking a new one—something more uplifting that has everyone at the bar screaming and clapping in encouragement. That's when I sense someone stopping beside me, way too close to my shoulder to be considered socially acceptable for a person who is here accompanied.

"What's a fine face like yourself doing alone in a bar?" the man asks me, his vodka breath almost knocking me off my stool. I wrinkle my nose, leaning back to move away from him without being too obvious.

"I'm not alone," I tell him bluntly, leaving no room for misinterpretations. "My boyfriend is in the bathroom." The word comes out of my mouth without me even thinking about it. But to be fair, this is the best explanation I can give a man who seems to have no clue he's being an inconvenience.

"'Your 'boyfriend,'" he air quotes in a very aggressive way, "is stupid to leave you here by yourself, darling."

I narrow my eyes at him, noticing he's not backing away. In fact, he's leaning forward again, closing the space I created between us. I'm almost falling off the stool, but I lift my chin in defiance, almost challenging him to try something. He's so drunk off of his ass that I wonder, if I push him, will he fall on his ass in the middle of the bar?

However, I do not like the look in his eyes or the way he's smirking at me, almost as if the alcohol can't coat his bad intentions.

"I think you're the stupid one to not realize you're being rude as hell," I hiss through clenched teeth. "You should take a hint and step away from me."

The guy is starting to give me the ick. I thought I could defend myself, but he's leaning too close, and no one seems to be noticing it. I don't think he'll try to do anything with a bunch of people around him, but it doesn't make him look less creepy.

"I love a feisty woman, I'll tell you that," he muses in a disgusting tone.

But before I can come up with another retort, an imposing frame steps in between us, momentarily blocking my view from the repulsive man.

"I think she told you to step away from her," Spencer snarls in a low voice—so low I barely hear him. I can feel the rage radiating from his muscled back, but he seems to be containing it quite well so far. His fists are clenched at his sides, but I fear what might happen if the guy keeps pushing. A bar fight is the last thing we need right now.

And even though I know Spencer is not the kind of guy to get into a physical fight like this, I'm also not sure what he can do if someone keeps hitting on me in front of him like that. It's not like we've been through this before in our relationship. Our high school years don't count since we were both kids at the time.

"Come on, man. No need for all that protective postering," the drunk guy blurts, his voice coming out staggering enough for me to have to perk my ears to understand him.

"Either you get out of my sight by yourself, or I'll make you leave," Spencer adds, his back still turned to me. I feel more relaxed now that I have him protecting me, but I'm not so comfortable with the way he's still frozen to the floor as if waiting for the guy to make a wrong move so he can dart at him.

"Come on, Spencer. It's not worth it," I plead softly in his ear, my hand reaching for his arm. I caress him, gently squeezing his bicep to get his attention. "Let's go back to the cabin," I press, suddenly eager to leave this place.

It takes him almost an entire minute staring into the guy's face to finally let go and turn to me. His eyes are darkened in a way I have never seen before, but he also looks hot as hell being all protective.

I can't say I don't like it.

"Let's go," I insist, taking him by the hand and pulling him toward the exit.

The drunk guy screams something at us, but I'm glad the squeaking girls are singing loudly again so we can't hear what he's saying.

Only when we get back to the resort do I feel Spencer finally starting to relax. His shoulders are still tense, though, and by the time we get inside our cottage, I'm feeling in the mood enough to try and make him snap out of it.

When he finishes taking off his coat, I push him onto the couch and climb on top of him, straddling him.

Spencer's body immediately stiffens but this time for the right reasons. His hands immediately dart to my thighs as I scoop myself forward, closer to him.

"You seem a bit tense, don't you think?"

I see him swallowing down, his hands gripping my legs and trapping me to his lap.

"Yeah? What are you going to do about it then?"

CHAPTER SIXTEEN

I smirk at Spencer, getting myself even closer to him—so close there's no space left between us.

"I have something in mind," I reply in a whisper, placing kisses on his neck, up to his jaw and then his ear. "You're really hot when you're all protective, you know that? It got me wondering if you think you own me or something."

His fingers grip my thighs harder, the slight pain sending a burning sensation to my core. "Careful, Jenkins," he warns in a hoarse voice.

"Or what?" I challenge. "You know, you got me really turned on back there."

A low rumble resonates in his chest, and I feel his hands sliding up until they reach my ass. Spencer pulls me hard against him, and a soft moan escapes my lips when I feel him hard against me. I scold myself inwardly for putting on jeans before leaving the cabin, so now I can't take them off easily or feel Spencer's fingers on my skin.

But that doesn't seem to bother him that much as he shoots his brows up and stares into my eyes. "Is that right? That's funny because you seemed really scared that I'd disfigure that guy's face."

He's right about that. But I don't want to think about that right now. I just want to think about the way he looked possessive and dominant as if I was his.

Which, honestly, I think I always have been. Even when I was with other men, I never truly felt like I belonged to any of them. Not in the way I feel like I belong to Spencer.

Suddenly, the jeans and the layers of my tricot sweater feel too itchy and uncomfortable for me to keep wearing them. I climb off his lap, noticing his eyes widening with surprise—and maybe disappointment.

But before he has the chance to complain or say anything, I grab the hem of my sweater, pulling it over my head and revealing the lingerie set I'm glad Lauren convinced me to wear. Its half cup accentuates my small breasts, making them look juicer and sexier than they actually are. The delicate black lace covers my skin like silk, definitely making me feel comfortable but also confident.

Spencer's eyes are so dark as he watches me undress that I momentarily forget they are as blue as the ocean. His hair is falling over them, slightly hiding his gaze, and I have to focus on what I'm doing so I don't surrender myself completely to him.

As I step out of my jeans, Spencer scans my long legs up and down, shifting on the couch slightly, his hands balled into fists beside him. I wonder for a moment if he's going to get up and pin me to a wall or something, but when he doesn't move, I take a few steps forward, straddling him again.

He still has his clothes on, which bothers me a bit, but being almost naked makes me feel more sensitive to his touch and to the slight cold breeze in the room, despite the heater being on.

I don't give him time or space to say anything, I just cup his face in my hands and bring his lips to mine. He tastes so good. His lips are so soft, his tongue playing with mine, making me squirm on top of him in a way I can't begin to comprehend.

How can he make me feel like this?

His fingers are gripping my thighs with such pressure that I'm sure they'll leave a mark the next day, but I couldn't care less. For all I know, I don't even need to leave this room tomorrow, so he can do whatever he wants with me tonight.

My hands find his hoodie, and I pull it off in a blink of an eye, desperate to see more of his perfectly toned abs. I didn't get enough of him the other night. I don't think I'll ever have enough of him.

As I caress his hard chest, Spencer cups my breasts, squeezing them over my bra, making me melt under his touch. I close my eyes, enjoying the way he touches me, and I don't even realize it when he pulls it down and takes one of my nipples into his mouth, licking it as if he's savoring the most delicious dish in the world.

I drop my head back, allowing him to take all of me, my breath becoming erratic and heavy as I feel like I'm not going to be able to go on like this forever. I need some release to be able to last enough for him to claim me completely. I rock my hips back and forth, needing some friction, anything that can put me out of my misery.

Spencer grabs my ass again, pulling me hard against his body, and the feel of his manhood pressing against my sensitive spot makes me delusional with pleasure.

"Spencer, I need you out of these clothes. Now," I order, although my voice sounds more desperate and pleading than commanding.

He chuckles against my breast, but does nothing to remove his clothing which frustrates me. However, before I have the time to complain, one of his hands darts to my panties, his fingers sliding under the thin fabric and finding me wet and slick for him.

He groans against my skin but doesn't stop savoring my breasts as his fingers start toying with me in a slow, but delicious, dance. I find myself rocking my hips harder against them, feeling that electric current taking over my entire body, from my toes to my head, leaving me completely numb and disoriented.

My nails dig into his shoulders as I try to steady myself on top of him, waiting for the orgasmic wave to fade. My limbs and my core are still buzzing with dopamine, and I lean my head on his shoulder, trying to calm my breathing.

"Shit, that was really good," I manage to whisper, feeling his fingers still inside of me. Spencer isn't making any moves though, waiting for me to compose myself.

I can still feel him hard against me, and I know this is far from over. I just need a moment to get myself back together.

"Glad to be at your service, ma'am." He chuckles, removing his hands from inside my panties. A moan of complaint almost slips out of my lips, but I manage to hold it in.

Spencer is watching me intently as I straighten myself up on his lap. I suddenly feel so empty that it bothers me.

"You were supposed to take your clothes off," I grumble, narrowing my eyes at him.

"I had some other things to take care of first." He smirks at me, holding me by the waist and setting me on my feet on the floor as he gets up from the couch. "Are you ready for the second round?" Spencer asks, kissing the nape of my neck.

Another current of pleasure rushes through me, and I feel aroused again as if I haven't just been pleasured a minute ago.

"Only if you are," I tell him with a grin, even though he can't see me, his mouth still nibbling on my neck.

While kissing me, Spencer leads us to the bedroom, tossing me on the enormous California king bed. If possible, the mattress is even softer than his back in Missoula, and I feel like I'm being hugged by it. But Spencer makes me forget about it as quickly as possible because, the next thing I know, he's stripping out of his pants and boxers, leaving me thirsty for him.

"It took you long enough," I say, sitting up on the bed so I can unclasp my bra. I toss it over Spencer's head but don't even get the chance to see where it lands because he is on top of me again before I know it.

He kisses me once more, this time with more hunger and urgency than before. I guess he's controlled himself long enough. His hands are roaming over my entire body, and I reach between us, finding his hardness and squeezing it with my small, slender fingers. But that doesn't seem to be an issue because Spencer groans against my mouth, clearly enjoying my ministrations.

This does seem to wear his patience, though, because he suddenly finds the straps of my panties and pulls them down in one go, not even caring if he rips them apart or not.

I can't find it in me to complain either, now that I have nothing in the way of getting what I so desperately want.

Spreading my legs apart enough for Spencer to fit, and still holding him in my hands, I guide the tip of his dick to my slick folds, using it to massage my sensitive spot. We both moan at the same time, too over our heads to think of what we're doing anymore. It's just pure, animal instincts now.

I remember what he said when we had sex in his house a few days ago—that he made love to me, not fucked me.

I loved that; I loved how romantic he can be. But I also like it rough sometimes. And right now, that's exactly what I want.

"So, if I recall correctly, you said you could fuck me if I wanted," I blurt out, barely able to control my breathing. Spencer's body stiffens above me, and he pulls away from me just enough so he can stare in my eyes. I smirk mischievously, blinking my lashes at him. "Is that offer still standing?" I ask, squeezing him harder between my fingers.

Spencer growls, tossing his head back and taking a deep breath. "You asked for it, Jenkins," he warns, looking back at me with a huge grin on his lips.

Before I know it, he's adjusting himself at my entrance and thrusting himself so hard into me that I need to bite the sheets so as not to make a sound. I definitely do not want anyone complaining that there are guests being too loud inside their cabins, not allowing them to sleep. I'd die of embarrassment if that happened.

Surprisingly—and proudly enough—Spencer and I manage to go three more rounds before we're finally exhausted and drained. I don't think I've ever been this horny before, but I guess that's what happens when you're in the desert for too long, thirsty for some water.

When you find yourself a gallon, it's hard to let go.

But even though I feel like I won't be able to move tomorrow–let alone stand and walk, my body and my core too sore from all the exercises we just got–I can't sleep.

My eyes are wide open as I stare at the wooden ceiling, one of Spencer's arms under my head and the other wrapped around my waist, keeping me close to his warm chest. I can't move, but I'm so utterly happy that I'm afraid my heart might burst from my chest at any moment now.

How is it possible for just one person to make you feel so complete? I could die now, and I wouldn't complain about a thing.

Sure, I've had my ups and downs in life—geez, I am jobless—but at his moment, that doesn't seem to be an issue. As I contemplate my life and every blessing I've received, I find myself feeling like the luckiest woman in the world. I have an amazing family, an incredible best friend, and the most caring and kind man in the world beside me.

What else could I possibly want?

"Are you okay?" Spencer asks in a quiet voice. I'm still too tired to answer with proper words, so I just hum in response, squeezing his arm for emphasis. "Are you sure?" he adds. "You're so quiet, and it's been long enough since our last round."

I chuckle softly, turning on my side to look at him. His hair is a mess—but a beautiful one nonetheless. I can't express how I love the way his strands fall over his eyes, making him look boyish but manly at the same time. His blue eyes are studying my face intently, as if trying to find something here I can't comprehend.

"I'm perfect," I manage to say, mostly because I don't want him to worry. I'm quiet because I can't put into words how elated I feel. "Just thinking about my life."

His brows furrow almost imperceptibly, but his arm tightens around my body. "Do you want to talk about it?"

I had originally pictured our conversation being more formal, almost as if we were in a meeting, deciding what would be the best thing to do with our relationship. But honestly, there is no better place or situation to be in to have this conversation other than in Spencer's arms in this amazing cottage.

"Okay, sure, yeah…" I say, a bit uncertain. I'm not even sure where to begin this conversation, and if I'm being completely honest, I'm afraid whatever we talk about might burst this bubble of happiness we find ourselves in before the sun even rises outside.

"Is there anything you want to ask me?" Spencer starts, his eyes still searching my face. "Anything about my past, or I don't know, about the present…anything at all?"

I ponder his question. Do I? Do I want to know about his ex-girl-friends or anything that happened while we were apart? Will that do me any good? Knowing myself, I know it will just make me paranoid.

And what good could this bring? If it's in the past, it's supposed to stay there, right?

"Hays, talk to me," he insists, brushing a strand of my hair behind my ear gently.

"I don't know. I'm just deciding if I want to know about it or not. It feels like digging up seven years might be a bit overwhelming, don't you think?" I reply, caressing his arm with my fingers. "Do *you* want to know anything?"

He shakes his head slightly and smiles at me. "Not really. I already told you there's been no one in my life other than you. And that's all that matters to me."

It's incredible how Spencer can still soothe my feelings without me even having to ask him to.

I smile at him, grateful for his explanation. "The same goes for me."

Spencer pulls me tighter against him. "I won't be surprised by another Jake Monroe, will I?"

I laugh—really loud this time—because he catches me off guard. "Oh, God. No! That was the lowest I've been in my life. Or maybe there was another one or two who could compare. But no one's made my heart flutter the way you do."

He leans forward, kissing my lips softly. "Good."

I clear my throat, still uneasy about one thing though.

"Just ask away, Hays. This is what we came here for, isn't it?" Spencer chuckles.

"I thought we came here so you could fuck me without having my brother punching you in the face," I muse, getting tickled back as response. "Okay, fine, fine!" I plead, pushing Spencer away so I can catch my breath. "I guess I'm just wondering what will be like for us now. Are we dating or what?"

Spencer's brows crease. "Isn't that obvious? Should I make it official? I'm honestly not really sure how it's done these days. I haven't dated anyone seriously in a long time," he explains, a bit embarrassed.

It's endearing. How is it fair that he looks cute even when he doesn't seem to know what to do? God!

I slap him on the arm. "Of course not. I'm just making sure I'm not misinterpreting anything, that's all."

"How could you misinterpret anything? I literally told you there's no one else in this life for me other than you. So, can you please trust me, trust us, and just snap out of whatever is holding you back?" he asks in a kind, sweet voice.

His eyes are soft as he looks at me, waiting for a response. Whatever doubts I had when coming here, the way he holds me expectantly and stares at me makes me reprimand myself for being so scared and insecure. I trust him. I trust his feelings for me. I guess whatever is holding me back is something that I need to deal with myself.

But I shouldn't allow it to prevent me from finding my happiness with the man I love. It's been so long since I've been trying to find someone who completes me as much as Spencer, and God seems to have given me a second chance with him because I could never find anyone I'd love more in my life than him.

"Hays," Spencer calls me in a whisper, his voice barely audible. I look up again, held in his gaze like I'm being hypnotized. "I love you."

I feel like I'm about to die.

It's not like I didn't know. I can feel his love in his words, his actions, his stares. But hearing these three words being said out loud does have its power.

It has my entire body going numb again, and my brain seems to have melted under my skull in a way that prevents me from thinking.

Spencer loves me.

Still.

After all this time apart.

After everything that has been done and said between us.

Life separated us, allowed us to try and find our other halves in other people, but it didn't work because we're meant to be together.

And right now, being in his arms like this, I don't know what I had been thinking.

Spencer has always been the one for me. There could never be anyone else. I was simply trying to fill the void he left when he walked out of my life. And looking at it now, I don't know how I've been so stupid to allow him to leave one day.

Gulping and trying to prevent myself from crying, I pull him into a kiss, my hand darting to the nape of his neck and bringing him closer to me.

"I love you," I whisper against his mouth. "I always have, and I always will."

CHAPTER SEVENTEEN

ay too soon, we are back home. I wasn't ready to return to normal life, but Spencer has so much to do before his record label's launch party (and I have to figure out what to do with my life) that staying away for too long felt wrong, although magical.

I never thought I'd be able to experience such delightful and unforgettable days again in my life. Especially not with Spencer.

But life always finds a way to surprise us, I guess.

For the next few days, Spencer and I barely see each other. He has so much to put in order—he's bought an office downtown, but according to him, even though the place is great, some adjustments and renovations need to be made before it can officially function as his record label.

Not only the fact that he's busy keeps me from seeing him, but I am actually keeping myself occupied, helping my mom and Alice at the bakery. Surprisingly enough, I love it. Way more than I thought I would. I used to help Mom every once in a while back when I was in school, but at that time, I hated being forced to work instead of just going home and doing whatever my teenage self liked to do.

But welcoming people into my mother's cozy shop is way more

fun than I remembered it being. It's nice to see familiar faces, talk to the customers while they wait for their food, and also get to know tourists and people from all over the world. It astonishes me that they end up visiting such a small place like our hometown, but it's so exciting to hear their stories.

It actually inspires me and gives me some ideas for my book.

Which is also something that I restarted writing as soon as I was back from my trip with Spencer.

Turns out I decided to start everything from scratch. The draft I had from several years ago had nothing to do with who I am now, and it's not a story I want to tell anymore. So, one night, I decided to write down some new ideas for plots and characters that I want to bring to life.

I don't have as much time to do it as I want to, but when I'm back home from working at the bakery and helping Dad with the ranch chores, I feel so exhausted and drained that all I care to do is eat something, take a hot shower, and collapse in my bed.

And that's exactly what I did when I got home earlier tonight.

My room is pitch black since I closed the blackout curtains and wrapped myself in a warm, fluffy blanket, but as I close my eyes to try and fall asleep, I can sense my phone screen lightening up the room after buzzing slightly on my nightstand. I groan, contemplating if I should just ignore it and check whatever it is in the morning.

I assume it's Poppy sending me messages to tell me all about the office's gossip of the day. Since we don't see each other daily anymore, she said she feels obliged to keep me updated on what is going on at the newspaper. I pondered telling her I don't want to know, but to be fair, that'd be a partial lie. I kind of want to hear her say that Kayla's having a hard time without me. I haven't heard that, but Poppy did tell me that my former boss seems more stressed out than ever, so it made me feel a bit less upset.

I know it's selfish, but I'm still feeling a bit sour about the way she treated me and fired me so heartlessly.

However, it could also be Spencer texting me. It's not every night that he does so, but he makes sure to at least text me a 'good night' before going to bed if it's not extremely late when he gets finished with his day. I'm exhausted, but not enough to completely ignore him.

Blindly trying to grab my phone, I almost knock over the glass of water beside it, but luckily, it stands still enough so as not to make a mess. I would die if it splashed on the floor, or worse, on my phone.

The light momentarily blinds me as I open my eyes to check the screen. When my sight adjusts to it, sure enough, there's a message from Spencer.

'Sleeping already?'

I smile softly to myself before replying to him.

'Almost, but not yet.'

'I want to hear your voice. Can I call you? I swear I won't talk for long. I just miss you,' he texts back.

My heart jumps in my chest as I read his words. He's so sweet and romantic. I miss him too. After returning from our trip, it feels a bit odd to be away from him for too long. And since we don't have a lot of free time, it's been hard to even find a moment to talk over the phone.

I don't even reply to his message, deciding to call him right away. He picks up on the first ring.

"Hey, baby," I greet him, my voice low and hoarse from being quiet for a while now.

"Hey… are you sure you weren't sleeping?" Spencer asks, his voice full of concern.

"Yeah, I just laid down actually," I tell him, closing my eyes again and just focusing on his beautiful voice. "Is everything okay?"

Spencer hums, but doesn't say anything else. I frown.

"Are you sure?" I press. "You don't sound like it is."

"I'm just tired, that's all. I had some issues to handle this afternoon, and it wore me out a bit. I wanted to go and see you before you left the bakery, but I got caught up with one thing after the other," he explains, frustrated. "I can't wait for this to be done and over soon."

"Just hang in there a bit longer. I'm sure it'll be worth it." I know my words are not the encouragement he needs right now, but it's all I can offer from a distance.

"Guess you're right. How was your day?" he asks, changing the subject.

"It was all right. I'm having way more fun with the customers than helping Mom in the kitchen, but hopefully, she doesn't notice it," I joke, recalling the way she looked at me a few days back when I leaned against a table to entertain this young couple from Lisbon who was telling me about their plans to visit fifty countries before they turn forty. Their stories were so nice that I almost took a seat beside them to listen to them.

My mom simply shook her head and carried on with whatever she was doing, but after that, I tried to be more discreet.

"Yeah, well, let's hope you're not too obvious about it. Otherwise, you could get fired again. And by your mom this time," Spencer teases me, and I bite down a bitter reply.

"You're lucky I'm too tired to come up with a nice retort for you, mister," I tell him in a warning tone.

Spencer chuckles on the other end of the line and clears his throat right after. "I'll let you sleep now. I called to hear your voice, but also, I wanted to ask if you're free on Sunday. Aubrie wants to have a barbecue lunch with the fam, and she asked me to invite you. And by asked, I mean she forced me and won't shut up about it ever since we returned from Hot Springs."

It is my turn to laugh. "Of course I'll be there."

Spencer sighs with relief. "Good, thank you. I can't take another meal with her inquiring about you. It'll be nice to have someone to share the burden with."

"Is this an invitation for a barbecue or a guillotine? You're not being convincing enough," I ask, although I'm smiling from ear to ear.

"No, I promise you'll love it. As long as you ignore Aubrie." His voice is sarcastic and teasing, but I know there's some truth to what he's saying. I'm sure Aubrie will find a way to take me aside and ask about my relationship with Spencer, but truth be told, I'm not *that* apprehensive.

But maybe I should be.

Spencer picks me up on Sunday to take us to his sister's house. Funny enough, I'm equally excited and nervous to be with his family. They are people I already know, but still, it feels so official to be there with him after so long that I can't help but feel like this. The last time I went to this house, we were still in high school, when they lived with their grandma after their parents' death. It's Aubrie and her family's house now as their grandparents have also passed.

Before he can turn off the car or even begin to get out of it, his niece Caitlin shows up at the front door, rushing toward her uncle with her cute, curly blonde hair bobbing over her shoulders, her little arms stretched in front of her. Spencer hurries out of the car and squats down to hold her, and she wraps her arms around his neck, her bright blue eyes—the Bailey family's signature—shyly on me.

She looks exactly like her father, except for her eyes and her bubbly personality. I'm positive she took that from the Baileys as well.

I offer her a soft smile.

"Hey, little girl. How have you been?" Spencer asks while still holding her.

"I'm fine," Caitlin answers, her eyes still on me. I can sense her curiosity from where I'm standing, and if I could bet, I'd swear the wheels are turning inside her brain with all the questions she probably wants to ask me now. "Mommy said you were bringing a guest." She pulls away to stare at Spencer, finally breaking eye contact with me.

"Yeah, I did. I think you already know her, actually," Spencer says while putting Caitlin back on the ground. Even though she's four, very tiny and cute, she's also super smart for her age, so it's easy to forget she's so young sometimes.

"I do know you." Caitlin turns to me, looking up at me through her lashes. Her eyes look just the same as Spencer's, which amazes me. They are so blue sometimes—especially in the sunlight—it feels like I'm staring into the ocean.

It's my time to squat down. I smile at Caitlin again. "And I know you. Do you remember where from?" I ask her.

She studies my face, her hand darting to her chin while she racks her brain for memories of me.

"Do you need a hint?" I offer, tilting my head to the side.

Caitlin nods eagerly, her eyes widening ever so slightly. "Just one." She pops her little finger up to emphasize it.

She's so cute it should be a crime.

"Okay… well, you saw me at a wedding a while ago."

That seems to revive her memories as she widens her eyes even more, her mouth agape. "Yes, you were very pretty in a green dress."

I nod proudly. "You are correct. And thank you for calling me pretty. You're very pretty too."

She blushes and turns to look at Spencer again. She waves her hand at him, gesturing for him to lower to her level again, and when he does, she whispers in his ear, her other hand covering her mouth in an attempt to keep me from hearing what she's saying. But I do anyway.

"Is she your girlfriend? Mommy said she is."

Spencer chuckles, glancing up at me with a smile on his lips. "Yes, she is. This is Hayden."

"I saw you at my mommy's store too," Caitlin notes conversationally, looking at me.

"Oh, you're right. I go there sometimes to buy some books. I love them!" I tell her. She looked very shy at first, but now I can sense she's opening up and letting me in by taking the initiative to talk to me.

"What books do you like? I have a lot in my room. My mommy always buys them for me."

"Why don't we get inside first, Cait? You can show Hayden your books after lunch. What do you think?" Spencer suggests, grabbing my hand and guiding us inside the house.

Caitlin darts inside without even answering him, yelling at her mom that she's going to show me her room and her books after we eat. I chuckle, receiving an encouraging smile from Spencer in return.

As soon as we step inside, a feeling of nostalgia hits me as I stare into their living room. I spent so much time here in the past that it leaves me disoriented for a second. It looks exactly as I remembered it, except for some different paintings on the wall and Caitlin's dolls and toys spread on the floor. The TV is on, some cartoon Caitlin was probably watching before we arrived, and I allow myself to get lost in this feeling for a moment.

Spencer's home always felt cozy and inviting, having the same family atmosphere mine has always had. Both of us are lucky to have a close family where everyone likes to be together and gather for meals, or just to do anything, really. After his parents died, I remember how gloomy and sad the house was, and it made me feel uneasy whenever I came to spend some time with the Baileys.

"Everything okay?" Spencer murmurs in my ear, jolting me back to reality.

I clear my throat, shaking my head and turning to look at him. "Yes. Just took a trip down memory lane for a second. Everything here still looks the same."

He shoots me a warm smile, his hand darting to my lower back and guiding me toward the backyard where Thomas is probably working on the grill. "Come on. I'll get both of us a beer. I'm sure you'll need it for my sister's inquisition," he jokes.

"I heard that." A feminine, sweet voice comes from the patio before we even step into it. Aubrie's voice is threatening, although I can sense the teasing tone in it. "Very funny, but also cliché, to turn me into the villain, brother."

Aubrie is looking at us by the time we step outside, her bright blue eyes piercing through her brother's skull. She has a grin on her lips, her dark hair—the same color as Spencer's—tied into a french braid. She is wearing a floral summer dress and a beige cardigan on top of it since it's windy and slightly chill out here.

"Don't pout, sis. I'm only stating the truth and preparing Hayden for what's ahead of her."

Aubrie scoffs, walking toward us. "As if she doesn't already know me. You can't pretend you're the saint here." She wraps her arms around me, pulling me into a tight embrace. "It's so good to see you, Hayden."

"It is so good to see you," I repeat, trying to emphasize how happy I feel to be here. It feels different to see Aubrie outside of her book-store. She has always been kind to me, but now that I'm her brother's girlfriend again, it seems like there's an invisible rope bringing us closer to one another.

As if… I'm part of the family.

"Don't worry, I know Spencer is being overly dramatic," I tell her, watching her turn to her brother and grin at him. It feels like I'm watching two kids banter, but again, who am I to talk when I do the exact same thing with Chad? I guess siblings never really do grow up.

I glance at Spencer, who feigns being offended, and then allow Aubrie to guide me toward the grill where Thomas seems to be preparing food for an entire battalion.

"Thomas, you do remember Hayden, right?" she asks, catching the attention of her husband. Except for his eyes, he looks just like his daughter, his blond hair neatly styled even though he's facing the heat from the grill. He's a tall man, with a confident posture, something I figure he must have learned from his job as a real estate developer. He's a bit quieter than the rest of the family, a bit too serious even, but I know he has a kind heart from the way I've seen him treat Caitlin and Aubrie.

He's also always treated me well whenever we bump into each other in town, so I have nothing bad to say about the guy. I like Thomas.

"Of course. Welcome, Hayden. It's so good to have you join us."

"Thank you, Thomas. It's very nice to be here."

"Okay, so you go over there with Spencer to distract Caitlin while Thomas and I finish preparing the food," Aubrie urges me, pushing me toward Spencer and Caitlin, who are now focused on some toy she's showing her uncle in the living room.

"Oh, it's fine, I can help you. What can I do?" I offer, already knowing she won't allow me to do anything.

Aubrie shakes her head eagerly, forcing her hand on my shoulder and guiding me back inside. "Absolutely not. You're our guest today. I must say, though, handling Caitlin might be worse than chopping onions sometimes, so I apologize in advance for that." She chuckles, turning her back to me and walking inside the kitchen.

I ponder insisting on helping, but I simply know she won't let me do it. I can't blame her because, if this was the Jenkins household, my mom would be flipping out on me if I allowed a guest to do any work.

I take a deep breath, turning on my heel to go and meet Spencer and Caitlin. I thought I'd be more emotionally overwhelmed, but when Spencer looks up at me, and our eyes meet, I feel like I'm exactly where I'm supposed to be.

This feels like home. A different one, but equally as loving and caring as the one I have back at the ranch. It makes me feel so lucky. How did I end up being so blessed?

"Hayden, come see what my daddy got me for my birthday. It's a xylophone that lights up in the dark," Caitlin yells, waving at me enthusiastically as I approach them.

I bite down on my lower lip to prevent myself from laughing at how cutely she pronounced the word 'xylophone', and instead, I widen my eyes, squatting down in front of her. "Oh, wow. Does it really? That seems like the most incredible xylophone ever."

Spencer wraps his arm around my back, pulling me close to him as we both pay attention to Caitlin while she starts playing a song she apparently just learned from YouTube. I swear the kid seems to be in her twenties with how smart and self-reliant she is.

"You have no idea how much it means to me that you're here," Spencer whispers in my ear, causing my entire body to shiver with how close he suddenly is. It also helps that he's been the sweetest guy on earth by acknowledging how happy he is that I'm at his family's house with him.

I turn slightly to look at him, not wanting to be disrespectful to Caitlin's presentation. "It means even more to me that you want me here."

CHAPTER EIGHTEEN

*I*n the end, being questioned by Aubrie wasn't as bad as Spencer made me believe it would be. I had actually forgotten how witty and funny she is since we barely see each other in a lighter environment. She's usually working and so busy when I come by the bookstore that it's just not the same.

Aubrie was very nice when she cornered me leaving the bathroom and cautiously asked about my relationship with Spencer and how serious we were. If anything, she seemed more concerned about her brother than anything else, and I didn't mind her questions. I knew she was just looking after him. I assure her I'm in this for all the right reasons, and I truly care about her brother.

Once the week starts, Spencer and I are back to our busy routines at work. However, I manage to find a moment to visit his office since I haven't had the chance to do it yet, and I wanted to do it before he officially opened it. The launch party is happening tomorrow night, so things have been chaotic lately. I also feel like offering my help, even though I have no idea what I can do for him other than offer moral support.

When my shift at the bakery ends, I grab my stuff and head toward his office, which is a couple of streets away from my mom's shop. It's a nice, chilly night, so I wear my cardigan over my jeans and shirt, but it's actually enjoyable outside as I walk through the streets.

Before even getting to the corner, my phone rings in my purse, and I struggle to find it among so many of the things inside like my wallet, a couple of books I'm trying to finish reading, laptop, keys, and a bottle of water. When I finally find it, Poppy's name is flashing on the screen, and I smile to myself, already knowing she's dying to tell me what happened during her work day.

"You know, you should work for a British tabloid or something," I say by way of greeting, cackling when she curses me on the other end of the line. "I'm serious. No one would be able to beat you with how fast you spread gossip."

"Don't act like you don't like hearing it, Hayden Jenkins." I can almost see her rolling her eyes at me. "Do you want to hear it or not? I can always find someone else to share it with. I'm sure they will be more receptive than you."

I chuckle, pressing the phone harder against my ear. "Don't be so sensitive. I'm just teasing you. Of course, I want to hear it. Unless you're going to tell me that Kayla was promoted, or worse, got herself a billionaire or something."

"Ew, no!" Poppy replied. "She can kiss my ass. I couldn't care less. Anyway...so, do you remember that pop rock band we watched at Coachella a couple of years ago with the cute bass player and the hot singer?" she asks, her voice way too excited for me to keep up.

I rack my brain, trying to remember what she's referring to, and it doesn't take me that long to figure out what band it is. "Oh, yeah. I do remember. They sounded amazing. I remember you swore to yourself you'd marry the guy or whatever, but I guess it didn't turn out the way you planned."

"Ha, ha, very funny. I didn't say when, and guess what? I just heard they're going to sign with a new label for their next album," Poppy tells me.

"That's...cool?" I'm not sure where she's going with this, and I honestly don't feel as excited as my friend sounds at this moment.

"Girl, keep up with me here, please? They are signing with Bailey

Records!" she squeaks, making me pull the phone away from my ear for a moment.

"Spencer's record label?" I repeat, finally understanding what she's trying to say.

"Yes! And apparently they will be here for the launch party tomorrow, as will a lot of other celebrities. I can't believe you haven't told me," Poppy complains, sounding offended.

"Honestly, I didn't know. Spencer is not really sharing every detail with me. He's been so busy lately that we're barely seeing each other. And I don't want to be all over him, asking who is coming to his party."

"Well, because you're a lame friend, that's why."

"Are you getting somewhere with this?" I ask Poppy.

But before she can answer me, I turn the corner to the street where Spencer's office is and am abruptly stopped by the scene unfolding in front of me. A beautiful, elegant brunette is stepping out of a black luxury car and walking toward Spencer's office, her black heels tapping lightly on the concrete. She's wearing black pants and a black turtleneck sweater, her golden earrings and necklace sparkling in contrast to her dark outfit. Her hair falls in waves over her shoulders down her back, her tanned skin glowing even though the sun is already setting behind the mountains. Her green eyes—or are they blue—scan her surroundings while she holds her phone against her ear, stopping in front of the front door of Bailey's Records.

"Hayden, are you still there?" Poppy's voice echoes in my ear, bringing me back to real life.

"What?" I muse, unable to drag my eyes away from the stunning woman apparently waiting for Spencer.

"I said I need to write an article about the record label, so do you think Spencer could give me an exclusive?" she asks, but her tone indicates she's repeating herself. Which I'm sure she is since I didn't listen to anything she said while I watched the woman climbing out of her car.

Who is she? Is she one of Spencer's clients? I don't remember her from the news or the Internet, so I don't think she's a singer or anything, but I also don't know anyone in the music industry.

She could literally be anyone. Why should I care?

Why do I care?

I was never jealous before… Okay, I have been. Seeing Spencer with that Millie woman at my brother's wedding wasn't my best moment, but I was caught off guard. Sure, the woman looked like a model, and it made me feel even less confident about myself, but the woman across from me now, waiting for my boyfriend, makes me feel completely threatened, even though I have no reason to be.

Just because someone is stunning and hard to look away from doesn't mean I should feel intimidated. Right?

Right?

Get your shit together, Hayden!

What is going on with me? I'm with Spencer now. We're happy. We figured things out. I shouldn't be feeling like this.

"Shit, seriously, Hayden? I'm talking to you. What's going on?" Poppy insists, and I consider not telling her about my insecurities. They are stupid, and I know she will tell me I'm just being paranoid.

But when I see Spencer opening the door, looking slightly alarmed by this woman in front of him, I just know something is wrong. I feel it in my gut. The woman takes a step closer to him, and when I see her lips touching his cheek while she greets him with a kiss, I snap.

"Poppy?" I call, making sure she's still hearing me since I've been quiet for a while now.

"Yes? What's going on, Hayden? You're scaring me."

"I was coming to visit Spencer at his office before heading home. And now I'm watching the most beautiful woman walk into his office. I don't know what it is, I'm probably freaking out for nothing, but there's something telling me he wasn't expecting her here. Am I reading too much into this? Tell me I am," I plead, looking away as Spencer lets the woman inside and closes the door behind him.

My heart is pounding like crazy against my chest, and I feel like I'm falling into a spiral.

"Hayden, chill out. I have no idea what you saw, but it's probably nothing," Poppy assures me, her voice low and serious now. It seems like I'm talking to a different person all of a sudden. "You don't want to ruin what you have with Spencer because you're jumping to conclusions."

She's right. I definitely do not want to do that. So, why am I feeling like my stomach just dropped to my feet, and I can't breathe? Why am I imagining all these scenarios inside my head?

I trust Spencer. He'd never do anything to hurt me.

"Girl, listen to me. Don't overthink this, okay? Let's just do something together to distract you, and then later, you can ask Spencer if you want. Or even wait to see if he tells you something himself," my friend suggests.

It's the wisest thing to do. But I just know I won't be able to get this out of my head, even though I saw nothing incriminating. Spencer can meet whoever he wants, whether it's a man or a woman. I'm not that controlling. I don't ever want to be that person.

"Okay, fine. You're probably right. I'm just intimidated by her presence and beauty, that's all. Should I still go there and offer my help, though?"

"What if this is an important meeting? You don't want to ruin things for him, do you?" Poppy retorts, making me be reasonable. This is one of the many reasons I love having her by my side. She always makes me see the light and be rational instead of emotional—something I often do.

"Sure, yeah. So, should we do something?" Then I remember I didn't answer her. "About the exclusive, I'm sure Spencer will be happy to grant that to you. I'll talk to him later about it."

"Yay, great. Thanks, girl. I love you," Poppy muses, returning to her normal, cheery self.

"What would you do without me, huh?" I tease, grateful for the distraction she's already giving me.

We decide to watch a movie while drinking wine at the ranch. By the time I get home after getting some groceries, Mom and Dad are on the couch watching the local news, while Chad and Lauren play Monopoly on the living room table.

"Don't you guys work anymore?" I ask in a judging tone, eyeing my siblings as they look up at me. I'm just teasing them, of course, but it's funny to see them getting offended by it and quick to defend themselves.

"I'm off duty tonight, sis," Chad replies bitterly. "Not that I need to give you any explanation about my life."

"Ouch!" I put my hand on my chest to pretend like he hurt me.

"And I don't know if you remember, but I was involved in a fire incident. I'm still recovering," Lauren muses, throwing the dice and turning her attention back to the game.

I chuckle to myself, collapsing on the couch between Mom and Dad.

"What took you so long to get home?" my mom asks kindly, turning to look at me. "You left the bakery before me."

I consider lying to her, but I can't make myself do it. At least, not completely.

"I went to visit Spencer at his office but decided against it since I thought he might be too busy. Then Poppy called me, and we decided to watch a movie and drink some wine, so I stopped by the market to get something for us to eat," I tell her, ignoring the way Chad gives me a sideways glance.

Whatever he thinks he's looking for in my face, he won't find it.

"Can I join you?" Lauren asks, her puppy eyes turned to me. "I'm bored out of my mind in this house."

"Hey! I've been getting my ass kicked at Monopoly for the last three hours just for you, sis. That's a very ungrateful thing to say," Chad whines.

"Don't be such a baby, big brother. You can both join us. I don't think Poppy will mind," I tell them.

"Of course she won't. She loves me," Chad muses, a cocky grin forming on his lips.

I bark out a laugh, throwing my head back.

"What? She does!" he argues.

Both Mom and Lauren join me in laughing at Chad, and even my dad is shaking his head at my brother, a small smile at the corner of his mouth.

"Son, it's not a good thing to fool yourself like this. Us men normally tend to come up short in our beliefs," my father jokes, making the rest of us laugh even louder.

Chad shifts in his seat, turning to fully face us on the couch. He raises an eyebrow at us, challenging.

"I could get Poppy if I wanted," he states.

"Get me to do what?" Poppy suddenly steps into the living room wearing sweatpants and a hoodie, her long auburn hair tied into a ponytail, with her glasses on, looking like the cutest thing on the planet. Her infectious energy can be felt as soon as she walks in, looking at us with an amused look on her face.

I know she heard our little conversation before walking in. That's why I can feel she's messing with my brother. They've always been like this, ever since we were kids, and at times in the past, I wished they had gotten together. But they became more friends than anything, and I thought the moment had passed.

But maybe...it hasn't? I honestly have no idea if they ever felt something for one another, but I do see some sparkle between them whenever they are teasing each other. Chad is a big flirt, and it's not like Poppy doesn't like men like him. I just feel like they tread carefully through these waters so as not to harm our friendship above all else.

"Chad was betting he could get you to himself if he wanted," Lauren blurts, making Chad snap his head toward her, almost breaking his neck in the process. He grimaces, rubbing the nape of his neck, slightly embarrassed.

"I just said you loved me," he explains defensively. "They just like to team up against me."

"Right, that's what it was," Mom muses in a low voice, turning her attention back to the TV.

"Sorry, Chad. Maybe in another lifetime, but now, my focus is on getting myself a hot singer from a band called Glitch," Poppy says excitedly as she walks over and sits on the armchair beside Lauren.

It doesn't go unnoticed by me the way Chad frowns at her, but it is so quick, I wonder if I imagined it.

"Or so you wish," I tease my friend, shooting her a smirk and being cursed in return.

"Sorry, Mr. and Mrs. Jenkins." Poppy turns to my parents, not looking apologetically at all. "The lack of faith from your daughter in my dating skills is preposterous," she adds dramatically, making Mom and Dad laugh.

We spend another hour bantering and talking about different things until my parents decide to go to bed. With that being my cue, I get up and walk to the kitchen, grabbing a wooden tray to cut the cheese I bought from the market while Poppy helps me to open the wine bottle and wash the glasses we're using.

Chad and Lauren have the arduous task of picking the movie we're watching, and judging by the way their voices are rising in the living room, I can tell they are already in disagreement.

"Are you all right?" Poppy bumps into my shoulder, eyeing me while opening the wine bottle.

I nod, focusing on the task at hand so I don't cut my finger off instead of slicing the cheese.

"Yep," I answer, popping the P.

"Any word from Spencer?" Poppy pries.

"Not yet. Not even a text," I tell her. "I am trying hard not to think about it. I know it's stupid, and we're not kids anymore, but… I don't know. I just feel insecure."

"You have no reason to be," my friend insists, leaning against the counter so she is facing me completely. "Look at me. Spencer loves you. So, stop looking for trouble, and just snap out of it. You have no reason to feel insecure or doubt him."

"I know, I know."

"And if you're too worried, just have a conversation with him about it. It doesn't do any good to jump to conclusions. It never ends well, and as a reader and a writer, you should know that better than anyone."

I smile at her, shoving her slightly. "Fine! Why are you always so wise? Ugh!"

Poppy straightens her shoulders, looking cocky all of a sudden. "My bad, I guess."

"Shut up!" I chuckle, grabbing the tray filled with cheese and turning toward the living room. "Let's go before those two kill each other."

After another fifteen minutes of debating about what we should watch, we settle for a stand-up comedy show on YouTube instead, which ends up being way funnier than we expected. Halfway through it, I've been to the bathroom three times so I don't pee my pants from laughing so hard.

It does wonders to be distracted like this around my siblings and my best friend, and for a couple of hours, I completely forget about Spencer and how bad I felt from seeing that woman clinging to his neck as if she was afraid he'd slip away from her grasp.

I go to bed feeling numb and slightly dizzy, my body so relaxed from the wine that I fear my legs will wobble beneath me while climbing the stairs to my room. Poppy decides to crash in the guest room since she's way too drunk to drive home, and Chad is sleeping on the couch already, so we didn't want to wake him up since he has to work tomorrow morning and probably needs all the rest he can get.

I go to my bathroom, brush my teeth, and put on my pajamas before climbing into my bed, feeling like I'm walking on clouds. I didn't realize I drank that much, but now that I lie down in my bed, I regret it a bit. My head is spinning more than I thought it would.

My phone buzzes on my nightstand, and I grab it to find a text message from Spencer, checking if I'm still awake.

I am dying to talk to him, to hear his voice, because I miss him like crazy.

But I also know I'm not in the right mindset right now, and adding alcohol to the mix is definitely not a good combination.

I don't want to ruin what we have fought so hard to build back, so with that thought in mind, I ignore his message and try to get some sleep.

CHAPTER NINETEEN

I wake up to find three new text messages from Spencer on my phone. After sleeping it off, I now feel completely guilty for ghosting him last night, even though I was too tired and slightly drunk from all the wine I had. It was very childish to feel the way I felt when I saw that woman, and even though people always tell us to trust our gut, I just don't think I had reason to act the way I did.

Poppy was right; it was nothing, and I overreacted.

Before even stretching, I open the messages, hoping Spencer isn't mad at me or anything like that. Today is a huge day for him. I should be the first one to support him.

'Are you sleeping?'

'Guess you are. Just got home now. Things at the office look okay. I really think tomorrow will be great. Fingers crossed.'

'I could never have done this without you. I love you.'

This last message feels like a punch in the stomach. I did nothing to help him. Offering moral support shouldn't count when I barely got to see him during the process. I feel awful, like the worst girlfriend in the world.

Maybe I should do something to make it up to him. I could go to the bakery and get something for him for breakfast. Maybe we could spend some time together this morning before he has to dive into CEO mode for the rest of the day. The party is scheduled for 8:00 P.M., but I just know Spencer will have things to do for the entire day since lots of people are coming to town to attend his party.

From what I heard, the hotels downtown are full, not to mention the reporters and media waiting to get an exclusive from him and the artists he's signing. Which reminds me that I should ask him about Poppy's interview before he promises to grant it to someone else.

I get up from bed, rushing to the bathroom to take a quick shower before heading out to get ourselves something to eat. It's too early for the bakery to be open yet, but I know my mom always leaves some goodies prepared overnight, so I should be able to grab something.

Alice is already at the bakery when I get there, so I walk inside, greeting her with a, "Good morning," and start looking for something that I can take that won't make my mom mad at me.

"Can I help you with anything, Hays?" Alice offers, seeing that I seem a bit unsure of what to get.

I clear my throat, turning to look at her. She has a warm smile on her face as she stares at me, amused, her hands on her hips as she waits for my answer. "Well, I was hoping there was something in here that I could take to Spencer for breakfast. I wanted to do something nice for him before the big party tonight."

Alice's smile widens even more as she walks past me, heading for a shelf filled with donuts, muffins and mini cakes. She grabs a kraft box, adding all sorts of things she can get her hands on. It's more than I need and certainly more than Spencer and I can handle, but I'm grateful she's doing this for me.

"Isn't Mom going to be mad that I'm taking all of this? It doesn't have to be too much, Alice," I tell her, watching as she grabs another box and fills it with some croissants and different types of bread, which is something I'm not complaining about because bread is one of my weaknesses.

"Of course not. She always makes much more than necessary. You know her. She's constantly asking me to take stuff home so it doesn't go bad, but Ryan and I are trying to eat a healthier diet," she explains, grimacing and rolling her eyes at me. "So, you'll be doing us a favor." She chuckles, putting down a second box filled to the brim.

I frown. "Why would you guys even need to diet?" Ryan and Alice might not each have a six pack, but they are pretty close to it. I honestly have no idea how they do it, but even after the wedding and their honeymoon, they still manage to keep their bodies something to envy and die for.

Alice laughs, tilting her head back slightly. "I'm not trying to lose weight, but it is hard to keep it as it is when we have your mom's delicious food at home every night. You'd know, right?"

I scoff. "You got me there." Damn right I know how hard it is to keep my hands—and mouth—away from stuff my mom makes. Sugar is something I find almost impossible to say no to.

"Anyway, just go and give your man a breakfast of champs. He certainly needs it today." Alice encourages me, putting the boxes into a single paper bag and shoving it into my hand.

"Thanks, Alice." I offer her a smile, hoping it expresses well enough how grateful I am for her help and encouragement. "You're coming tonight, right?"

"Of course." She nods enthusiastically. "Do you think I'd miss the chance to see a few celebrities in Missoula? How often do we see that happening?"

"You sound like Poppy." I groan, rolling my eyes. "Spencer will love to see you all there, though."

"I'm sure it will be a success. And we wouldn't miss it for the world. We need to show support as a family, right?"

My heart swells in my chest as I hear her mention Spencer as part of the family. Which, in a way, he already is. But still, I can't seem to control the way my body reacts to hearing Alice—who's not blood related to me, but that I consider my sister nonetheless—calling my boyfriend 'family.' "Thank you. Really."

The look in her eyes tells me that she knows what I'm thinking without me having to say it. Which I'm glad for. I might be good with words, but sometimes I struggle to say them. Writing them down is much easier than speaking them out loud sometimes.

I wave goodbye to Alice and drive to Spencer's house, hoping that he hasn't left yet. I wanted to surprise him, so I didn't tell him I was coming. His day might be swamped, so I'm hoping I can have him to myself for at least a few minutes so we can enjoy a peaceful breakfast together before all hell breaks loose.

A sigh of relief escapes from my mouth when I see his car parked near the garage. He's still at home. It takes him less than thirty seconds to answer the doorbell. It's a sight to keep in my memory for a long time. The way he opens the door, the gust of wind slightly making his damp hair flow over his eyes. He's wearing black chinos, a white button-up shirt with the sleeves rolled up to his elbows and slightly open in the chest—leaving room for my imagination to run wild—and a pair of white sneakers.

I let out a whistle, taking in the man in front of me from head to toe. His eyes sparkle mischievously as he grins at me, stepping to the side and making room for me to enter. "Sorry, ma'am, but I'm already taken."

His answer does something to my core that I don't have time to deal with right now, but he won't be getting rid of me tonight, that's for sure. I peck his lips as I step inside, passing by him with the bakery bag in my hand.

"Good answer," I joke, heading to the kitchen and setting the bag on the counter. "I know you have a full day, so I thought I'd surprise you and bring you some breakfast in order to wish you good luck tonight and also to enjoy some alone time with you before I have to share you with everyone else." I turn to look at him, my smile widening as I see him looking into the bag, beaming at the sight of so many good things.

"Good lord, you read my mind. I'm starving, and thankfully, I just made some coffee to go with this, so it's perfect." Spencer walks toward me, his arms snaking around my waist and pulling me closer to him. "Thank you for doing this. I missed you last night."

I smile at him, trying not to think about the real reason I didn't go to meet him yesterday, and hoping he doesn't notice something is off.

Which it's not. I'm over it, and today is all about Spencer and his record label. My stupid jealousy has no room here.

"Sorry. I intended to visit you, but I didn't want to disturb you. I know you were super busy," I say as an excuse. It's a poor one, and I hate that I wasn't more present for him during this period, but I also didn't know how to help. "Sorry I wasn't there for you more often."

He frowns at me, pulling me even closer to him. So close that I can feel his heart beating against my own. "You have nothing to apologize for. You've been my biggest supporter, and I could never have done this without you. And you'd never disturb me. Are you kidding me?"

I chuckle, shoving him slightly on the shoulder. "You know what I mean. And of course you'd be able to do this without me. You decided to come here and open your record label before we were even back together."

Spencer grins at me and kisses me softly on the lips before pulling away to stare into my eyes, his blue pools piercing into my soul. "We weren't back together, but you were the biggest reason why I returned. So, I guess you helped me big time, even if you didn't know it."

My cheeks feel like they are about to burst into flames, so I break free from his embrace—afraid I will never be able to if I don't talk some sense into myself—and step over to the kitchen counter to open the boxes and to pour us some black coffee.

"Smooth as ever, Bailey," I muse, hearing him chuckle behind me as he helps me set the table. "How are you feeling about tonight?" I ask, hoping we can change the subject, in desperate need of a distraction.

"I'm okay," he replies. "It's a bit mind-blowing to realize this is actually happening, but I feel like I'm in the right place, you know? It's different to work by myself. And it does help that I already have clients, so it doesn't feel like I'm starting anew."

I nod, sitting across from him at the table and grabbing a donut covered with a white layer of sugar from the box. "Before I forget," I begin, taking a bite from the donut, tasting its delicious flavor spreading across my tongue and mouth, "Poppy wanted me to ask you if you could give her an exclusive for the paper."

"Of course." Spencer nods, taking a sip from his coffee and picking out what to eat first. He decides on a croissant, spreading some butter on it before shoving half of it inside his mouth.

"Thanks. She will be very grateful. I'm sure she'll also ask you to introduce her to one of the guys from that band Glitch, but you don't have to do that if you don't want to," I tell him, biting back a smile, already knowing Poppy would kill me if she heard me saying this.

Spencer chuckles. "Noted."

Breakfast goes by quicker than I expected, and soon enough, Spencer is saying goodbye to me, climbing into his car and heading toward the office. I promised him I'd get to the party earlier so I can help with some last minute preparations, and also to be his sidekick with anything he needs during the event. With the amount of people coming tonight, I'm sure his head will be all over the place, so I'll be there to take care of him.

Spencer's office is bigger and cooler than I thought it'd be. He always had good taste, but looking at how spacious, modern, and unique it is makes my jaw drop. His personality shows through everywhere—from the concert posters and vinyl albums hanging on the walls, to the black leather couches spread across the room—everything screams Spencer.

I have no idea how he managed to get so many people inside it, though. It's a bit crowded and hard to move freely without bumping into someone, but not to the point where it's uncomfortable. If anything, it gets people to bond more easily. The atmosphere is friendly and cheerful, and I find myself relaxing a bit when I see that Spencer has everything handled.

He has given Poppy her exclusive interview already and also answered some reporters and media representatives. He's introduced me to all his clients—including the members from Glitch who turn out to be super fun and polite. For rock band members, I expected them to be more arrogant and full of themselves, but I couldn't be more wrong with my prejudgment.

Everyone from my family is present, even Mom and Dad who said they wouldn't miss it for the world. Seeing them here, supporting Spencer, means the world to me. Ryan and Alice are talking to Aubrie and Thomas, while Lauren and Poppy are in one of the corners gawking at Glitch's singer, who's talking to another guy I can't remember the name of. Chad is all over the place, greeting people he hasn't seen for years who studied with him and Spencer.

And that's when I spot the mysterious woman from the previous day. She looks even prettier tonight, wearing a tight black dress that emphasizes all her curves, with a slit that cuts all the way up to her right thigh. The Louboutin heels and the golden earrings only add to her look. I instantly feel self-conscious.

An arm snakes around my waist from behind me, pulling me flushed against a hard muscled chest. The woody, smokey fragrance hits my nostrils, and I look over my shoulder to see Spencer staring down at me with his blue eyes sparkling and a huge grin on his lips.

"So, I guess we can call this a success, right?" I muse in a low voice. Spencer leans down and pecks my lips for a brief second before pulling back.

"Hey, man," Chad greets us, patting Spencer on the shoulder, seemingly coming out of nowhere. "How does it feel to be the richest and most popular man in Missoula?" he teases, sipping from his glass of champagne.

Spencer grimaces at him, but before anyone has the chance to say anything else, the clicking of heels on the marble floor catches my attention, and I have to bite my lip so as not to make a face when I see the beautiful woman approaching our small circle. She has the biggest smile on her face as she walks toward us, stopping in front of me and Spencer. She barely regards me, pretending I'm not even here as she addresses him.

"You know, Spence, I knew you could do it, but I must confess, I wasn't expecting it to be such a smash," she purrs with her LA accent.

"I'm glad that the guys decided to follow you and get out of that awful label. I was having nightmares with how they were handling things with their contract. Thank God you decided to open your own thing."

Spence? Why is she calling him that? Are they that close?

"I'm happy to have them signed with my label too, Kendal. I'm very grateful that they decided to come with me," Spencer says. I don't know if it's just my paranoia speaking, or did his body just tense up against mine?

As if noticing my discomfort, my brother clears his throat, looking at Spencer with a look on his face I can't quite interpret.

What the hell is going on? What am I missing here?

There is no way this is all in my head.

"Er, Kendal, this is Hayden, my girlfriend," Spencer introduces me, his hand on my waist squeezing my skin slightly. "Hayden, this is Kendal. She's the manager of Glitch."

It doesn't go unnoticed by me the way Kendal winces at his words, as if he's hurt her somehow. Then she turns to me, the forced smile on her lips the only thing I can focus on as she tries to pretend she's not sizing me up. "Oh, sorry. It's a pleasure to meet you, Hayden." She reaches out a hand with perfectly manicured red nails toward me.

"Likewise," I reply, shaking her hand and doing my best not to show how I instantly don't like her. And this time, it has nothing to do with my jealousy and my inability to shove my insecurity down my throat.

"I didn't mean to make it awkward for you," she adds, her eyes darting to Spencer for a split second before they are back on my face.

I fight the urge to frown. I'm sure that's exactly what she intended by pretending she didn't see me literally leaning against Spencer, but I don't say it. Whatever she wants from me with this shit show she's putting on, she won't have it.

"Why would it be awkward?" I ask instead, challenging. In my peripheral vision, I can see Chad tensing up, and I don't even need to turn to look at Spencer to know he's holding his breath.

"Oh, you don't know who I am?" Kendal pretends to be shocked, her hand covering her chest in the fakest and worst performance I've ever seen.

"Kendal," Spencer calls in a warning tone. "This is not the time for this."

"What do you mean?" I hiss at Kendal, losing my composure for a second. I don't mean to cause a scene—and I won't—but it's getting on my nerves to be the only one who doesn't know what the hell is going on here.

"Well, I'm sorry," she sings, narrowing her eyes at Spencer as if she's confused. "I assumed that she'd have heard about me by now since I'm your ex-fiancée."

What.The.Actual.Fuck?

Fiancée?

Since when did Spencer get engaged to someone?

CHAPTER TWENTY

*H*oly shit.

She isn't lying.

Judging by the ridiculous and most uncomfortable silence that follows Kendal's statement, I know for sure that there's no way she's making this up.

I dare to glance at Chad, and then over my shoulder at Spencer, and by the way their brows are creased, and their jaws are tense and clenched, I know for a fact that she's telling the truth.

Her intentions are not the best—that much is obvious—but it doesn't matter now. Does it?

I don't want to show her how much this affects me, giving her the satisfaction she is clearly seeking. Kendal might be beautiful, but she's a snake. I can tell just by how dirty she's playing to have Spencer cornered in front of me. Of course, she knew he hadn't told me. How, I have no idea. But no one can convince me otherwise. Whatever the reason is for why he's kept this for me, I'll find out. But not now.

Right now, I will be the bigger person and just show her I'm not someone to be messed with. The Hayden from seven years ago would never be this mature, but thankfully, I learned a thing or two ever since.

"Oh, I don't think it was that important for Spencer to bother me with that kind of information. The past is in the past, right?" I finally reply, showing her my brightest and biggest smile. The sarcasm is dripping from my voice, though. "There's no need for us to waste time talking about it."

It is a lie, but she doesn't need to know that. To be honest, a heads-up from Spencer that I would be meeting his ex-fiancée would be nice. In fact, it would be nice to know he even had a fiancée at all. That isn't the type of news you keep from someone you're dating, right? Especially after everything we went through.

Kendal was clearly not expecting me to answer her at all, judging by the amount of times she blinks as she looks from me to Spencer and back.

She chuckles, trying to hide how her cheeks are reddening from embarrassment.

Good. I hope she chokes on her words.

Snake.

"I guess you're right. Why talk about that, huh?" She darts her eyes one last time at Spencer before clearing her throat and looking around, pretending to be looking for someone. "Well, it was nice to meet you. But I need to find the boys now. If you'll excuse me."

I don't bother answering her. Now that she's out of my sight, I can barely keep my self-control. I don't want to look at Spencer, or my brother, for that matter. All I want is to get away from here. It feels like the room has sucked all of the air from around me, and it feels like I can't breathe. I need to go outside and get some fresh air before I freak out or do something I will regret later.

"Hays…" Spencer's soft voice calls me, and I clench my teeth so I don't snap at him in front of his guests.

"Not now, Spencer," is the only thing I manage to say before walking out of his arms and away from him.

Chad tries to stop me, but I yank my arm free from his grip and head to the front door, hoping no one follows me on my way out. Hopefully, no one does, and I don't bump into anyone on the way, either. I only encounter the waiter with a tray filled with champagne glasses, which allows me to snatch one up. The gush of cold wind that hits me in the face as soon as I step outside is reinvigorating. I take a deep breath and swallow the uncomfortable feelings threatening to boil up my throat.

I shouldn't be feeling like this because of a stupid thing that seems to definitely be in the past. Yes, Kendal wanted to affect me, and to my distaste, she succeeded. Thankfully, it didn't seem like she noticed it. But I hate the fact that she did. I'm sure I'm overreacting, like I do every time, but it hurts. It fucking hurts to know Spencer had planned to marry someone else before me. It's not fair to think like that—we hadn't been together in years. For all he knew, there wasn't even a single chance that we'd cross each other's paths at all in the future. So, he might as well have been married to someone else, and I'd have no right to be mad at him for it.

So, why am I?

Maybe I'm romanticizing everything, wanting to be the only person in his life that he ever thought of having a family with. Wasn't that what he told me? That there was never anyone in his life but me? So, how come he has an ex-fiancée?

I chug down half of the champagne in my glass, closing my eyes to feel the liquid sliding down my throat. I just hope the alcohol kicks in sooner than later. I can't face this party sober anymore. In fact, I wish I could just go home.

"Hays?" Poppy's voice brings me back to reality, pulling me away from my excruciating thoughts.

"Yes?" I turn on my heel to look at her, finding her eyes narrowed at me and her brows creased with concern.

"Is everything okay? You passed by me like a rocket," she notes, stepping out onto the sidewalk and closing the door behind her.

I turn my back to her again, focusing on the cars passing by to distract myself. I'm still not calm enough to talk about it. And I appreciate the fact that Poppy seems to know that by standing beside me, her arms crossed in front of her chest while she looks ahead to mimic me, giving me the space I need.

"Spencer has a fucking ex-fiancée," I blurt out before I even know what I'm doing. So much for self-control.

Poppy almost chokes on her saliva as she looks at me, her mouth agape. "I beg your pardon?" she asks in a very dramatic voice, and if I wasn't so pissed, I'd be laughing at her reaction.

"Exactly. She's the woman I saw walking into his office yesterday that I told you about," I explain, drinking the rest of the champagne in my glass. I wish the waiter were serving outside, too, so I could grab another one. I don't want to go back inside and risk facing Spencer. Or anyone, for that matter. The last thing I need is my family asking me why I look like someone just pissed on my cereal.

"Shit," she hisses, blinking aggressively at me. I know she's trying to find the right words to say to me, not wanting to add fuel to the fire. "Judging by your reaction, you didn't know about her, right?"

I snort, unable to answer her properly.

Before Poppy has the chance to say anything else, the sound of chattering and the loud music blasting on the speakers inside grows louder as someone opens the door. I bite my tongue to prevent myself from cursing when I see Chad heading toward us. My friend seems to notice the instant tension that rises between us as she takes a step back and whispers, "I'll be inside if you want to talk. Or leave. Or both."

I smile softly at her, trying to show my gratitude without really saying it. Poppy walks back inside, nodding slightly at Chad as she passes by him. They exchange a glance I don't care to interpret right now.

"Hays, can we talk?" Chad asks, his voice low and cautious as he stops beside me.

"If you're going to lie to me, save your breath," I retort harshly.

"I didn't lie to you. You never asked me anything. How was I supposed to know you weren't aware of it?"

I turn to look at him, too astonished to form the right words. "I saw the look on your face when that woman came to talk to Spencer. You knew who she was, and you seemed very worried that she was getting close to me."

"Of course I was. I know Kendal. She doesn't play nice, and I feared she might want to cause a scene or something." Chad is making excuses. His explanation does make sense, judging by how I could see Kendal's true colors immediately, but it doesn't help his case. I'm still angry. He's just unlucky that he was there at the wrong moment. I don't feel selfless enough not to throw some of the blame on him right now. "Come on, Hayden. It wasn't my story to share. It's Spencer's past," he argues.

"You didn't seem to have a problem with that when I started seeing him again. You meddled in our lives just fine," I spit.

"I was just trying to protect you both from hurting each other again."

"Didn't you think it would be nice to warn me that Spencer had a fucking ex-fiancée? Who looks like that?" I gesture to the door of the office, my hand shaking slightly. I hate that I'm out of control, but I'm glad it's Chad on the other side receiving it and not Spencer. Even though I'm super mad at him for keeping this from me, I wouldn't want to ruin his important day by causing a scene and spitting mean words at his face like this.

"She's crazy, Hays. I'm not the one who should explain things to you, but don't be hard on Spencer. I mean, it's been years since they broke up, so..."

I bite my tongue again, swallowing hard so I don't say anything else I'll regret. I hate that Chad is being the voice of reason when all I want is to punch something--or someone—to vent my anger.

"Whatever, Chad. I don't want to talk about it anymore," I tell him. I wanted to come here to get some fresh air and maybe get my head in the right place, but for some stupid and immature reason, I can't. I can't stay here anymore. I can't face Spencer. And I can't pretend I'm okay, facing everyone and smiling at the guests when all I want is to be alone.

But I also can't go now. It would make people talk. Not that I care, but again, this is an important moment for Spencer. If this was me when we were dating back in high school, I just know I'd have been home by now, too hot headed to continue to be here. I wouldn't have cared about him. I would have just been selfish and thought about myself. But I'm different now, or at least I want to believe I am.

Sure, I won't pretend this didn't happen tomorrow, but trying to solve things when I'm too angry right now isn't helpful either. I know that.

"Fine. Are you coming back inside then?" Chad pries cautiously, afraid I'll snap at him.

But I just inhale and exhale slowly, deciding what to do.

"I guess I should. Just give a few minutes, all right? I don't want to fuck it up, so it's better that I calm myself down first," I explain, hoping he'll leave me alone for a moment.

Chad nods, shoving his hands into his pants pockets, suddenly looking awkward. "Look, I'm really sorry, okay? I didn't want to keep anything from you. You know that, right?"

His question makes me feel bad. I didn't want to snap at him. He's right, it wasn't his story to tell. It'd have been nice to know it, but he's not the one at fault here.

"It's okay, Chad. I'm not mad at you. I was just...caught off guard. That's all."

"I get that. I'd be fucking pissed too. I don't understand why Spencer didn't tell you, but maybe he has a reason? You guys should just talk about it," he suggests, studying my face.

I nod, not wanting to extend the conversation any longer. I'm suddenly feeling a terrible headache coming on, and this topic is only making it worse.

"I'll be inside if you need me," my brother tells me before heading back inside, finally leaving me alone with my own thoughts.

I stay on the sidewalk for a while, almost losing track of time. But when I hear people clapping and raising their voices as if they are getting ready for a toast, I take that as my cue to go back inside. I don't feel like it, but I need to be beside Spencer for this moment.

No one seems to have noticed my absence, and if they did, they don't say anything. I grab another glass of champagne on my way inside and spot Spencer raising his own at the audience, speaking a few words of gratitude for everyone present and how happy he is to be able to finally accomplish this dream to open his company in his hometown. My heart swells at his words when he turns to me and briefly mentions how I helped him take that next step, encouraging him to follow his dreams.

I smile at him, truthfully happy that I am somehow responsible for it. It takes my mind off things for a moment, allowing myself to just be happy for him. This is bigger than anything else going on right now. It's not like Spencer cheated on me or something. Or at least I hope not. Images of Kendal walking into his office last night invade my mind, and I'm momentarily paralyzed.

They couldn't be doing anything, could they?

Of course not, Hayden. It's Spencer. You know he would never do that to you.

But no matter how many times I repeat these words in my head, I just can't seem to make myself believe them.

After the toast, Spencer tries to reach out to me, but I step away from his hand, letting him know I'm not in the mood to talk. I manage to stay away from him as much as possible until I see people starting to say goodbye, congratulating him for his accomplishments, and saying that they expect him to have lots of success in the future. I step to one corner, finding an empty couch to sit on while I watch his guests leave one by one.

Lauren suddenly tosses herself by my side, the couch's cushion sinking slightly with her weight. Poppy sits on my other side, and I can feel her eyes on my face, but I don't look at her, choosing to keep my focus ahead, watching as Spencer talks to one of the singers he used to work with back in LA. I don't remember his name, but I remember seeing his face once or twice on my TV back home, when Mom and Dad were watching some show on a Sunday night. I guess he's a country singer, but I honestly can't remember.

The guy pats Spencer on the shoulder, smiling widely at him. I can't hear what they are saying, but it's evident from the look on this guy's face that he's thrilled to be here and working with Spencer. It fills my heart with pride.

"Is everything okay, pony? You look...weird," Lauren points out from beside me. I can now feel the other side of my face burning from her stare.

"Yep, everything is fine," I lie, not wanting to bring my sister into this mess. I know she'll find out eventually—I might be the one to tell her, even, when we're back at the ranch—but right now, I don't want to talk about it.

Poppy shifts uncomfortably by my side, but I ignore her. That's when I see Kendal heading toward Spencer like she's walking the fucking runway with her heels and long legs. My fists clench in my lap as I watch her throwing her arms around his neck, saying something in his ear. Spencer's body tenses immediately under her touch, and even from a distance, I can tell he's not comfortable. But it's not like he's just afraid that someone will see it, but he seems rather... disgusted by her approach.

In your face, Kendal. Try harder.

A grin spreads across my lips as I see Spencer grabbing her by the shoulder and pulling her away from him, creating a safe distance between them.

Poppy snorts by my side, clearly watching the same scene as me.

"Wouldn't want to be her right now," she muses in a low voice. Lauren seems distracted by something else, so she doesn't hear my friend, but it wouldn't be bad for my ego to hear my sister dissing that woman too.

"Are you ready to go home?" I ask them instead, looking from one side to the other to take in their expressions. Mom, Dad, Ryan, and Alice have left already, so I'm stuck with these two...and Chad, and I have no idea where he is. If I know my brother, he's probably somewhere getting wasted or trying to find himself a woman to spend the night with.

"Hell yeah," Lauren replies, leaning back on the couch and closing her eyes. "Why do I feel so tired? I thought I was bored out of my mind inside that house, but now that I'm here, I just want to go back to my bed." She chuckles, shaking her head.

"Well, staying at home is a point of no return, trust me," I tell her in a teasing tone. I would know since I love doing exactly that. Give me a night in with wine and a good book any time of the week, and I'm down.

"That's because you're boring," Poppy chimes in. "How can you find hot guys and good food while staying at home?"

"That's why people invented delivery," I reply with a sarcastic smile. "And as for hot guys, I'm not looking for one right now."

My friend rolls her eyes at me. "You selfish bitch. Not everyone is lucky enough to find a Spencer, know that?"

"What about the guy from Glitch? Weren't you planning on having him fall head over heels in love with you tonight?" I tease, receiving a slap on my arm in return.

"Shut up. I tried to, but you know what? He's probably gay."

That has me cackling so loud that people around look at me with judging eyes as if I'm off my face.

Poppy huffs, crossing her arms across her chest angrily.

"Ready to go, girls?" Chad asks, appearing out of nowhere, his hand dangling his car keys. "I'm taking you home."

I get to my feet, still affected by Poppy's comment. My sister and my best friend do the same, just about the time I spot Spencer coming toward us from behind Chad.

"You're coming, too, or are you staying at Spencer's?" my brother asks, still unaware of his friend behind him.

My eyes meet Spencer's from over Chad's shoulder, and the intensity in them leaves me speechless for a moment. But it also reminds me why I am so upset with him. That's why I look away, back to my brother's face, and tell him, "Actually, I'm going home tonight."

CHAPTER TWENTY-ONE

"Can we talk?" Spencer asks as I pass by him.

Chad, Lauren, and Poppy exchange a glance and tell me they will wait outside, and I'm thankful for it. I don't want them to listen to this. They would bombard me with questions on our way home, and I'm not in the mood for it. I'm sure that not staying at Spencer's house tonight is indicative enough that something is not right. Also, Lauren is the only one who still doesn't know what happened, so it's not like the damage control would be that exhausting. But if I could choose, I'd rather stay in silence the entire way.

"I don't think that's a good idea, Spencer," I tell him coldly. "I don't want to say the wrong thing to you. Not tonight. Everything was a success, so it's better to wait until I sleep it off," I explain with sincerity.

He opens and closes his mouth as if he wants to argue but decides against it. I feel bad for him. I really do. But I can't order my feelings to change and bend to my will whenever I want. That's not how it works, unfortunately.

"Okay, sure. Can I call you tomorrow?" he asks softly, his pleading eyes almost becoming the death of me. If Spencer wanted, he could make me forget about everything that happened in a second. That's how putty I am in his hands, under his puppy eyes. I hate the way my body reacts to his ocean blue eyes, almost as if it has a mind of its own. If Spencer insisted, I'd just give up on everything entirely. That's how his charms work on me.

But he's too respectful for that. He knows I need space, and he agrees to grant it as soon as I ask for it.

I don't know if I hate or love him for it now.

So, instead, I just nod at him in response.

But I don't answer him when he calls me the next morning. Nor during the afternoon. Or the evening. In fact, the entire weekend passes without me getting even close to my phone. I decided to leave it in my drawer so I don't get tempted to answer him. It's not that I'm running away or anything, I just need some time to myself, to put my thoughts in order and understand why the whole Kendal debacle got me so keyed up.

It's a *me* problem. I go over it several times during the weekend, and no matter how hard I try, there is no explanation for why I got so upset with his omission other than—I'm insecure. Too afraid to give myself entirely to him and our relationship. His past haunts me, even though it shouldn't.

Spencer is with me. He decided to stay with me. He moved back to goddamn Missoula *because* of me. It's ridiculous that I'm allowing this stupid discovery to get in between us, but somehow, I can't fight it.

I'm directly responsible for it, though. I was the one who didn't want to know about his past in the first place when he offered to tell me about it. I said it wouldn't do us any good, and I believed it. I just wasn't expecting his past to show up in the form of long legs, tanned skin, and a fucking model's body—Kendal. That did not help my insecurities at all.

Trying to stay shut away so my family doesn't feel the need to check on me every five seconds doesn't help me either. It's obvious they know something is wrong since I didn't leave my room for most of the weekend, and when I did, I chose to stay somewhere silent and isolated. I would go to the porch to write my book, or down by the horse stables so I could have their company instead as I tried to get somewhere with my novel. It's the only positive thing I can take out of this—creativity for my story. I channeled all my anger and frustration into my writing, and it turned out to be somewhat exciting and productive.

Seeing the words flying out of my fingers onto my keyboard put me in a better mood.

But whenever my mom, my dad, or even my siblings tried to pry into my life, asking about Spencer, I would go back to my bitter mood, telling them that everything was fine and that I was just working on my book. It was nothing to worry about. They didn't buy it, of course, but they respected me, which I was grateful for.

On Sunday evening, Poppy texts me, asking me about the River City Roots Festival happening next Saturday. We've made it our thing ever since we were young, going every year together to watch the concerts, drink beer, eat lots of festival food, and buy pottery and ceramics from local artists that we never really find use for. I love festivals, so I'm always excited for this time of the year. However, that's not the case this year.

With everything that happened with Spencer, I can't find it in me to want to go out and do all these activities. I just want to be alone and mope around all day. I'm making this a big deal, but I guess I'm mostly disappointed in myself for not handling this like a grown up. Why can't I just answer Spencer's calls and deal with this like a normal adult would? It's infuriating and frustrating.

Knowing Poppy will kill me if I tell her I'm not going, I reply to her saying that I can't wait, although she will probably see through my lie. As soon as I press the send button, another message appears on my screen, this time from Spencer. Even though I'm not answering his phone calls, I'm reading all of his messages. He sent a couple over the weekend, wanting to meet me so we could talk, but I ignored all of them. This time, though, I can't do the same. My heart starts beating rapidly in my chest as soon as I read his text.

I'm downstairs. We need to talk, and I won't leave until you come outside.'

"Shit!" I mutter under my breath, trying to find a way out of this. I don't want to talk to him now. I look…like I haven't been out of my room for two days. My hair is up on top of my head in a messy bun, I'm wearing my oldest pair of sweatpants and hoodie, and my socks are worn out and different from one another. I'm wearing my glasses because there's no need for me to wear my contact lenses at home and just be uncomfortable with them in all the time.

I don't want to discuss our relationship looking like this. Especially if we're talking about Kendal. That'd do wonders to my already low self-esteem.

I ponder what to do. Should I run to the bathroom and take a shower before heading downstairs even if I just took one a couple of hours ago? What if I apply some makeup just to try and look presentable? The bags under my eyes definitely need to be hidden. I look like a fucking panda. And not the cute type. Or maybe I should change into something less lazy that doesn't scream, "I'm moping at home all weekend after finding out my boyfriend had a fiancée who looks like a Victoria's Secret model."

Ugh! Why did he have to come all the way over here?

Deciding against all of this, I just jump out of my bed and rush down the stairs, ignoring the alerts going off in my head yelling at me that I look ridiculous. *Whatever.* Spencer has seen me at my best and worst, so it's not like he hasn't seen me like this before.

Thankfully, my parents don't seem to be anywhere around the house as I step into the living room. I look around, checking if they might be in the kitchen or maybe even on the porch, but judging by the silence that reigns around me at this moment, I'm assuming they have already retired to bed.

Good.

At least they won't be listening to me and Spencer. It's also encouraging to know that my siblings won't show up out of nowhere since Chad is at his apartment, and Lauren went back to work.

Opening the front door, I immediately spot Spencer leaning against the fence, his car parked a few feet away from him. He has his hands shoved into his jacket pockets, looking as handsome as ever. He's wearing a black cap, covering his eyes and casting a shadow over his beautiful features. His chiseled jawline is still visible, but the dimples I love so much are nowhere in sight. Instead, all I can focus on is the way he's clenching his teeth as if he's mad at something.

Or better yet, *someone.*

That someone being me, of course.

I'm momentarily distracted by the way his dark hair pops from under his cap and curls slightly at the nape of his neck.

"Glad to see you're still alive and didn't vanish into thin air like you made me believe for the past few days," Spencer notes, his voice deep and cold. It causes shivers to run down my spine.

I wrap my arms around my waist, protecting myself from the cold breeze outside, even though I still have my hoodie on, and the goosebumps I feel have nothing to do with the weather.

Spencer's athletic shoulders are tense under the fabric of his jacket, and he shows no intention of moving from where he's standing. I take a few steps forward, walking off the porch and crossing the dirt drive in front of the house to get closer to him. I know he wants to talk, and there's no need to act difficult anymore if I'm already out here. We might as well get this over and done with.

Whatever that means.

I swallow hard, trying to think of how to answer.

"I just needed some time," I finally say, studying his face even though I can't see much of it in the dark.

I see his dimple making a brief appearance as he sneers at my reply. "Of course you did. I just didn't think you'd need a whole weekend. I mean, it'd take you probably even more than that if I hadn't shown up here tonight."

I lower my head, staring at the way my UGG boots are drawing circles on the ground. "I'm sorry I acted childishly."

"Yeah..." Spencer retorts, and even though I'm not looking at him, I can feel he's not looking at me either. He sounds...annoyed and impatient. "I guess I'm the one to blame for believing you'd see this in a more mature way."

I snap my head up, certain that I heard him wrong. "Excuse me? What the hell is that supposed to mean?" I ask under my breath.

What is he implying with that?

"Well, if you had been mature enough to deal with it, you'd have come to my house or answered my calls so we could discuss this," he accuses in the same bitter tone. "But you didn't do that, did you? You hid in your room and avoided me so you wouldn't have to fix this."

"I don't have anything to fix," I hiss back, astounded. "You're the one who kept crucial information about your past from me."

"And I tried to explain myself to you, but you ran away. And don't act like it's my fault you didn't know about it. I asked if there was anything you wanted to know about me, or my past, and what did you say? You didn't want to know because it wouldn't do us any good. I respected your wishes, so don't put this on me, Hayden!" Spencer blurts out, his chest now moving heavily with his erratic breathing.

His eyes dart to my face, and I can tell they are dull and distant.

He has a point, and as much as it kills me to admit it, he is right. I didn't want to know. True, I didn't know what to expect, but I can't hold it against him. I take a deep breath, sensing where our conversation is going. I can tell Spencer is mad. If any trauma still remains from our bitter breakup in the past, this would be the time where I'd fear losing him.

And somehow, deep down, my heart is shrinking at the possibility of it.

"You said I was the only one for you," I finally whisper, looking away from him, still unable to hold his gaze. "You said there was never anyone that could compare."

Spencer sighs, and I notice that there are tears blurring my vision that I hadn't noticed until now. "And I meant it, Hayden. That was a stupid mistake, a dark moment in my life I wish I could forget. It meant nothing—"

"You were going to fucking marry her, Spencer. How can you tell me it meant nothing?" I interrupt, staring up at him, too worked up to even fathom what he is saying. "You don't get engaged to someone that means nothing to you."

"I said it was a dark period in my life, Hayden. What do you want me to say? It meant nothing. We ended things before it got more serious, and that's it. What else do you want me to tell you?" Spencer rubs his face in frustration. "I wasn't in a good place back then, and Kendal manipulated me. I got carried away. You had your fair share of bad choices, too, didn't you? This is mine."

"How do you expect me to take this? Up until a couple of days ago, I believed I was the only one for you," I cry out, aware that I sound childish and spoiled.

"And you still are. I'm with you, aren't I?" Spencer counters, shoving his hands into his pockets again, clearly unsure of what to do with them. He inhales sharply and licks his lips before continuing. "You know what the problem is with us? You don't trust me. You don't believe in us. You're constantly trying to find something to justify you distancing yourself from me. No matter what I do or say to you, it will never be enough, will it?"

His words feel like a physical blow to my face. It literally feels like he has just punched me.

I bite my lower lip to prevent myself from crying in front of him, but by the way my chin is trembling and my throat is itching, I can tell I'm not succeeding.

"That's not fair," I breathe out.

"I know. But it's the truth, isn't it? You know I'm right, Hayden. You're constantly trying to find excuses for us not to be together. The mistakes we made in the past are in the past. But you can't seem to accept that. It feels like you're constantly looking over your shoulder, waiting for our ghosts to come back and bite us in the ass."

"And can you blame me?" I snarl back in a loud voice. I instantly regret it, hoping I haven't woken up Mom and Dad. I don't need an audience.

"No, I don't blame you. But we talked about it, and I thought you had gotten past it by now. But I was wrong. And I can't make this… us," he points between us in a tiring gesture, "work all by myself. This is supposed to be a two way street, Hays. And you're not meeting me halfway here."

I swallow the bitter taste his accusation has left on my tongue and look away from him. I can't stare at him any longer. All I want to do is go back to my bed upstairs and curl up under my blanket until I fall asleep and pretend my love life isn't falling apart in front of my eyes.

What hurts me the most is to know Spencer is right, and I can't seem to find a way for my mind to make peace with it. Why can't I be more confident? Why can't I trust Spencer and our relationship completely? Why do I allow the fear of the past to haunt me and distance me from the man I love? We are not who we used to be back then. We have grown, faced hardships, and become stronger.

So, why am I boycotting us now?

"What does this mean for us then?" I ask, slowly looking back at Spencer. His eyes are still dark under his cap, but I can see the glint of sadness in them as he stares back at me.

"I don't know, Hays," he answers with a shrug. He looks and sounds tired, but more than that, he seems heartbroken. And I can't blame him because that's exactly how I feel. The only difference is that I'm responsible for this going off track. So off that I don't know if I can bring it back to the way it used to be before. "All I know is that you need to figure out what you want because I'm not going to fight for us alone."

Spencer steps away from the fence and climbs into his car before I have the chance to even make sense of what he's just told me. The loud roar of the engine is the only thing I can focus on as I watch him drive away from me, leaving me out here in the cold night by myself, my only companion the moon, shining over me as if mocking the pitch black darkness I feel inside my heart right now.

How come I'm the one who fucked this up?

CHAPTER TWENTY-TWO

he entire week goes by uneventfully. Every morning, I go to the bakery to work, leaving only when the sun has already set, and go back home to focus on my novel, which is miraculously halfway done by now.

It is the only thing keeping me excited after my bitter argument with Spencer on Sunday. I haven't talked to him at all since, and he hasn't tried to contact me either. Not that I was expecting him to. He made it pretty obvious that he was mad and done with me when he walked away from me that night.

Poppy, Lauren, and even Chad tried to snoop around, separately cornering me to see if I would blurt something out, but I wasn't ready to tell them that I screwed everything up. In fact, I'm not ready to face the new reality of my life yet—that being that I have no idea if Spencer and I are still together.

He didn't break up with me—or at least not that I know of—but I need to try and fix this. However, I have no idea how to do it. The whole thing with Kendal feels stupid now that I look at it with a clear mind, even if it still hurts me a little to know I'm not going to be the first and only person that Spencer ever proposes to.

But I need to accept it and make peace with it because it's just how things are. I can't change the past, no matter how much I'd love to.

And on top of everything, I don't want to lose Spencer.

Now that I got him back, I can't begin to imagine what it'd be like to not have him in my life anymore.

A knock on my bedroom door pulls me back from my thoughts. I look up to see my mom's head peeking through the door gap as she stares kindly at me.

"Can I come in?" she asks softly.

I smile at her, nodding slightly. "Of course, Mom." I put aside my laptop and scoot over so she can sit beside me in bed. "Is everything okay?" I ask, even though it's obvious she just came to check on me.

"I should be the one asking you that question," she replies, her expression soft and comforting. "You don't need to talk if you don't want to, but it is my duty as your mom to ask."

I reach for her hand and squeeze it, offering her another smile. "I know, and I appreciate you for caring, Mom. I do." I close my eyes and take a deep breath. "I guess I'm just trying to make sense of my feelings and thoughts right now."

"You don't have to go through that alone. I know you need to make the decision for yourself, but sometimes, it's okay to ask for help," she tells me. "And even though you have Poppy and your siblings for that, a mother's advice might be just what you need. We do have a superpower, you know?" Mom chuckles, bumping me in the shoulder.

"Yeah?" I indulge her, raising my brows.

"Hmm," she muses proudly. "The whole experience, more mature, 'I've been in your shoes' kind of thing," she explains with amusement.

"Right..." I consider what to say. My mother has always been a good friend to me–and an amazing listener. She always gives me the best advice, and when I went through my first breakup with Spencer, she was there for me the whole time, even when I just needed a shoulder to cry on. I guess I was just too young and self-absorbed back then to cherish and value her support as I should. "I don't know how to fix my mess. I don't know how to teach myself to trust someone completely, to give myself away entirely to someone else. What if I end up getting hurt again? What if this time I'm broken beyond repair?" I finally ask.

My mom nods, offering me a reassuring smile. "That's what living means, Hays. Risking and carrying that constant fear that something might not work out."

"Well, that sucks," I grumble, rolling my eyes.

"Real life sucks sometimes, but the good moments we live, the great memories we create, they are worth it," Mom says. "And choosing to trust someone else with your heart, that's not an easy thing to do. It takes a lot of courage to give your most precious possession to another person."

"How did you do it? How did you know Dad was the right one for you?" I never really cared to ask her about this before, mainly because I thought it'd be weird to have this conversation with my mother. But now, it just feels… right.

If anything, my mother's answer will be something I'll hold dear to my heart. Her marriage with Dad isn't perfect, but is any marriage?

The most important thing—and that is what I consider crucial in a marriage—is that they respect each other, they are there for each other no matter what, and they are ready to face whatever life throws at them–together.

Their companionship is enviable. Something anyone would die to have in a marriage.

And to be fair, it's something I always had with Spencer.

"You just know it. I know it's cliché to say this, and not very help-ful, but it just feels different. It just…clicks. You realize you want to share every single aspect of your life with that one person. Even the bad aspects. Especially the bad ones. You can't imagine sharing them with anyone else," my mother answers. And even though it is not what I wanted, or expected, to hear, every single word makes sense to me.

Because that's how I feel about Spencer.

I never doubted he was the one for me, but now, I couldn't be more sure of it.

I have a huge mess to clean up, and I hope he's still willing to forgive me for being so childish and immature about the whole situation with Kendal.

The ranch is remarkably quiet on the day of the festival, even though my mom decided to participate by selling pastries and cakes. It's not every year that she does it, but since this is an event that values the local businesses, she told me that she had to set an example for the "young kids," whatever that means.

I, for one, have nothing against it. I just wasn't expecting to have to work during it. But as I help her and Alice set everything up, I distract myself with the bands doing their soundchecks on the main stage while drinking some of the craft beer from the food stalls next to ours.

When I told Poppy I'd have to work, I expected her to be sulky and complain about not having my company during the festival as we had planned, but I was wrong. She squeaked on the phone and offered to help, saying it'd be nice to talk to customers and just have a different experience at the festival.

I swear this girl never ceases to surprise me.

"Isn't it just weird to have beer with bacon flavor? Who one day came to the conclusion that this might be good? I mean," Poppy points out, taking another sip from her beer and rolling the liquid on her tongue to savor it, "it *is* unexpectedly good, but also weird."

I chuckle, setting aside a tray filled with salted caramel brownies. My beer is long gone by now, since I was extremely thirsty when Poppy brought me a glass a couple of minutes ago.

"It is good, but not my favorite. I like the orange one better," I tell her.

"Ew, no! You have an odd taste for things," Poppy murmurs.

"Look who's talking," I say back, rolling my eyes at my friend.

She turns to my mom, choosing to ignore my retort, and shows her stupidly white teeth in a smile. "Mrs. Jenkins, do you mind if

Hayden and I take a break during the Glitch concert? I promise we'll be back to help out as soon as it's over."

"Of course!" my mom answers cheerfully. "You don't have to stay here the entire day. We can all take turns. Chad, Ryan, and Oscar will also be here later to help out."

Right... I forgot that Spencer's band will be doing a special presentation tonight. I didn't find out about it through him, though. Poppy was the one who called me during the week to tell me that they had been invited to play and were now going to be the main attraction. Surprisingly, they have a huge fanbase, and from where I'm standing, I can already see some fans camping out at the front row barrier to get the best view of their favorite idols.

To imagine I was like one of them back in the day when I used to obsess over the Backstreet Boys. I still love them to this day, but I definitely do not have the energy to wait on my feet for hours just to be closer to them.

I can't see Spencer, however. He hasn't spoken to me ever since he left my house, and I haven't had the courage to call him yet. I'm trying to think of what to say to him. Poppy thinks I should just rip off the band aid and get it over with, but I'm too much of a coward for that. Truth be told, I'm just scared of the potential outcome. What if Spencer decides he doesn't want to be with me anymore? What if he breaks things off between us?

I'm not ready to give up on him—on us.

That's the only thing making me procrastinate and delay our conversation.

"Hello, fam!" Chad's cheerful voice echoes through our stall as my brother approaches us, wearing his Sentinel's cap, a glass of beer in hand. For a moment, I hold my breath, expecting to see Spencer by his side, but he's nowhere in sight. My tongue itches to ask my brother where his friend is, but I control myself. I don't want to sound desperate. "Need a hand there, Mom?" he offers, leaning against the shelf I'm working on to organize the muffins and mini lime pies.

I slap his hand when he tries to grab one, narrowing my eyes at him and silently mouthing for him to step away. Chad grimaces at me but doesn't move from where he's standing.

"No need, son. I already have a lot of hands helping me out for now," Mom replies, dismissing him with a wave of her hand. "Later I will, though."

Chad finally seems to notice Poppy amongst us and frowns. "Aren't you supposed to be working today?"

My friend shrugs. "Nah, Kayla asked someone else to cover the festival this time. Which I'm glad about. I just want to enjoy myself instead of having to write for that bit—"

"Poppy!" I call in a warning tone, afraid she might be heard by someone else. Living in a small town is already dangerous enough for gossipers like Poppy. She doesn't need to be fired for dissing her boss at a local festival.

She doesn't seem affected though. She simply shrugs and gets back to her task.

"You're not really enjoying it, though, are you? You're still work-ing," Chad points out, taking a sip from his beer.

"Not really working when I get to spend time with my favorite family. Besides, Mrs. Jenkins said we can leave to watch Glitch play, and that you'll be here to help." Poppy offers my brother the best sarcastic smile she can, and I bite my lip not to laugh at my brother's expression of disgust.

"That band sucks," he grumbles, but I know he doesn't mean it. He's just jealous of the attention their members get from women— especially Poppy.

"You're just jealous they're cuter than you," Poppy muses, teasing him.

As much as I love to watch them banter, I'm not in the mood for this platonic relationship today. It just reminds me of how screwed my love life is right now.

"Well, hello there," Ryan greets us as he walks in with our dad on his tail. Both of them look country enough, wearing matching flannel shirts, jeans, and boots. He goes to Alice, giving her a kiss on the cheek as she barely looks up from her hard task of piling up the blueberry muffins.

Dad does the same with Mom, and I look around, missing someone.

"Where's Lauren?" I ask.

"She came with Chad, didn't she?" Ryan retorts, turning to look at our brother.

Chad shrugs, rolling his eyes dramatically. "She stopped to speak with whoever that guy is that she works with. Jason? Jack? Josh?"

"James," I correct, narrowing my eyes at him. "What's wrong with James now? You used to like him."

"Yeah, until I found out he wants to sleep with my sister," my brother replies in a bitter tone.

"What? James is into Lauren?" I squeak, shocked. "Oh, my God!"

"Who is James again?" Poppy chimes in, suddenly interested in our conversation, her task of organizing the napkins long forgotten.

"The cute guy with green eyes and dimples? Girl, Lauren has won the lottery," I muse. James has been my sister's coworker since she got into the fire department. At first, he was just this shy guy who helped show her around, but after one summer, he simply became this…hot, guy-next-door kind of boy, so cute I barely recognized him when I saw him at one of Lauren's work parties.

"Oh, that James…" my friend murmurs dreamily. "You go, Lauren!"

"Whatever, he's not all that," Chad grumbles.

"Yeah, right…" I tease, offering him a mocking smile. "You're just jealous because you can't get yourself a nice girl."

Chad straightens up, turning to look at me. "Who told you that? For your information, I'm quite popular, sis. I'm single because I want to be, not because I don't have options. And you should be focusing on your love life instead of dissing mine, don't you think?" He grins at me, stepping aside just in time to dodge my punch.

That was a low blow, and I curse him when he takes a couple of steps backward, still laughing at me.

"Don't be rude to your sister, Chad," Mom scolds, pointing a finger at him.

He throws his hands in the air, feigning innocence. "Just stating the facts, Mom."

"Shut up if you don't want to miss your chance at having kids one day in the future," I warn him through gritted teeth.

"When are you guys going to grow up?" Ryan interjects, apparently too mature and serious to be affected by our sibling banter.

"Don't act like you didn't just step out from under Mom's wing," I snap at him.

"Yep, and fell right into your wife's lap. Not that big of a change," Chad adds, getting flipped off by our older brother.

Ryan looks shocked, glancing at Alice with his mouth agape.

"You asked for it, sweetie," Alice remarks with a shrug and a gentle smile, making us all howl with laughter.

It takes us all more than five minutes to compose ourselves and get back to finishing our tasks before the festival officially starts. But when we finally do, I'm too focused to notice someone approaching just outside the stall. It's only when I hear the sound of a guitar string starting to play on the stage and the loud, high-pitched fans yelling at the members of Glitch arriving at their soundcheck that I look up and spot Spencer talking to my brother.

It's been just one week since I last saw him, but no matter how much time has passed, whenever I see Spencer, I feel as if it's the first time ever. I'm always astounded by how handsome he is. And today is no different. He's wearing a denim outfit, with a matching jacket and pants, and a white T-shirt. His hair is slightly wet and combed back, and his beautiful blue eyes are covered by sunglasses. His dimples are on full display as he laughs at something Chad said, and I am momentarily in awe, just knocked dead staring at him.

He looks like a fucking supermodel.

I, on the other hand, didn't put too much effort into my outfit when I left home this morning. I slept in and got up late, so I had to rush to take a shower and help my mom pack the truck with the bakery boxes to bring to the festival. Thankfully, I had picked out what to wear last night, so I didn't have to grab whatever came to mind, but I still don't look as good as Spencer. My plain black pants, white shirt, and oversized jacket doesn't do his outfit justice. Good thing I decided to braid my long hair, so I do look kind of cute. At least that's what Poppy told me when she saw me earlier today.

And right now, I choose to trust my friend's judgment.

Because Spencer is looking over here, and I suddenly forgot how to speak. I need to trust my appearance, at least.

"You know, this would be a good time for you to solve your problem," Poppy whispers in my ear, nudging me in the ribs while she stares at the same spot as me.

"I can't, I need to finish this," I lie, pretending I still have something left to do. The bakery stall looks amazing, and no matter how hard I try, I can't find anything out of place or needing a last touch to keep myself occupied.

"Come on, Hays. You need to step up and stop being afraid. It's just Spencer," she insists, turning to face me. Her eyes are encouraging, and her smile is reassuring, but I still feel my throat and mouth dry as I ponder what could go wrong.

What if Spencer doesn't want to speak to me?

"That's the problem, isn't it? He probably hates my guts, Pops."

My friend snorts, rolling her eyes at me. "I don't believe that, and you don't believe that either. Spencer could never hate you. Now, stop whining and just go talk to him."

She shoves me out of the stall, and I almost trip over, my boots getting stuck in the dried mud on the ground. I turn and shoot Poppy a deathly glare before straightening up and taking a deep breath. My friend is right. I better just get this over with. I've put this off for a long time already.

With renewed determination, I walk toward my brother and Spencer, who is now looking at me. I can't see his eyes clearly, but he seems to have noticed me, and by the way his jaw and his posture are relaxed, I don't think he's angry.

At least, that's what I'm hoping.

"Can I talk to you for a sec?" I ask softly, approaching from behind

Chad's back and making my brother turn on his heel, slightly alarmed with my sudden presence.

I don't look at him, though. I have my eyes set on Spencer, and I don't dare to blink until I see him nodding at me and slapping my brother on the back, saying he'll meet him later. He then gestures at me to follow him.

CHAPTER TWENTY-THREE

e walk for a few minutes in silence as Spencer guides me to the back of the stage, away from prying eyes and the crowd at the festival. Surely, this isn't the best place for us to have this conversation, but I couldn't wait anymore, and Poppy also didn't give much of a choice. I'm actually grateful that she forced me to do it because I don't know if I would have done it by myself.

Spencer and I walk between some trailers, and he nods at some people who recognize him—probably the production crew and some equipment technicians—but he doesn't stop until we get to the wire fence that marks the terrain of the park. The day is colder than usual during this time of year, but thankfully, my oversized jacket is doing its job, protecting me from the wind. I'm already uncomfortable enough with this situation as it is. I don't need the weather to make it worse.

Spencer suddenly halts and turns to me, his arms crossed over his chest as he takes me in, his eyes still covered by his sunglasses. I can't decide if I prefer it this way or not. On one hand, staring at his beautiful blue eyes is one of the things I love the most, but on the other, it'd just make me more nervous, so maybe it's better that they are covered.

"So..." Spencer trails off, waiting for me to start. Since I'm the one who asked to talk to him, it's only fair that I'm the one to begin the conversation.

I clear my throat, trying to put my thoughts together, and think about the best way to bring this up.

"I'm... sorry I didn't call you this week. I... my head... uh... has been all over the place lately," I stammer, closing my eyes tight and cursing myself inwardly. Why can't I speak clearly? It's so frustrating. I sound like a child trying to apologize for doing something wrong. "I...that is not what I want to talk about, though. I've been thinking, and I wanted to apologize for how I dealt with the whole...thing with Kendal. On the day of your party and all, it wasn't cool, and I'm truly sorry for it."

That's not what I was planning to say–nor how I planned to say it–but the words just blurt out of my mouth before I can stop them. My hands are suddenly sweaty, and I can't remain still, shifting uncomfortably on my feet as I stare at Spencer, then my shoes, and back at his face. His stoic expression is not helpful, either. I have no idea what he's thinking, and it's driving me crazy.

"You already apologized for that," he points out with a shrug. "That's not what the problem is, though, is it?"

I nod. "Yeah, well, there's a lot of apologies I need to make."

"I don't want your apologies, Hays. I just want you to trust me. I can't be with you if you're not going to be with me fully. Can't you understand that?"

"I can," I argue. "I was getting there. I just wanted to apologize for everything else first. I was really hurt when I found out about you and Kendal, Spencer. I get that I didn't deal with it in the best way possible, but I also don't think it was fair that you kept that from me. Can't you imagine how I felt?"

He inhales sharply, his hands darting to his hair as he runs his fingers through it in frustration. "I know. I'm not proud of it either. I...I guess I just didn't feel the need to bring it up since you didn't want to know about my past. I meant it when I said it was a dark part of my past, Hayden. I didn't want to think about it anymore because I *don't* think about it. At all. It's like it never happened. Kendal is nothing more than a coworker now."

"Did you ever…love her?" The words taste like copper in my mouth, but saying that out loud makes me realize that I still fear that it might be true. The fact that I never loved anyone else other than him makes me afraid to even consider that he might have loved someone else other than me.

His head snaps to me, and even though I can't see his eyes, I can feel their intensity from behind the sunglasses. "I've never loved anyone but you. And if you need me to tell you that every day, I will. Okay? How can you not see it when everyone else can? *You* are the one I want. *You* are the only one I've always wanted. Anyone else was just…a way to try and forget you."

My eyes sting as I hear his confession, and I have to swallow hard to choke down my tears.

"I know I haven't been mature enough. I thought I had improved, had become better at this whole relationship stuff, but the thing is, with you… I just can't seem to make it right," I confess. "I guess I was just afraid that I'd be heartbroken again, and I ruined it with my insecurities. You were right; I didn't trust you or believe in us. But I *want* to. I really do, Spencer. I can't be away from you."

He takes a step forward, pushing his sunglasses up onto his head. His blue eyes are finally staring back at me as he closes the distance between us, his hands darting to my waist and bringing me closer to him. I instantly feel at ease as his woodsy scent invades my nostrils, and his warmth radiates through me. I melt under his touch, thankful he's holding me.

"I don't blame you for being afraid, Hays. I've been scared shitless, too, you know? To open up my heart to you again? To risk it all over again? But being with you made me realize that there's no other place I'd rather be. Nothing makes sense without you in my life," Spencer whispers to me, our foreheads touching. "And I know we can make this work. As long as both of us lay our hearts bare on the table. That means being vulnerable and trusting each other completely."

I nod eagerly, shoving away the tears threatening to fall. "I'd really like that. I promise I'll be better at it. I'll work on my trust issues and stop behaving like a teenager all the time." I sniff, chuckling awkwardly.

"Good, because I need my wife to trust me. I can't have you turning my kids against me whenever we have a fight," Spencer notes, a joking tone in his voice and a grin on his lips.

Him calling me his wife and the mention of us having kids one day makes my stomach do a backflip and my core tighten so hard that I struggle to breathe.

"Your wife?" I let out in a whisper.

Spencer's arms tighten around me, and he pulls me flush against his hard chest. "Yes, because that's what you're going to be. Soon."

My eyes widen, and my jaw drops as I stare up at him. What is he saying?

"That's your way of proposing to me?" I ask curiously, biting down on my lower lip.

"I'm just stating the facts. It remains a secret when it'll happen. I guess I'll just surprise you–eventually." And before I say anything else as a response, Spencer claims my lips with his, kissing me like he hasn't kissed me in a long time. I melt in his arms, relishing the way my entire body molds to him, the way his tongue plays with mine, and the way my brain stops functioning when he softly bites my lip. I moan quietly against his mouth, throwing my arms around his neck and pulling him nearer.

"I missed you so much," he murmurs against my lips.

"I missed you more," I reply, resuming our kiss until someone clears their throat behind us, and we're forced to pull away from each other. I feel my cheeks burning up as I see a man I don't recognize, wearing a shirt that reads PRODUCTION on the front, looking anywhere but at us as he waits for Spencer to acknowledge him.

"We need you for the last adjustments, Mr. Bailey," the guy says, clearly uncomfortable and regretful for interrupting us.

"Of course. I'll be right there, Mark. Thank you," Spencer answers, straightening his hair and trying to make it look presentable again. I guess I messed it up more than I intended.

I smile softly at him when he turns to me, self-conscious of what just happened. "That was… disconcerting," I note, amused.

Spencer chuckles, pulling me toward him once more and pecking my lips. "Can we talk later? I need to help them out, but maybe we can continue this tonight? My bed feels really big without you in it. Maybe you could solve that."

I blush ferociously. Spencer has always been straightforward about what he wants, and unexpectedly, I still get caught off guard by it.

"I'll take that as a yes," he adds before turning on his heel and walking back toward the stage.

I need a couple more minutes to compose myself, but when I finally return to my mom's stall, I need to control my stupid grin from giving me away to my family.

It takes me a couple more months to finally write 'the end' in my first novel. I stare at the last page, the cursor still blinking lazily on my laptop screen as I realize I really did it.

I finished my first book!

A scream escapes my mouth before I realize it, and Chad jumps at my side on the couch, cursing at me when he splashes his cereal and milk all over the shirt of his uniform.

"Fuck, Hays! That was my last clean shirt," my brother grumbles, rushing to the kitchen to grab a towel. He comes back, still rubbing the wet stain from his chest, staring at me with wide eyes. "What the hell was that about?"

"I finished my novel," I tell him excitedly, too worked up to control myself.

"Okay…congratulations. But next time, try to give me a heads up. You almost gave me a heart attack."

"Sorry." I offer him a sympathetic smile. "I'll make it up to you when I get my first royalties from this. Although, it is partially your fault since you shouldn't be eating cereal before breakfast anyway," I tease.

Chad grimaces, turning back to the kitchen, but I know he's happy for me. He's been nothing but supportive this whole time. I can't say anything bad about him when all he's done is keep me company and even give me some ideas whenever I was dealing with writer's block.

Most days, I stayed at Spencer's, but since he had to go to Los Angeles to take care of some new contracts, I came back home to spend time with my family and focus on my book. It was really easy to get…distracted whenever I was with Spencer, and I needed to finish this story before the end of the month because I plan on submitting this book for a summer program for aspiring authors. Spencer told me about it when he heard from a friend in the market back in New York, and I thought it was the perfect opportunity for me to get into the industry on my own merits. Spencer offered to help by introducing me to a few people he knows, but for now, I want to give it a try by myself first. If it doesn't work out, maybe he can give me a hand. I won't say no to good networking.

"I think we need to go out tonight and celebrate. Spencer is coming back from LA, and he can meet us there," I suggest, walking to the kitchen to see Chad still trying to get his uniform clean. I gesture for him to give me the shirt so I can do it. He grumbles in complaint but does as I ask, and I use my cleaning skills to save his last uniform before he has to leave for wok.

"I'm off duty tonight, so I'm down for a beer," he finally answers, sitting on the stool in front of me as I apply some detergent to the stain. "Who else are you calling?"

I look up at him, narrowing my eyes as I study him. His expressionless face pisses me off, but he's only doing this out of spite. "Why do you want to know?" I ask.

"Am I not allowed to know who I'm hanging out with?" he argues back.

"Yes, but you sounded too interested in who I'm bringing."

"So?" He raises his eyebrows at me.

"Do you want to know if Poppy is coming?" I tease, noticing his eyes twitch almost imperceptibly.

"Why would I want to know that?" Chad shoots back, but his eyes dart to the shirt in my hand, and that's the giveaway I needed.

"Aha!" I point a finger accusingly at him. "You're into her! I knew it!"

"No, I'm not," Chad denies vehemently. "Where did you get that nonsense from?"

"You are! You are so into her. I can see it in your eyes," I yell, rejoicing at my brother's reaction. His face is so red, up to his forehead, even making his light brown hair look red.

"Who's into who?" Ryan walks in, followed by Alice and Lauren, who's obviously just gotten off work since she's still wearing her bright orange firefighter jumpsuit, her hair tied up in a ponytail.

"Chad likes Poppy," I blurt out, dodging a slap from my brother. I chuckle, running behind Ryan to protect myself from Chad's fury.

"She is just babbling stupidity, as always," my younger brother snarls, his eyes narrowed to slits as he shoots me a deathly glare.

"Oh, is that even news around here?" Lauren muses, heading to the fridge and grabbing a bottle of water. "You'd need to be blind not to see it."

I pretend I didn't have my doubts about it this whole time and just use this opportunity to keep making fun of Chad.

"That was pretty obvious," Alice agrees with a nod, sitting at the table and pouring herself some coffee.

Chad stops his pursuit of me and halts abruptly, staring flabbergasted at our sister-in-law.

"What?" she asks, surprised. "I didn't even know it was a secret," she adds, making us all laugh at the way Chad winces in embarrassment.

"I can't say I paid attention to it before, but now that you mention it...it was really obvious," Ryan agrees, sitting beside his wife.

"Come on, brother. Denying it will only make it worse," Lauren teases, becoming the new focus of Chad's fury.

"Well, if you're worried about it, I'm glad to tell you that you have my blessing," I say, causing Chad's head to snap to me. "Just don't hurt my friend, or I swear I'll chop your balls off," I warn, pointing my finger at him.

"I wouldn't ignore her on that," Lauren jokes, bumping Chad in the shoulder as she passes by him to sit at the table.

Mom and Dad are still nowhere in sight, but we're all expected to gather for breakfast, so I'm sure they will show up at any time now. Spencer was supposed to be here, too, but since he's still in Los Angeles, I guess I have to accept he'll come next time. The Jenkins breakfast has become a tradition for a while, and I love that Spencer gets to be a part of it now.

"Changing the subject… I was talking to Chad about going out tonight to celebrate." I turn to my siblings and my sister-in-law, grinning at them. "I finished my first novel," I announce excitedly.

Lauren and Alice jump from their seats, rushing to hug and congratulate me. Ryan smiles at me from his seat, giving me a thumbs up and nodding proudly at me. "Good job, sis. I'm sure you'll be the next J.K. Rowling."

"That's a stretch, but thanks, Ryan," I reply, accepting another hug from Lauren.

"I'm so proud of you, pony. I knew you could do it."

"Thank you, guys. It means a lot. So, we're all up for some karaoke tonight?" I suggest.

"Oh, hell yeah!" Alice claps her hands, delighted. If there's anyone in this world that turns into a complete maniac when it comes to karaoke, that someone is her. You would never imagine that someone as sweet and gentle as Alice becomes a freak whenever a couple of beers and Toni Braxton are involved.

"Oh, good Lord," Ryan mumbles, slapping his forehead dramatically. "Do we really have to?"

I guess he must be the one who suffers the most from Alice's excitement, but I can't say I blame her. Karaoke is just so much fun.

"Regretting the wedded life already, brother?" Chad teases, getting himself a cup of coffee. I can see him getting impatient with Mom and Dad's delay, his eyes darting several times to the orange cake at the corner of the table.

"Not quite," Ryan bites back. "And you should watch your mouth. You could be next. And if I remember correctly, Poppy is quite the competitor when it comes to karaoke. Right, baby?" He looks at Alice, looking for support.

He's right. After Alice, my best friend is the karaoke bar nightmare.

Chad curses my brother at the exact moment my mom walks into the kitchen, being followed by my father.

"Do I need to wash your mouth out with soap, mister? What kind of language is that inside this house?" Mom scolds, but by the way her lips are curling up on the side, I know she's just messing with Chad. Dad looks away, hiding his face so no one sees him laughing, but we're all used to this scene, so it's no secret that he's enjoying the exchange.

"You should be defending me, Mom. They're teaming up against me," Chad whines, getting up from his seat and hugging her, pretending to be hurt by our teasing.

I smile, feeling joy and love spread through my heart. Watching this scene makes me realize that this is exactly what a Jenkins gathering is about.

And I wouldn't change this for anything in the world.

Maybe Missoula is a small town. Maybe my future isn't promised to hold far-fetched accomplishments and grand dreams. Maybe this is all this huge world can offer me.

And I'm okay with that.

Because I have everything I need right here.

Friends that support me.

A family that is here for me no matter what.

And a love that would walk through fire and water to make me happy.

What else could I possibly want?

EPILOGUE

WO YEARS LATER...

"Honey, aren't you ready yet? We're going to be late," Spencer yells from the living room at the exact moment I finish buckling my shoe. Before I can reply, he shows up by the door, eyeing me up and down as I stand from the bed, straightening my flower print dress and wrapping a beige cardigan around myself.

It's still fall, but the wind is not merciful when the sun starts to set, so I don't want to risk freezing to death when it's nighttime.

"You look... perfect. But are you sure you want to wear heels?" Spencer frowns as his eyes fall to my feet.

I chuckle, walking toward him and wrapping my arms around his neck. "Baby, I'm pregnant, not injured. Besides, they are square toe heels, so I'll hardly struggle with them."

That doesn't seem to convince him, though. Ever since I told him I was pregnant, he's been constantly overprotective and making sure I have everything I need–and more. Not that I'm complaining about the extra attention, but sometimes he goes over the top.

A year after the launch of his record label, Spencer and I went on a trip to celebrate Bailey's Records one year anniversary, and that's when he proposed to me. I knew he was going to do it one day, but he still managed to surprise me.

A few months later, we got married, and life has been chaotic ever since, in the good sense of the word.

I published my first book with a traditional publisher. I ended up not winning the competition for the summer program, so Spencer introduced me to that friend of his who works at a publishing company in New York. She is now my editor, and I'm planning to start writing my third title. We also moved to the ranch's guest house. Turns out, Spencer's house downtown was rented, and after pondering what to do once we got married, he suggested we move to the ranch.

Truthfully, I think he knew I never really wanted to leave my family's house. I would never ask him to move there with me since my parents still live in the main house, but he told me it's not like we'd live under the same roof. We'd still have privacy, but be able to live on the ranch either way, which made me so happy. I still wanted to be amongst my family, the animals, not to mention it'd be easier to help Dad out with the chores.

Someone will have to take over one day, and I am sure my siblings won't want to deal with that since they have their jobs elsewhere.

Now, I'm more than happy to know my kid will be raised in the same place as me, to experience the same things I did, and live amongst nature and animals the same way I did.

Spencer sighs, squeezing me into his arms. "Fine, sorry. Are you ready to go now? Aubrie will kill me if I get there after the guests."

"I know, I know. Let's go," I tell him, smiling as I picture his sister scolding him for being a lousy uncle, arriving late for his niece's birthday party.

Caitlin is turning six today, and she decided she wanted a picnic kind of party. She invited her school friends and family friends, and at first, it was supposed to be something more intimate. But Spencer, being the overindulgent uncle he is, told Caitlin he'd rent inflatable bounce houses and cotton candy machines as his contribution to the party. The squeak that came out of that little girl's throat when she heard that is something I'll never forget.

If Spencer is spoiling his niece so badly, I can only imagine what he'll do to our kid once he's born.

Yes, it's a boy! But he doesn't know that yet.

I'm waiting for the right moment to tell him, and I'm already feeling the butterflies anxiously flapping their wings in my stomach just at the thought of seeing his reaction to the news.

We head to the car, and Spencer opens the passenger door for me. I climb inside, buckling the seat belt and waiting for him to get into the driver's seat. He drives in silence for a few minutes, apparently focused on something inside his head. I enjoy the peaceful atmosphere, watching the streets blur in front of my eyes while listening to whatever new pop song is playing on the radio. I don't pay much attention to it. I just cherish this nice moment.

"So, have you thought about what you want to do for your birthday this year?" Spencer suddenly asks, and I snap my head to the side to look at him.

He still has his focus on the road, though, so I look out the window again, considering his question. There's still a couple of months until my 30th birthday, but by then, I'll be six months pregnant, so I have no idea if I'll be in the mood for a big party. Probably not.

"I don't know, maybe something more intimate with just the family? We could have it at the ranch, I don't care for having anything big. Maybe a game night?" I suggest, asking for his opinion. Honestly, I haven't thought about it until now. Everything in my mind lately is related to the baby, so I haven't thought about myself for a while.

"That sounds nice," he agrees. "I was also thinking we could celebrate our anniversary a bit earlier this year and go on a trip before... you know, things get harder and heavier," he chuckles, side-eyeing me.

"That's actually a good idea. I don't think we'll be able to travel for at least a year after the baby is born. Where do you think we should go?"

"Anywhere you'd like," Spencer answers. "I'll be glad to take you anywhere in the world."

"Ohhh, that sounds promising…and expensive," I tell him with a grin on my lips. "I can be quite a handful as a wife, Mr. Bailey. You shouldn't indulge me like this," I joke.

Spencer's smile widens, but he keeps his eyes on the road. "Yeah, I know. But you deserve much more than that. Also, I just signed another contract with this band from Nashville, so…" he trails off, leaving me in suspense.

"So? Is this a big contract?"

"Yep," he answers, popping the 'p'. "They are quite famous."

I squeal, clapping my hands like a little girl who just got her first Barbie doll. "Congratulations, baby!"

"Thank you," he muses shyly. His humbleness is one of the things that still impresses me. Spencer knows how good of a businessman he is, but he still gets shy and awkward whenever someone brings that up or compliments him. "So, you have that to decide by the end of the week. I was thinking we could go before you start writing your next novel, and I have my plate full for the new month."

I nod, already feeling excited about our next adventure. I have no idea where I want to go, but I do have a huge bucket list I want to start checking off, so I have a big task on my hands to work on once I'm back from Caitlin's party.

When we get to the Bailey-Walsh's residence, we find it still empty except for some of Caitlin's neighbor friends. My dad's truck is already here, though, since he drove my mom earlier so she could bring the cake she made. Aubrie said she didn't want anyone else's cake other than my mom's. I couldn't blame her.

Spencer and I walk inside, and we're immediately bombarded with greetings and questions from our family. Surprisingly, besides my parents, Chad, Lauren, Ryan, and Alice are already here too.

"Uncle Spencer! Aunt Hayden! Finally!" Caitlin is the first one to get to us, jumping into Spencer's arms, even though she's grown so much in the past couple of years. I hear him chuckling nervously as he tries to hold her weight, and I bite my lip so as not to laugh, focusing on Aubrie's hug instead.

"Aren't you the cutest pregnant woman on the planet?" she muses sweetly, pulling away from me and glancing at my not-so-visible belly.

"I'm barely showing yet, Aubrie," I say in a cheerful tone.

"Ah, but you definitely have that glow in your favor. I, on the other hand, remember being the ugliest, most annoying bitch while I was pregnant," she grumbles, receiving a disapproving shake of the head from her husband.

"I doubt that is true," I tell her. "I remember you being so cool about it, still working until the day your water broke."

Aubrie dismisses me with a wave of her hand, gesturing for us to come inside.

I greet my siblings, and a few minutes later, we're all settled at the table, eating and drinking—I have to settle for a glass of flavored sparkling water—the party is already crowded and at full power. Poppy arrived a few minutes after Spencer and I, and our table is now complete—except for Thomas and Aubrie who need to socialize with their guests.

By the time the moon is up, the last traces of the sunset painting the sky in that beautiful pinkish orange tone, everyone seated around the table is slightly drunk from all the beers, whiskey, and wine they drank. Apparently, I'll be the designated driver tonight since Spencer decided to show his "alcohol tolerance" and prove he can drink a whole bottle of Black Label without getting drunk.

My two brothers are wasted, but somehow, they manage to remain with their stoic expressions, unbothered. I just know they are past their alcohol limit because Ryan's cheeks are redder than normal, and Chad's hazel eyes have this sluggish gaze as he talks to Alice. Lauren is...something else entirely. My sister drank so many different cocktails that I lost count of them after the tenth glass. She's chattier than usual, and that's saying a lot. For at least fifteen minutes, she's been talking about this argument that blew up between a couple of her coworkers that left one of them with a black eye and a scratched face.

Poppy and Alice are the only ones who can be considered only slightly buzzed, sipping lazily on their wine.

Thankfully, Mom and Dad are talking to Valerie and Bob at their table, so at the moment, it's just us here.

"Oh, I have another piece of hot gossip to share..." Lauren continues, her eyes widening in surprise as if she has just remembered something really important. "A little bird told me this thing the other day..." she trails off with suspense, taking in everyone's faces before continuing.

I can see Poppy straightening up on her seat, already itching to hear the gossip.

My brothers don't seem to be that interested, rolling their eyes at our sister, and Alice is just listening politely. I can't tell if she's eager to hear it or not.

Spencer leans back in his seat, feigning indifference, but I know he wants to know whatever Lauren has to say. I swear the man loves some gossip sometimes.

"There you go again," Chad complains from the other side of the table. "Don't you ever get tired of spreading stuff that doesn't concern you?"

"I'm not 'spreading stuff,' brother," Lauren retorts through clenched teeth, narrowing her eyes at him. "And it actually concerns me...indirectly. If I were you, I'd be more concerned about this as well, since it involves *your* little ass."

Chad seems to sober up immediately, his eyes slightly widening at her. "What do you mean? Whatever you heard, I'm sure it's a lie."

"Is it?" Lauren threatens. "It also involves someone else at this table."

My head snaps from one side to the other, trying to put the pieces together by myself, but everyone seems to be just as confused as I am.

Lauren grins, obviously proud for getting the reaction she intended.

"So, the little bird told me they saw you, brother," my sister points at Chad, "and Poppy," she turns to my friend, "kissing at the bar the other night," Lauren spills, looking delighted with the information she just dumped on us.

Poppy chokes on her wine, and Chad almost falls out of his chair. The scene is hilarious, but I'm so shocked that I can't even find it in me to laugh at it. Ryan cracks up, Alice is stifling her laugh, and Spencer is drinking from his glass, nodding at my brother as if saying, "Good job, man." My jaw is literally hanging open, and I'm speechless.

"Apparently," Lauren continues, "this has been going on for quite some time now."

"Oh, my God!" I turn to look at Poppy with an accusatory look. "And you kept this from me?"

I'm not mad. I'm not even the slightest angry at them. I'm finding this so funny, and I'm so happy for them that whatever is going on between them can wait to be explained. I had given up on waiting for them to realize they liked each other, but not in a million years would I have imagined they were just getting on with it behind our backs.

"I-I…that's not what it seems, Hays, I…" my friend stammers, and I turn to look at Chad, who's stood from his chair and looks like someone who just got caught doing something they shouldn't be doing. A giggle blurts out of my lips, and suddenly, I can't control myself anymore. My head tilts back, and I need to hold onto my stomach, trying to keep it from hurting as I'm laughing so hard.

"Don't you guys have anything to say?" Lauren presses, clearly enjoying the embarrassment from our brother and my best friend.

"Don't be mean to them, Lauren," Alice chimes in, but her tone also indicates she's enjoying this more than she'd like to admit. "They obviously didn't want to get caught. Maybe the thrill of hiding their relationship excited them."

That makes me laugh even more when I see how Chad opens and closes his mouth, trying to decide whether he should reply to our sister-in-law or not. He opts against it, but I can tell he would have reacted completely different if it had been me saying that.

"We should have made that bet when we had the chance," Ryan notes, bringing up a conversation we had a long time ago when we were discussing our opinions on Poppy and Chad. They weren't present, of course, and my oldest brother had suggested that we bet on it, but Lauren and I just thought Chad was too scared to try anything with her, so we ended up not doing it.

"I would have lost it anyway. I never thought our brother would finally make a move," I say, breathing slowly so I can compose myself after bursting out laughing.

The look on my best friend's face is priceless and the one on my brother's even more so.

"I would have bet on you, man," Spencer points out with feigned support, teasing Chad, who flips him off.

Then his eyes dart to Poppy for a split second, as if he's trying to check on her and see if she's all right. It's so cute that he cares for her like this, and I don't know if I should tease them or just feel happy for them.

"Can we shut up about it and talk about something else?" Chad protests, turning to our sister. "You should be worried about *your* reputation, sis, or are you going to pretend you weren't sneaking around with James during lunch break the other day? I saw you getting in his car while I was on patrol."

Lauren shrugs, not the least bit bothered about his revelation. "At least it didn't take me thirty years to make a move on someone, unlike other people."

Everyone around reacts with audible 'oohs' after hearing her roast Chad. Sensing this might get ugly, I interrupt, raising my hand and deciding to change the subject.

"Okay, guys, I do have something nicer to talk about. I have some news to share too," I begin, glancing at Spencer to make sure he's paying attention to me. I was going to wait until I shared this, maybe tell him when we were alone, but I just feel so comfortable and happy right now that I can't wait any longer. It's a pity Mom and Dad are not here, but I can tell them later. It's not like it will remain a secret for long, anyway. Not after everyone here knows about it.

As if on cue, Aubrie and Thomas approach our table.

"Oh, it's great that you guys are here too," I add, waving at them.

"What's going on?" Aubrie asks curiously, looking around the table as if trying to understand what she's missed.

"Hayden is about to share something important, apparently," Lauren explains, turning in her seat to face me.

I swallow, preparing myself to share the most important news I have with my family.

I reach for Spencer's hand under the table, squeezing it slightly as I look at him.

"We're having a boy," I finally announce.

Everyone around me erupts in screams and claps, too much excitement for me to make sense of. Their celebration fades to the background, though, as I stare into Spencer's beautiful eyes that are shining with so much love and appreciation that it takes my breath away.

"We're having a boy?" he repeats in a whisper, leaning in and bringing our foreheads together.

I nod, too emotional to speak. The tears are blurring my vision, my throat is starting to burn, and I feel like I might explode with happiness at any moment now.

"I was thinking we could name him Ben, after your dad." The thought occurred to me as soon as I found out the sex of the baby, and I figured Spencer would love the idea.

And I was right.

By the way he's looking at me, his smile so wide I fear it might split his face in half, I know I was right to think like that.

"That'd be really nice, baby. I love you," he adds, kissing my lips, barely containing his elation. "You make me the happiest man alive."

I giggle, too overwhelmed to think of what to say.

Chad is yelling at our parents to share the news, but I can't bring myself to look at them. All my focus is on my husband, the man I chose to love, to share my life with, and to build a family together.

Surrounded by the people I love the most in this world, I feel like *I'm* the happiest human alive.

"I love you too," I tell Spencer. "Thank you for making all of my dreams come true."